THE PATRON SAINT

OF UNMARRIED WOMEN

KARL
ACKERMAN

THE PATRON SAINT OF UNMARRIED WOMEN

ST. MARTIN'S GRIFFIN

NEW YORK

This novel is a work of fiction. All of the events, characters,
names, and places depicted in this novel are entirely fictitious
or are used fictitiously. No representation that any statement
made in this novel is true or that any incident depicted in this
novel actually occurred is intended or should be inferred by
the reader.

The extract on page 176 from "The Throne of the Third
Heaven of the Nations' Millenium General Assembly," ©
1992 Smithsonian Institution, is reprinted with permission.

Excerpt on page 95 from *Truck Song* by Diane Siebert.
Copyright © 1984 by Diane Siebert. Reprinted by permission
of HarperCollins Publishers, Inc.

Library of Congress Cataloging-in-Publication Data

Ackerman, Karl.
    The patron saint of unmarried women / Karl Ackerman.
        p.   cm.
    ISBN 0-312-13142-9
    1. Man-woman relationships—Washington (D.C.)
—Fiction.   2. Single woman—Washington (D.C.)
—Fiction.   I. Title.
PS3551.C487P3   1995
813'.54—dc20   95-9862
                                                          CIP

First published in the United States by St. Martin's Press

First St. Martin's Griffin Edition: June 1995

              10 9 8 7 6 5 4 3 2 1

Books are available in quantity for promotional or premium
use. Write to Director of Special Sales, St. Martin's Press,
175 Fifth Avenue, New York, N.Y. 10010, for information
on discounts and terms, or call toll-free (800) 221-7945. In
New York, call (212) 674-5151 (ext. 645).

FOR JENNY
AND LITTLE Z

What is irritating about love is that it is a crime
that requires an accomplice.

BAUDELAIRE

THE GOSPEL
ACCORDING
TO MARIE

In the heat of battle it seemed important to me to hang with Marie step for step. By turns I was upbeat, sorrowful, angry at Nina, angry at myself, sullen, logical, defiant. Nothing worked. The conversation ended up as a modern reenactment of the Spanish Inquisition with Marie Lawrence in the role of Torquemada while I played the disbelieving fool. "Jack," she cried to the heavens. "The two of you are as stubborn as a couple of mules." "Marie, in real life, just because people fall in love doesn't mean they live happily ever after." "In real life, Mr. Smartie Pants, people fall in love and get married and *then* live together." "And ten years down the road half of them are divorced." "Not the Catholics," she snapped.

On and on it went:

"My little girl's a mess. She's falling apart."

"I talked to her this morning. She sounded fine."

"She's an actress."

"Nina is *not* an actress."

"She's upset, Jack."

"We're both upset."

"Then knock off the nonsense."

"This isn't nonsense, Marie. What can I say to make you see that?"

"Two dumb kids are what I see—two dumb kids who were meant for each other and don't for the world know how good they've got it. That's the whole story, buster. You can take my word for it."

I wouldn't. As confused as I was at that moment, I thought that Marie was wrong. And I said that. But when I tried to give her a reasoned analysis of why my relationship with her daughter had fallen apart, she nearly tossed me out the front door. The grim expression on her face and the white polyester scarf knotted like a tourniquet at her chin indicated that she was preparing to pay a visit to the Church of the Little Flower. She would make a novena. "To Saint Anne," she said darkly.

Saint Anne is the patron saint of unmarried women.

That was June.

In July and August I nursed my obsession for Nina Lawrence through the torn-Achilles-tendon phase of emotional trauma into the groin-pull phase. When the telephone rang, I hoped it would be Nina. Then the thought that it *might* be Nina would fill me with dread. And I would let the phone ring, let my answering machine field a plaintive message from someone whose maple tree was dropping leaves or whose zoysia grass was mottled with rust spots. By September I was limping through the ankle-sprain phase of my recovery and had at last begun to consider the idea that it might be best for both of us if Nina *didn't* call.

Which, of course, is exactly when she did.

The news is that Marie wants to see me again. About landscaping, Nina says.

"I know it's a huge favor, but would you do it?"

Of course I will do it. I will be there within the hour. But a second voice, speaking from the depths of my Waspy brain, reminds me that the passage of time has already taken Nina and me well past the huge-favor stage.

"Landscaping," I say.

Silence. Then Nina says, "It does sound like bullshit, doesn't it?"

I can see her sitting on the floor beside her bed. It is hot outside; she is definitely wearing shorts. A white tank top. Tanned shoulders. Her dark hair is piled on top of her head. I see the soft, curly hair on her neck. The line of her back: straight, strong—a swimmer's back.

"Jack, I'm really sorry. It was pretty dumb of me to let that woman talk me into this. And the truth is that it didn't take much of an effort. I wanted to call. To talk to you . . . see how you were doing. I guess I wasn't thinking."

I don't know what to say.

"Please don't crucify me. It's not like it's a huge mistake."

"So what's the news from Saint Lawrence Basilica?"

Nina's sigh indicates that we have reached solid ground. A lengthy discussion about the latest storm rocking her family has always been our safe harbor.

"You won't believe the latest."

"Of course I'll believe it. I'll believe anything."

"It's Barb. She walked."

"No!"

"The big Adios."

"And then there were nine. How's Marie taking it?"

"Valium and rosaries. She saw it coming but that didn't make it any easier."

"This landscaping consultation—I hope it's not going to include an effort to nab my eternal soul. As an attempt to even the score."

"She's an optimist, Jack. She's not a nut."

"I might be an easy mark."

Nina laughs. "She misses you. The whole family misses you."

"The *whole* family?"

There is a long moment of silence.

"Oh, Jack."

At the entrance to the Lawrences' driveway, I stop my van alongside a rusty milk can, which is attached like a torpedo to a rotting tree stump. Scrawled across it in black paint are the letters "Richter L," the foot of the L extending like a wriggly snake toward the lip of the can. Dan, my border collie, climbs into the passenger seat. He lets loose a tortured yawn, perfectly expressing my own state of mind. I give some thought to bailing out. In two minutes I could be on the Beltway; by lunchtime I could be lost in the Blue Ridge. Dan yawns again. I open my door. He leaps over me and disappears into the dense underbrush.

Nina's father is an architect, the sort of man who's at his best when he's up to his ankles in sawdust. His business and passion is buying and fixing up old houses. Thus, the Lawrences have moved like bedouins from one rehab project to the next. This lifestyle has allowed Richter to put away a bundle of money; it has also earned him the enmity of his entire family. Their current home in Mohican Hills is a pale yellow cement château with peaked roof and gables that looks as though it was built by someone with fond memories of Normandy, circa 1945. In these leafy days of summer, all I can see of the place from the street is a multicolored slate rooftop and a yellow chimney. But I hear hammering: the doctor is in. I turn into the driveway and wind down through the gulley separating Richter's manse from the street.

Dan has planted himself on the last remaining patch of grass in what was once the Lawrences' front lawn. From the look of the place, we could be anywhere in the third world. The old house, the bales of straw, the muddy tire ruts, the pickup truck propped on cinder blocks, the cement-caked wheelbarrow: all that's missing from this scene is a clutch of chickens scrabbling in the dirt and an old *paisano* perched on a stone wall eating a hard-boiled egg.

Richter is standing atop a rickety scaffolding, his thinning gray hair swept back like the crest of a great blue heron. I gun the engine to get his attention before shutting it off.

"Captain Jack!"

I tip an imaginary cap and wave him away from the length of rope hanging from the chimney. The last thing in the world I want to see is Richter Lawrence *père* rappelling down the fissured wall of his home.

He calls, "What brings you to our neck of the woods?"

"A summons! A consultation about landscaping, I understand."

"Landscaping, you say?" His worried gaze takes in the wall of forest in front of the house.

I don't think this man owns a lawnmower. Certainly he doesn't need one, with the yard transformed into a parking lot and the rest of the property covered with dense stands of tulip trees and enough bamboo to feed the remaining population of wild panda bears.

"Is Marie home?"

"Upstairs. The door's open."

He means this literally. I step around a pallet of flagstones and climb the warped sheets of plywood that cover the front steps. Inside the foyer I smell basil and garlic. A television blares in the living room. From the heavens comes the keening sound of an ancient vacuum cleaner. I call out, "Anyone home?"

"Jack! My God, is that you?"

Joan appears in the kitchen doorway. She's wearing a green rubberized apron and a purple bandanna. Both hands are covered with whiskers of humus. Whereas Nina has inherited a lean frame from Richter, sister Joan is all Marie: shorter than Nina, stockier, and well-muscled enough to wrench my neck when she grabs my head and pulls my face to her lips.

Joanie Lawrence and I are allies, *compañeros* of the soil. Out back is a greenhouse from which she supplies most of the health food stores in the area with alfalfa and mung bean sprouts. Select restaurants in our nation's capital receive their daily supply of oregano, basil, dill, cilantro, and a dozen other herbs from her impressive garden.

" 'His coming was in the nature of a welcome disturbance; it seemed to furnish a new direction for her emotions,' " she says brightly, apparently still mired in a Kate Chopin phase.

"So what's new in your life?" I ask.

"A feeling of abandonment. You have become like a stranger."

"Joans, I was dumped. I was sent off into the night with my tail tucked between my legs. To crawl back would have brought dishonor upon my whole family."

"We miss you, Jackie."

"I miss you, too."

"Well, come around." She takes hold of my hands and rubs the knuckles with her thumbs. "You okay?"

I shrug.

"If you ask me, that sister of mine has her head up her ass."

"Careful how you talk about my old girlfriend."

"What's she up to, Jack?"

"I didn't know she was up to anything."

Joan's eyes widen in surprise.

"Why the summons?" I ask. "What's on Marie's mind?"

"Anger, shame, disgrace."

"Might this be old news or new news?"

" 'Tis as hoary as last year's cheese, mi'lord."

"I spoke to Nina yesterday—"

"She didn't tell you?"

"Tell me what?"

"Brace yourself, lad." Joan goes to the stairway. "Mother!" she calls. "Don Giovanni has returned!"

The vacuum cleaner shuts down with an extended death rattle.

"*JAAAAAACCK!*"—three . . . four . . . five seconds.

God, it's comforting to hear a proper scream. My eardrums ache with pleasure. Shortly, Marie rumbles down the steps, her right hand riding above an ample bosom, as if to slow herself down. "You're so good to come, Jack. We can always count on him, can't we, darling?"

"That Jack is one straight arrow," Joan replies.

"He looks parched. Honey, get him something cold to drink."

The instant Joan shows us her back, Marie leans toward me and whispers: "John's Place in fifteen minutes."

"I thought this was about landscaping."

She scowls. "Don't be thick, Jack."

The road to John's Place takes me past the Defense Mapping Agency, a windowless brick fortress surrounded by barbed wire and landscaped in a style that can only be described as military-industrial school: lampposts instead of trees, acres of gently undulating pavement, with only enough lawn in the circle to justify the purchase of a riding mower. This complex is one of the white-collar factories in the greater Washington metropolitan area, and John's Place, a cafeteria on the ground floor of a small shopping center across the street, is where the salarymen take their meals.

The sign on the door says "No Bag Lunches." I wait for Marie beside a row of dart boards and survey the crowd: mostly men, all with laminated ID cards hanging from their necks on beaded chains. Across the room, two fellows with shiny red ties sit facing each other beneath a shellacked blue marlin. Every conversation in the room seems to concern computers.

"With the PA&E and the DRC—we need to bring in someone who has a background in those systems. . . . I wish there were more guys like that. He gets *inside* the software. . . . Every morning I have to go down there and boot the thing myself. . . . On 464, I have to assume we never levied anything on them. . . ." An older man stands. "Is it a true MPTR-MBF? I think not."

Two tables break up simultaneously and I expect to hear a whistle blow.

A hand settles on my arm. I turn to find Marie wearing a red-and-white-checkered scarf and Jackie O. sunglasses. She is in disguise. We head for the food line and make our way past cans of juice resting in shaved ice and a hideously encrusted nacho cheese pot. I order what Marie orders—BLT and a large Bud—and pay for both of us. Settling into a table near the front window, we are as nonchalant as a couple of spies preparing to pass bootleg maps of Pyongyang beneath the elbow-worn Formica.

I know what she's up to.

I'll tell you when I knew: on the telephone with Nina. That was as good a warning scene as the second act of *Andrea Chénier*, when Chénier's friend slips him a passport and tells him to get the hell out of Paris. Like Chénier, I will have none of it.

"Jack, tell me about the family."

I run through the list of characters, starting where Marie would want me to start, with my sister's kids. Then on to sister Ellen, husband Evan, my father. I am doling out small bits of what I hope will sound like gossip.

"You left out your mother." Marie is Cold War grim behind the sunglasses.

She's right. The sad fact is that I don't have much to say about my mother. After my parents were divorced six years ago, my mother remarried and moved to Philadelphia. I see her about once a year. Our infrequent telephone conversations are characterized by long stretches of accusatory silence.

I say, "Ellen tells me she's making a bundle selling real estate."

"It's nice to hear that someone is."

"She sold a church to an avant-garde theater company last month."

"Catholic?"

"The theater company?"

Marie frowns. "The church," she says.

I nod.

Her expression relaxes and her voice goes soft. "I didn't think they could sell churches."

"It was deconsecrated."

"Oh." She dips to take a swallow of beer and emerges with a little Vincent Price mustache of foam.

"Jackie," she says wearily. "Let me tell you something. God tests all of us. Sometimes in the strangest ways."

Experience tells me that we've moved on to a new subject, one allied to, but more painful than, the mere deconsecration and sale of sacred property.

My eyes are fixed on Marie as I tear into the sandwich. "Is this about Barb?"

She nods gravely. "You heard?"

I nod gravely. "Nina told me."

Last year Nina's eldest sister shocked the family to its Italian roots by marrying into the Jewish faith. The day before yesterday Marie got word that Barb has converted.

"Jack, why in the world would she do it?"

I understand her to mean, why would a thirty-three-year-old woman of sound mind leave a perfectly good religion—the self-proclaimed "One True Faith"—for one that seems so, well, *peculiar*. Strange food, strange clothes, strange language, strange holidays, strange haircuts. And no Savior, to boot! Marie views Barb's decision to convert as a step backward—like trading a late model Cadillac for a '66 Chevy Impala, straight up. What really frosts her, I think, is the suspicion that Barb quit the Catholic Church because Judaism seemed to her a thornier path to salvation. Leave it to Barb to spite her mother by donning the hairiest of hair shirts.

A group of men take the adjacent table. I look around the room. There is one black guy in the whole place, sitting alone. The five men at the table beside ours are all leaning forward on their elbows, consuming their sandwiches like ears of corn. Marie stirs. The topic is about to shift again. A more delicate person would set her BLT on the paper plate, dab the corners of her lips with a napkin, and say, "But of course I didn't ask you here to burden you with talk about my daughter's distressing conversion." Not Marie. She takes a huge bite out of the sandwich and has barely worked the food to one side of her mouth before blurting from the other, "I still don't understand why you did it, Jack."

To this day and forever, evidence and sworn testimony not-withstanding, Marie insists that I threw Nina over, not vice versa. This makes for a sadder story—the story of Manon Lescaut and a thousand like her. Bereft of honor, these wronged women are left with three options: the convent, exile, or death.

Marie swallows. "By the way, I spoke to Angie this morning. Did she call me? *No.* Did she call me last week? *No.* Am I complaining? *Yes.* I'm worried sick about that girl. What's going to become of her? She has such a delicate constitution." Nina has the constitution of a musk ox, but Marie prefers to see her Angie as Violetta in *La Traviata,* helpless in the full grip of consumption. "Jack, when are you going to come to your senses and admit your mistake?"

If Nina is Violetta, then I am cold-hearted Eugene Onegin.

"How many times do I have to remind you that this was her decision?"

"You walked out."

Technically this is true. But consider the situation. I had just finished a big landscaping job and was out celebrating with my Salvadoran crew—a big paycheck requires a small fiesta. Toasting the brave *muchachos* of the FMLN, the time got away from me; I arrived home two hours late. Nina was pacing. Her hair looked like it had been coiffed with a rake. Dan had shut himself in the bathroom, a very bad sign.

I tried the apology angle.

"Don't!" she cried. "You aren't married to me. You aren't responsible for the fact that I have been behaving like a crazy housewife. This is my problem, Jack. Tonight I lost it. Why did I lose it? Why didn't I spend the evening painting?"

I made an effort to think. "Because you kept imagining that I had been gunned down in a stinky alley in Adams Morgan?"

"Nooooo!" More pacing, more hair raking. "I just figured it out. Just now. As you were walking up the steps. I didn't paint because I couldn't paint, and I couldn't paint because I knew that you might walk in at any moment." She paused. "Don't you see what that means?"

I didn't. I couldn't. At that particular moment, my mind was resolutely focused on one extremely taut bladder.

"God was sending me a message."

"What sort of message?"

"A sign."

"A sign?"

"That it's over, Jack."

"What's over?"

"Jack, don't act like we've never talked about this before."

"You're not serious, are you?"

"Dead serious."

From the bathroom I called out, "Maybe we ought to run this by Him in the morning before we make any decisions. Just to be on the safe side." Silence. "I mean, doesn't this seem a little drastic? If I'd left right after the first toast to Farabundo Martí we'd be sitting in bed laughing right now."

"You haven't heard a *word* I've said."

It sounds funny now but at the time it wasn't funny at all. For the umpteenth time Nina had latched onto the idea that our living together was smothering both of us, and I knew that any attempt to discuss the issue further that night was doomed. We needed a cooling-off period, which meant that someone had to leave. Since the apartment was originally Nina's, that someone was me. I wasn't thrilled about going. After loading a gym bag with underwear and socks and a wrinkled shirt, I drove to Ellen's house. It wasn't until I was parked out front that I considered the embarrassment of turning up on my sister's doorstep at midnight, with tears in my eyes and beer on my breath. That night Dan and I slept in the van. The next day Nina and I talked, but things just got worse. The fatal moment came when I began cross-examining her about the logic behind her decision. She walked out. That night I slept on the guest futon on the living-room floor. Day three I moved into Ellen's spare bedroom. Day four I went back to the apartment to pick up the dog food and the rest of my clothes. I gave brief consideration to barricading myself in the bathroom. But I went to retrieve my shaving tools and took a good look at the place, and knew that the cops would have had me out of there in fifteen seconds.

Nina was crying when I left and I wasn't. Only later, while Dan and I were walking alongside the C&O Canal, did it occur to me that Nina and I had played that scene backwards. Which is when I started to cry. I found a bench and sat down and bawled like a child. The trigger wasn't the prospect of losing Nina—I hadn't even begun to consider *that* possibility—but the realization that I was suddenly alone. There wasn't a soul in the world I wanted to talk to. There is no feeling of aloneness to match the feeling of one who, for all intents and purposes, is living in the back of a van.

I let time go by, too much time, and when Nina finally called me, her voice was edgy and official-sounding. At the instant she said my name, a feeling of dread settled over me, and we navigated the conversation by feigning the politeness of strangers. That was a new trick for us, and that we pulled it off seemed like the worst sort of news. Nina and I have had separations before, but none had lasted more than a couple of days. Three months feels like an eternity. Like Marie, I can't seem to accept the possibility that this last eruption might have been the big one, the terminal event that my interpersonal seismologist of a sister has been predicting for some time.

Marie strokes the lone whisker on her chin. Her eyes are glazed. She is eavesdropping on a nearby conversation. I tune in in time to hear a grandfatherly voice say, ". . . but after we left, everything went to pieces. Andy came home early and found the nanny crying in the kitchen. Don't get me wrong; she's a nice kid. But right off I knew something had to be wrong. An attractive young woman without a family life—it just didn't make any sense."

Marie says, "Jack, you shared Angie's bed for what?"

"Three years."

"Three years, four months, and ten days." She crosses her meaty arms. "You still love her?"

"You don't quit loving someone just because you stop living with her."

"Do you love her?"

"Of course I love her."

"Then ask the poor girl to marry you."

"Marie, we tried that."

Last year Nina and I took a stab at getting married. We sailed through the pre-Cana grilling by Marie's priest, a dapper young fellow with high, obliquely angled, razor-sharp sideburns. I lied and claimed to be Roman Catholic. Nina and I promised to raise all ten of our children in the Church. Father Mike signed off on the application. Little Flower published the banns. The invitations went out. Then, a couple of months before the wedding, we bailed out. I'm not sure if it was marriage per se that suddenly seemed too daunting or the Catholic wedding itself. I must confess to an aversion to priests that dates back at least to the first time I saw *Aïda*.

Marie takes a final swallow of beer. "If you want to know what I think, I think you should ask her again."

I shake my head. "It won't work. Nina swears that she isn't getting married for another five years."

Marie rolls her eyes; even behind the sunglasses the gesture is apparent. "What planet were you born on, Jack? *All* women want to get married. They want a man to sweep them off their feet right now and carry them off on a white horse."

"Is that what happened to you?"

She leans forward and whispers, "I *had* to get married, and we'll leave it at that." She shakes her head. "We had to scramble to get Richey, Sr., into the Church before I was showing. God, what madness." Her lip catches on an eyetooth and she smiles ferociously. "A bottle of Chianti, a dozen red roses, a little Sinatra," she adds quietly. A quick burst of cafeteria origami has transformed a paper napkin into the shape of a manger.

"And then what?"

"Then you talk to Father Mike."

"Again?"

"You didn't finish the job."

At one point during my conversation with Father Mike, he started pressing me for details about my sex life. He wanted to know if I had ever masturbated, and Nina tried to interject a note of levity into the discussion by saying, "You mean *how often* don't you, Father?" And I said, "Look, Mike, I'll tell you if you tell me." He blushed to his sideburns and labored to explain that he didn't have any *personal* interest in this information. It was just that couples sometimes have difficulty dealing with such *personal* issues. But given the ease with which the two of us talked about this, er, subject, he figured we didn't, so maybe we could just move on to the next question: "Jack, what does it mean to you to be a soldier of Christ?"

"Talk to me," says Marie.

Why am I so determined to postpone confirmation of the obvious? Am I afraid of the emasculating nature of the specific words that will soon be uttered? Do I fear that I might go off the deep end like Renato in *Un Ballo in Maschera*? No, it's stranger than that. Weirder. Sitting here with the Source, I can feel Nina's presence. For this reason alone I want this scene to drag out all afternoon. I want to feel wounded or jealous or vengeful—I'm hoping it's the latter. Right now I don't feel much of anything but a vague scrotal uneasiness. You see, I had a hydrocele corrected when I was a kid. The operation was a success, but I was left with scar tissue that always seems to announce its presence in anticipation of bad news. It is my emotional barometer.

"Jackie, I'm depending on you," Marie says. "Talk some sense into that girl. *Please.*"

I have no doubt that Marie and Nina love each other, but you wouldn't know this to see them together. They argue constantly. About art, religion, politics, the meaning of life, a woman's role in the family, you name it. Lately, the childbearing issue has gotten very hot. Marie takes Nina's refusal to settle down—that is, marry and produce a houseful of kids—as a personal affront. What's worse, she is convinced that this stance is a clear sign that Nina is headed for trouble. "Maybe you don't know it," Marie remarked to me during a tête-à-tête in the pantry some years ago, "but Angie's the sort of girl who could end up in a tragedy."

Visions of Anna Karenina throwing herself under the train filled my head. I knew that Nina was impulsive, but was she *unbalanced?* It took months—nay, years—before I had a sure enough grasp of the Laurentian tongue to realize that a woman "ends up in a tragedy" when she reaches age thirty unwed. Marie holds with Rigoletto's view that disaster is certain to strike any attractive young woman who allows herself to be guided by the stirrings of her own heart. Add to this scenario that the young woman in question lives alone in a dangerous metropolis, and she must certainly be doomed.

Marie drums the Formica. "Let's get down to brass tacks, Jack. What do we do about this unfortunate turn of events?"

I am actively avoiding her gaze.

"Give me your hand," she says.

I do so with great reluctance. Marie runs her fingertips across my palm and repeats the question. Hooked into a foolproof Calabrian lie detector, I can't dissemble. So I take a different tack. "Are we talking about Nina?"

"Have we spent the past forty-five minutes talking about Lady Di?"

"I've spoken to Nina once in the last two months. Yesterday. Mostly what we talked about was my coming to see you."

"And why do you suppose that I asked to see you?"

"I have a clue—"

"Thank God."

"But it's none of my business. Not anymore."

Marie addresses the fluorescent tubes: "He admits that he loves my little girl, but who she is seeing is none of his business." The sword buried in my breast, she heads back to the food line. In a moment she returns with coffee and a wiggly slice of lemon meringue pie. Dropping into her seat, she says, "Jack, this is not a good match."

"How serious is it?"

"Angie brought him to the *house* last weekend." Marie consumes half the pie in one bite.

A vein in my forehead begins to thump.

"Um, anybody we know?"

She motions to her mouth with a fork, not that a mouthful of food has ever stopped her from talking before. Finishing, she says, "A fancy-pants lawyer, of all things."

"Marie, your *son* is a lawyer."

"Richey, Jr., has been a stranger to me since the day he left for Charlottesville."

"Okay, besides practicing law, what else is wrong with this guy?"

She squirms. She does a little air dance with her fork. Finally, she says, "He's not from the area."

The way she says this makes it sound like he's from Beirut, but a bit of probing reveals that Nina's new paramour hails from Short Hills, New Jersey.

"Do I know him?"

"In this town you've seen a thousand like him."

John's Place is empty. A woman is shifting tables to open up lanes for the evening dart-throwing crowd. The source of Marie's discontent is suddenly clear to me. I rear up on my elbows and whisper, "Let me guess. He's not a Catholic."

Marie begins to rock. Her bosom trembles. She crushes a wadded-up hanky to her nose. O faithless offspring who make alliances with the sons of Shem! I help her to her feet and we stagger outside into bright yellow sunlight.

"He's never set *foot* inside a Catholic church," she whispers. "He won't. On principle, he tells me. Not until he gets an apology from the Pope. For what? I ask. For something that happened almost fifty years ago. *Fifty years!* Jack, what kind of a world would we live in if everyone held grudges for fifty years?" I steer her toward the wheelchair ramp and we stumble into the parking lot. "He comes from a broken home," she adds.

"Marie, I come from a broken home, too."

"Your parents had troubles," she says sharply. "His have psychological problems. *Both* of them remarried psychiatrists."

When Marie grips my arm as we plod across the hot, spongy asphalt and says, "Trust me, it just won't work," she is admitting that a good Italian mama like herself stands as much a chance of converting Nina's new beau as she would a drawerful of *australes*. With the soul of Jack the Unbaptized, on the other hand, there is still room for the miracle of prayer.

We stand at the door of Marie's boat-sized Ford Toronado.

The green metallic paint is pitted with rust, making it look as if the car has been raked by machine-gun fire. I reach through the open window and unlock the door.

"You know something, Jack? There are some men in the world who would take news like this as a personal insult."

"It's her life, Marie."

"So it's the Pontius Pilate routine." She faces a large blue dumpster across the lot. "God gave him a pair of hands and he has decided to sit on them. Beautiful."

A truck exiting the parking lot climbs a long incline. In the rumble of its engine I can hear the first notes of the basso profundo strain of the Marie theme. Bile suddenly rises in my throat. Either I'm hopping mad or my stomach is having trouble digesting the raft of purple bacon I've just consumed. I take a deep breath.

It's not the bacon.

Marie has me in her pocket. The tight smile playing at the corner of her lips as she settles in behind the huge steering wheel indicates that she knows she's got me in her pocket.

"Let's get on with it," I say. "Give me a name."

Her cunning expression all but whispers, "I have seen Desdemona's handkerchief in Cassio's hand lately." But when she speaks, she feigns indignance. "Upon my word, Jack Townsend! I'm sure I've said too much already. After all, this isn't any of my business, either."

O Iago, dressing now in a red-checkered kerchief!

MAD SCENES

Sometime after midnight I see myself creeping along a hedge outside Nina's apartment. I study the play of light and shadow in her window and learn absolutely nothing. What am I doing here? Hoping to get a make on the new fellow? Planning to scare the wits out of everyone in the neighborhood? Later I am in a fencing class. Bright lights, mirrored walls, padded floor with a light dusting of talcum powder. The other students stand planted like young oaks, sparring with the effort it would take to whisk an egg white. Not me. I'm all over the place, howling like a Marine. I wake up shooting foul shots with my brother, Ray. He's at the line; I stand beneath the net and feed him the ball. Ray is a solid kid with a lock of sandy hair hanging across his forehead. His face wears a faintly ironic smirk to let me know that he is the master of this situation. He can't miss:

34 . . . 35 . . . 36 in a row. "The secret," he tells me, the older brother who can't shoot free throws to save his life, "is to shoot with your legs. And don't give a damn. The instant you start to care, you're sunk. End of lesson, John." He is imitating our father and has captured the nasal quality of the voice so well I have to smile: 46 . . . 47 . . . 48 in a row.

I can't bring myself to open my eyes.

Reason tells me to let Nina go, but my heart says baloney to that, and for once I am certain that my heart is right. It is. It really is. I still love this woman. I miss her. I miss the sound of her voice and the smell of her skin and the sex beneath a crucifix as big as an aircraft carrier. *O soave fanciulla!* I miss our life together. I miss the evening reports on the latest tremor rocking the Lawrence household. I miss the beeswax candle that Nina would burn on Catholic holy days. I miss her Virgin Mary collection and the frosty box of Mrs. Paul's fish sticks that she keeps at the back of the freezer like a spiritual first-aid kit.

My sister would not in a thousand years understand my current frame of mind. Ellen and I are sprung from the same genetic supermarket, but from different aisles altogether: she is Lean Cuisine and flavored seltzer water; I'm Gravy Train and bulk laundry detergent. Ellen refuses to accept this difference in our characters, which goes a long way toward explaining why she sends me a postcard nearly every week, a Matisse cutout or a big-bottomed Degas *fille* with a tidy aphorism scribbled on the back in Ellen's loopy hand: "Plain cooking cannot be entrusted to plain cooks." Or: "What they call 'heart' is located far lower than the fourth waistcoat button." Or, opposite the reproduction of one of Thomas Eakins's weary rowers that arrived in yesterday's mail: "There are few sorrows, however poignant, in which a good income is of no avail."

To reinforce these messages, Ellen invites me to her elegant Victorian home every few weeks for lunch and a chat. Inevitably, we end up talking about what Ellen calls my "lifestyle." My lifestyle troubles her. For one thing, she finds it disturbing that I'm always free for lunch. If I was serious about my landscaping business, I would spend lunch hours rustling up new clients or badgering bank officers for a loan to open a branch office in Potomac. (Never mind that I don't have a *main* office.) I would dress like a businessman (my wardrobe favors khaki) and carry a bulging leather-bound appointment book instead of jotting my schedule on the backs of tattered envelopes.

This morning the Cleveland Park chautauqua includes Ellen and me and Mrs. Stubbs, her housekeeper. The kids are at a play group. Evan is down on K Street, multiplying his net worth. The chicken is boneless and skinless; the wine white, Californian, and cold. The conversation is one we've had a thousand times, but with all the enthusiasm my big sister brings to it, I wouldn't dare make an attempt to change the subject. Often I come away from these discussions with the feeling that Ellen should be out there directing my crew and cutting deals for me, and I should stay at home raising her children. Her interest in the vicissitudes of the lawn-care industry seems inexhaustible.

She aligns knife and fork on the plate, then presses a napkin to her lips. "Did you see the real estate page this morning? Housing units are way up in northern Virginia. They're building like crazy in Vienna. Why not set up shop there?"

"I get lost every time I cross the Potomac."

"Hon," she says gently, "there are maps."

"The point is, I don't want any more work. I'm booked solid for the next three months."

"Sounds like it's time to hire a few more people and expand the operation."

"And I get to spend my days in traffic going from job to job. No thank you."

"That would be temporary. Once things were running smoothly you could hire someone to sit in traffic for you."

"And what would I do?"

"Look into franchising?"

T-shirts, videos, a line of gardening tools, Jack Townsend salad dressing—if Ellen were running this show I'd have an 800 number and a thirty-second commercial running constantly on late night TV. How can I convince her that I like my life the way it is? I enjoy my work. I'm learning Spanish and putting away a tidy sum at the end of every month. Adolfo and his four brothers and I are recognized as one of the top landscaping crews in the city. "Hire Adolfo's uncles and cousins and nephews and make it a *better* crew," Ellen would say. "Isn't that what America is all about?"

"Dearheart," says Mrs. Stubbs, the lilt of Jamaica rolling off her tongue. "You must lairn to listen to your sister. She is con-cairned wit' your welfare. You can't keep keeping on as you have been going, wit'out a thought about the future. It's time you had a family. But tell me, dearheart, how are you going to suppart a family in this expainsive town?"

Ellen and Mrs. Stubbs have a program for me. If only they could persuade me to shave every day and get serious about a real job (glass-box office, generous benefits, the prospect of a six-figure salary), start a family, and enter into a long-term relationship with a federally insured bank. If only I would open a charge account with Arthur Adler, buy a silver Volvo, and sign up for season tickets with the National Symphony Orchestra and Arena Stage—not the Washington Opera, mind you.

My love of opera worries Ellen. That I came to this passion while living with Nina only reinforces her conviction that opera glorifies the lives of unbalanced people. She can't get past the stories. Last year I took her to see *Manon Lescaut* and she came out of the theater saying: "In act one, the heroine falls in love and elopes. But by the next act she's living with a different man in Paris. Then she gets arrested and she and the first beau are shipped to New Orleans, where they both die. The end." She turned to me and with a straight face said, "Hon, it just seemed so unnecessary."

Ray would have hated opera but applauded my love for it.

Opera, it turns out, is just the tonic that he was always trying to prescribe for me. "Just pay attention to how something makes you feel and what you think about it won't make a damn bit of difference," he once said. This from a kid of sixteen.

A few months ago Ellen and I went to see a Georgia O'Keeffe exhibit at the East Wing of the National Gallery. Room after room of colors exploding off the walls. Nina's artwork is nothing like O'Keeffe's. Her paintings tend to be finely drawn, richly colored figures of toys or household objects set up in such a way as to please the eye at first, then disturb. Last fall Ellen bought one of Nina's paintings, a piece called *Bienvenido*. It's a view of the inside of a kitchen drawer: carrot peeler, corkscrew, a bag of twisties that look like dried pasta, nutcracker, cheese slicer turned sideways, garlic press with a few whiskers of garlic, barbecue skewers bound like a quiver of arrows, melon baller in the knife slot. The whole thing is very realistic.

But gaze at that painting for a while and it puts you off balance. The drawer is pulled out too far. Or it's too full. And it seems alive, like a drawerful of bugs. I lived with that scene for seven months and I still can't pin down what makes it so affecting. Ellen raved about the painting at the show and bought it on the spot. She told Nina that she thought it was "gritty" and announced that she would hang it in her kitchen. A week later I received a summons to Cleveland Park. "Honestly, Jack, I thought you were on my side. You really should have warned me. I've had this painting in my house for exactly six and one-half days, and I can't bear to look at it anymore. This is not a happy picture."

At the East Wing, Ellen would gaze for a moment at one of O'Keeffe's southwestern landscapes and then shake her head sadly. "Hon, do you think it was worth it? I mean her going off to live by herself in the desert and all? She wasn't much to be around from what I've heard."

I got the message.

The comparison isn't fair but I knew better than to try to

argue this point with Ellen. God only knows what prompted O'Keeffe to paint. As for Nina, I have always sensed that the time she spends at the easel satisfies a lost religious impulse. She once told me that painting kept her sane. At heart, she is a self-doubter and a worrier. Without art these destructive impulses would probably claim her soul and she would feel compelled to guide her life according to the tenets laid out in the *Washington Post* Personal Finance insert, or those insidious life insurance commercials showing young couples joshing around and then being sternly reminded that life is not a humorous business: the only thing that gives meaning to our earthly existence, admonishes the voice of God, is the accumulation and protection of capital. Nina picked up this particular worry from her mother, who often behaves as if she were put on this earth to act out the last scene of some Ellis Island tragedy. Next to the Bible (blessed by Pius XII) on Marie's bedstand sits the latest U.S. Labor Department Occupational Outlook Survey (blessed by Alan Greenspan, I suppose).

The combination of a good income and steadily accruing, well-diversified assets are as important to Marie as seeing her daughters wed in a Catholic church. Thus, Nina's oddly affecting painting of a kitchen drawer, which brought $500, doesn't hold a candle in Marie's mind to the books Nina designs for the National Geographic Society. In fact, that Nina insists on calling herself an artist is something of an embarrassment to Marie—as if, say, Richey, Jr., the lawyer, were to spend his weekends in the backyard working on a split-fingered fastball and talking up his chances of getting a tryout with the Orioles.

Still, Marie could suffer greater embarrassments than these. The conversion of one of her own to Judaism, for example.

Downtown, the wind has picked up. A white plastic bag sails into traffic at Dupont Circle. On 17th Street, the leaves on a row of lindens are flipping like pinwheels. This is the first late-summer day with a hint of autumn in the air. Women in sleeveless dresses hurry down the sidewalk clutching their arms. A uniformed man stands at the door of a tour bus, tapping a walkie-talkie against his leg. I am parked in the no-parking zone in front of the National Geographic Society when Nina comes through the polished bronze doors. Heads turn as she descends the steps, arms swinging, every bit the vision of a lanky, lovely Palestinian in checkered kaffiyeh, bomber jacket, black tights, and black Reebok hightops.

My first inclination is to roll down the passenger window, crank up the Grand March from *Aïda,* and stop her in her tracks. But I don't. It isn't necessary. Nina spots me right away and her posture changes instantly. A complicated smile comes to her face as she approaches the van. Dan is in the front seat now, his tail slapping molto scherzando against my arm.

"Well," she says. "Hello."

"Um, good morning."

Her expression grows a bit wary. "Jack, I don't want to get into a fight or anything right off, so please don't tell me that you just happened to be in the neighborhood."

"I was on my way—"

"Marie called this morning at six A.M. to tell me that she had a wonderful, wonderful conversation with you yesterday but wouldn't give me a clue as to what it was about."

"She drilled me. I'm lucky to be alive."

"The two of you are as thick as thieves, and if you want know the honest-to-God truth, I don't care."

"Not even a little bit?"

She turns away.

"Actually I'm here because it's time to pay a visit to the world's largest frog suspended in the world's largest jar of formaldehyde."

"It's off display," she says.

"I'm here for the 'People of the Mud' exhibit?"

She gives me her sideways skeptical expression.

"Okay, I'm here because I am hoping to talk you into inviting Dan and me to your place for lunch, and if that doesn't work, to ask you to help me take on a lady in Georgetown who has begun to put up a fight to save a hydrangea."

"I'm sorry, Jack."

"I'll pay you this time."

"It's not that."

"Please don't make me beg."

"Then don't lean on me," she says wearily. "Look, they've about got me chained to my desk. I've got deadlines hanging over me like the Sword of Damocles."

"You're freelance; they don't own you."

"Not yet."

"Not *yet?*"

She studies the Coal Association building across the street. "There's an opening on the magazine. I put in an application."

"Nina!" (Full-time at NGS means death to art!)

"I know, Jack, I know. But right now I could really use the extra cash and the benefits package."

"Excuse me?" Never in my life have I heard this woman use the term "benefits package."

"Knock it off with the sarcasm, okay?"

"Sorry."

"No you're not."

"Okay, I'm not. But please tell me that you don't want this job."

"I just might," she says.

She doesn't. A woman serious about a permanent position at National Geographic does not dress like she just got back from an interview with the PLO.

"Nina, I know it's none of my business, but as an old friend I feel obligated to remind you that it was just last spring that you said that you would submit to torture before you would take a full-time job inside Mao's tomb."

She expels all the air from her lungs in one great disbelieving *huff.* I am on thin ice now. The shouting could commence at any moment: packed into Nina's slender frame is the distilled temper of three centuries of Calabrian peasants. To tell the truth, I am pushing her. I miss those outbursts. When Nina screams it means she cares.

Softly, she says, "Well, you're right. It is absolutely none of your business."

With that, she turns on her heels and heads up 17th Street. When she darts across M Street, I follow, a foot on the brake as we move together separated by a line of parked cars. Nina walks with a loose, rolling gait.

A half block farther, I call out, "Does the fact that you haven't said anything about lunch mean that I'm invited?"

Her eyes stay straight ahead.

"Maybe we should head out to Little Flower and light some candles. Is Matthew the patron saint of employment—or does he just take care of CPAs?"

Her shoulders drop. She slows.

"Or is it Saint Luke? He handles artists, which would probably include graphic designers, right?"

Eyes ahead, she calls, "Would you please tell me why it is that every time you have a conversation with Marie, you come away sounding like you were raised in a monastery?"

"You're asking *me?*"

"I haven't been to Mass in over seven and a half months. I forgot everything I ever knew."

"Patron saint of barren women, lost articles, and the poor?"

"Antony of Padua."

"Midwives and the falsely accused?"

"Raymund Nonnatus. Knock it off."

"Happy death, carpenters, and real estate sales?"

"Saint Joseph. Jack, everybody in the *world* knows that." She picks up the pace; we've reached idle speed. Her arm is swinging like a metronome.

"Who was pope before John the Twenty-third?"

"Pius the Twelfth."

"And before him?"

"I haven't a clue."

"Take a guess."

"Pius the Eleventh?"

"Bravo! Before him?"

We are stopped at the corner in front of the B'nai B'rith building. Nina comes to the window. "Okay, Saint John the Divine, dazzle me."

I cut the engine and take a breath: "Benedict the Fifteenth, Pius the Tenth, Leo the Thirteenth, Pius the Ninth, Gregory the Sixteenth, Pius the Eighth, Leo the Twelfth, Pius the Seventh and the Sixth, Clement the Fourteenth, Clem the Thirteenth, Benny the Fourteenth, Clem the Twelfth, Benny the Thirteenth, Innocent the Thirteenth—"

"What year are we at?

"1721."

"You're a nut. You're a complete nut." She muscles Dan into the back of the van and climbs in beside me. "I have to know one thing. Did you memorize the popes of the last two hundred years in order to impress me?"

"Four hundred years. But it wasn't just to impress you. Catholicism is my avocation. You know that. Why do you think I read Joyce and attempt to train Dan according to the rules laid down by the monks of New Skete?"

It's true. Shortly after I met Nina I took it upon myself to read the Bible cover to cover. I wanted to understand the Lawrencian dinner table quips and allusions (once her sister Anna mentioned the Infant of Prague and I thought she was talking about a new punk band). For months I assumed that the Assumption of the Virgin Mary referred to a miraculous inference. When sister Liza mentioned visiting the Capuchin House, I thought she was talking about a trip to the National Zoo. Anyway, Marie caught wind of my ecclesiastical studies and has decided that I will turn out like Saint Paul, made devout when God knocked him off his horse on the road to Damascus. Which in my case means I'll probably get rear-ended on Route 270 on the way to a tree farm in Damascus, Maryland.

The engine cranks for a few moments, then roars to life.

Nina says, "I take it it went okay yesterday?"

"Piece of cake."

"Thanks a lot, Jack."

"No problem."

At Massachusetts Avenue, a Latino woman in a full-length fur coat stands on the front steps of the Peruvian Embassy with a tough-looking hombre at her side. His fierce expression and the cords of muscle that wrap around his neck suggest that he would welcome the opportunity to defend this lady from a cadre of *Sendero Luminoso*. You see this sort of scene up and down Embassy Row: the guards at the Turkish embassy alert for vengeful Armenians, the Brits keeping an eye out for murderous Irishmen, the South Africans watching everybody.

Nina says, "So what exactly did Marie want?"

"The usual. Cut-rate azaleas, peace from her children, my eternal soul."

"That's it?"

"More or less."

We pass a black man with a white beard carrying a backpack fashioned from a plastic garbage bag. He wears a tattered army jacket and is pulling a two-wheeled shopping basket. Walking in front of him is a young white guy with a black bag slung from his shoulder. Nina and I roll along in silence. Her eyebrows are knit. It would seem that the tacit luncheon invitation requires as a quid pro quo a full report of yesterday's gossip.

"As I understand it, Marie seems to have worked herself into a panic over the fact that she has another daughter on the cusp of thirty without marriage prospects. She thinks I ought to make you an honest woman."

"Oh, God. She swore up and down that she had gotten past all that. She promised me, Jack. I can't trust a thing she says anymore. What did she say? Was she rough?"

"I touched her up a little, but she finally knocked me down in the sixth round."

"What did you say?"

"The usual obsequious stuff."

"I don't believe that for a second."

"Basically I said that you are a big girl and I am a big boy and we are entitled to screw up our respective lives if that's what we choose."

"And what did she say to that?"

"Not much. I think she's planning to get Nonna working on us."

"That's it. That's the last straw. Never again. I'm really sorry, Jack."

Passing the familiar trees and wrought-iron fences and parked cars and real estate signs that constitute my old block, I can't help but add, "Me, too."

I climb the steps to Nina's third-floor apartment and get to thinking about the living room as I left it: the bucket seat that tips backwards almost to the floor, the huge black walnut coffee table I bought from a high school friend who drifted off to work in the coal mines of West Virginia and came back a wood-carver, Nina's mammoth print cabinet wedged between the two bookshelves I built from scrap oak, a love seat with torn armrests that always reminded me of a weight-lifter with bulging biceps.

The place is clean, too clean. The print cabinet, once a sacred repository of dust and fingerprints, gleams with lemon-scented polish. A beautiful old quilt covers the tattered love seat. The bookshelves have been stained a somber brown. The monstrous coffee table is gone. In its place is a functional little rosewood table with a glass top that Dan nearly knocks apart with a sweep of the tail. He races around his old home, his nose to the parquet floor.

I follow in much the same frame of mind. Only I am making an effort to look nonchalant.

I take a peek into the front closet, looking for an unfamiliar coat (brand-new wooden hangers, of all things!), scan the bathroom for a second toothbrush (nope), or whiskers in the sink (not a chance—even the mirror, lightly stuccoed in my day, now gleams). Using little more than strong detergent and a new design scheme, Nina has made this place her own. Dan noses open the door to the small patio and I see a miniature white table and four chairs where once sat a scarred old church pew. *Addio, del passato!*

I crack the door to Nina's studio. It's a mess, a wonderfully reassuring mess. Against my better judgment, I step into the bedroom—Nina's bedroom, I remind myself, though the faint scent of Dr. Bronner's almond soap tells me that I am home. I don't want Nina to pick up my wistful state of mind. She has unfailing intuition for such emotional slips. I am speaking here of matrilineal Calabrian voodoo. As a girl, Nina apprenticed herself to her grandmother, who instructed her in the fine art of tuning the left ear to tingle whenever someone was talking about you. She couldn't have found a better teacher. The redoubtable Nonna Romano (née Strepponi) has mastered this ear-tingling technique to the extent that she can tell you the sex of the speaker and whether the conversation is taking place in the New World or the Old.

"Jack? Everything okay?" The call comes from the kitchen.

"Fine. You have somebody coming in to clean?" No answer. "Nina?"

"Salad and bread okay with you?"

"Wonderful."

Dan emerges from beneath the bed carrying an old toy, a red rubber doughnut. He shoots past me into the living room.

"Help yourself to a beer if you want it," Nina says.

I open the fridge to a six-pack of St. Pauli Girl. To think that once the occupants of this household were satisfied with Rolling Rock!

The telephone rings. Nina lunges for it and moves into the hallway. "Yes, yes," I hear her whisper. The bedroom door closes. I gnaw on a stick of celery. Freelance designer that she is, it's entirely possible that she has disappeared into the bedroom because she doesn't want me to overhear a banal conversation about the logo for a stock-fund newsletter or the cover-photo possibilities for a trade association annual report. That's what I would like to think. But another part of my brain considers that Nina might be chatting with a breezy gent who she met on the subway and who is now hitting her up for cappuccino at Kramerbooks.

Dan leans into my leg to be petted. "Where is she?" I whisper. "Where's Nina? Go see her." He trots into the hallway and knocks open the bedroom door. "Sure," I hear her say. "That's fine. Let's talk then. Ciao." She hangs up the phone and is soon lifting Dan off his front paws by the scruff of his neck, gently shaking him. He goes limp; his head rolls to the side, tongue lolling from his open mouth.

I stand in the kitchen doorway, sipping another man's beer, madly considering the many ways to read Nina's use of the word "ciao." She is at the counter, chopping vegetables. Her shoulders the picture of tension, she takes thin slices from a fat carrot with a precise yet ferocious stroke that leaves a hollow, damaged sensation somewhere below my fourth waistcoat button.

"Place looks great," I say.

Not a sound, not even a sigh. All my comments about the look of the apartment have been received as disapproval. (An *artiste* with a clean abode is no *artiste* at all!) That I haven't said a word about the paintings lined up in the hallway means I don't like them. That I am not giving her a full account of yesterday's *scena e duetto* with Marie means I have something to hide.

"I ran into Joanie at your folks' place," I say.

"Talked to her last night." Chop, chop, chop; shoulders riding up around the ears. "She went on and on about what a wonderful guy you are, Jack."

"I guess there's always a chance she might be right."

"Hmm."

Nina pulls dishes from a cupboard, two placemats from the top of the refrigerator, knives and forks from a drawer. She shoots past me carrying a tray.

We sit in silence on the porch, perched like game show contestants on those wobbly little chairs. Dan barks the whole time at a cat spread out on the roof of a pickup truck across the street. Notwithstanding Ellen's Chicken Dijonnaise resting in my stomach like a small pile of stones, I eat with an appetite, tearing off hunks of bread to mop up the dressing. Throughout the meal, Nina gazes at something far beyond the most distant rooftop.

"So when do you hear about the new job?"

"Next week, the week after."

"I'll keep my fingers crossed."

She sighs. "To tell you the truth, a new job is probably the last thing I need right now."

"There's no law that says you have to take it."

She regards the ragged tips of her fingernails. "You'd think this was the last design job on the planet the way everyone around me is carrying on about what an opportunity it is."

"Not everyone."

A smile. A small blessed smile.

"Don't forget that in a pinch, you could be planting dogwoods tomorrow. Big bucks digging holes."

A grin!

"I'm up to my eyeballs with that place, Jack. It's gotten so much worse."

"How could it get any worse?"

"The money starts drying up, the intrigue gets smellier, the old men at the top don't retire."

"So what's the hurry to get back there this afternoon?"

"Duty," she intones.

I frown.

"Okay, okay. Guilt or some other ridiculous feeling."

"Fresh air is the only cure for that."

She rolls her eyes. "How long in Georgetown?"

"You'll do it?"

"Depends."

Suddenly I can see a long blissful afternoon stretching before me like the scene on a medieval tapestry. "Thirty minutes. If it goes longer than forty you have permission to throw an artistic temper tantrum and storm out."

"No English," she says.

"I'll introduce you as Contessa Pignoli."

She smiles. "And then what?"

This is an old game of ours. Nina wants the afternoon scenario laid out before her like a bouquet of roses. She wants to savor the details.

We will repair to the van. Dan will scramble atop a dented metal cooler and hang his head out Nina's window. On P Street, he will bark ferociously at the statue of Taras Shevchenko, bard of the Ukraine, executed in the grand neo-Fascist style. Entering Georgetown, he will sigh deeply as we pass one of his favorite Frisbee fields. Mrs. Dalton will meet me in jodhpurs and riding boots at the tradesmen's entrance of her N Street mansion. She will shrink into the shadows when Nina emerges from the van wearing red sunglasses, red silk scarf and white shirt, red lipstick, and black leather pants. Even that nervous little dog of hers with the terrific underbite will be cowed to silence as we make our way through the sunroom to the garden. The hydrangea is history. There will be no arguments about my plans for a low stone wall and a fish pond. The first mention of rhododendrons and day lilies will bring a quick nervous nod. Mrs. D. will sign her maiden name to the deposit check by mistake. Afterward, Nina and I will stroll over to Cyclepro on M Street and test ride a couple of $800 Cannondale touring bikes. We will pedal across Key Bridge toward the magic kingdom of Rosslyn. Heading west, Nina will ride in front of me, the wind in her hair, her long torso hovering over the handlebars and compact derrière floating above the gel-cap seat. *O don fatale!*

"And then what?"

"We return the bikes and drive out to the Palisades and you spend the afternoon at my place."

She frowns.

"Painting," I say.

The frown doesn't budge.

"Huge living room. Floor-to-ceiling windows looking down on the Potomac. Incredible light."

There is a flicker of interest in her coal black eyes.

"Painting," she says.

"You know, you dip a small brush into different colors, and stroke the color on a gessoed canvas."

"You know I can't just pick up the canvas I'm working on like it's a suitcase and carry it across town," she says with some irritation.

"Then we'll come back here."

"I don't want to come back here."

"Then we'll go to my place and not paint."

"Well," she says slowly, "that won't work either."

"Why not?"

"Because of *Beasts*, for one thing."

"Beasts?"

"*Our Amazing Beasts of the Jungle*. A new pop-up book. This afternoon I'm supposed to make some sketches of a chimpanzee swinging across the center spread."

"You can do it at my place. I'll be your model."

Her lips purse.

"I guess it would seem a little sleazy if I started carrying on now about Hank and Sylvia's sound system and their devotion to La Divina."

Nina is on me like Sparafucile in the last act of *Rigoletto*. "What do they have?"

"Only the latest reissue of *everything: Lucia, Tosca, La Gioconda, La Trav, La Bohème*—this morning I was listening to a collection of some of Callas's great mad scenes."

"Jack!"

"Of course, most of it's mono."

"Remastered CDs?"

I nod.

Nina bites her lower lip. "I'd love to. I really would. I'd like to see where you're living." She stops. "But I shouldn't."

"Shouldn't?"

"I can't," she says.

Can't I can accept, but *shouldn't?* Shouldn't is not a reference to time that must be spent sketching chimps swinging in a cardboard jungle. Shouldn't is not work-related at all. Shouldn't is an expression of doubt about the wisdom of the two of us passing a quiet afternoon in an empty house with double beds on every floor. Shouldn't is a word sprung from the imagination of someone who is considering issues unrelated to the size of my plate glass windows and the quality of afternoon sunlight.

"I just don't think so," says Nina.

And there the saga should end, a rather anemic finale to our little post-Verdian opera. No one is murdered, no one drinks poison or gets buried alive in an empty tomb or dies of consumption. No one even tries to throw himself from the top of the Washington Monument. At the electric moment in the last act of *Jack e Nina*, the set just goes dark, and the tenor and soprano wander off in different directions.

But suddenly Nina brightens. "You know, the *Beast* sketches aren't due till tomorrow afternoon. And the canvas I've been working on isn't going anywhere. Maybe this is exactly what I *need*. To start something new. I really would like to see where you and Danny are living. And it's a perfect day for a bike ride. And *La Bohème*, well—"

J. TOWNSEND DOES NOT ADVERTISE

The day after Nina and I split up, Ellen started pressing me to rent a bachelor efficiency in one of those grand old apartment buildings on upper Connecticut Avenue. She said she was worried about me living alone. This way I could pop over for dinner at the last minute, see the kids, prune the trees, whatever. Actually, I think she wanted me close so that she could keep an eye on me, which was exactly what I *didn't* need at that moment. I telephoned around and found a friend who happened to know that friends of a friend were leaving that very week for a month in the Camargue. These folks were looking for a baby-sitter for their Vietnamese pot-bellied pig. Thus, June found me swimming laps beneath the stars in a twenty-five-meter pool in

McLean, while Dan and little Ho policed the squirrels and each other across four rolling acres of Virginia thicket and scrub.

July and August I would spend in my father's Watergate condo while he passed the hot months of the summer breaking in a pair of cowboy boots in Jackson Hole. But Dan and I bailed out after a month. There was something oppressive about that apartment. It was too quiet, for one thing. The air was stale. Nothing except toast has ever been cooked there, and the place smelled like a dry-cleaning plant run by a man addicted to Honduran cigars. Then there was the book collection, which must have come with the place—titles like *Our Man in Kinshasa, The Castro-Abu Nidal Connection,* and *The Myth of Nelson Mandela.* The Watergate is a haven for out-to-pasture CIA agents and right-wing dowagers. I think Dan disliked the apartment even more than I did. He refused to sleep inside, spending hours on the balcony, gazing at the muddy edges of Theodore Roosevelt Island across the river.

So I spread the word that I was on the house-sitting circuit again and soon received a call from Sylvia Roper. It turned out that Sylvia and husband Hank Snow, professors of anthropology and music, respectively, were planning an autumn sabbatical in the hill country of northern Thailand. Their glass box on the Palisades needed a caretaker. That is, Sylvia was looking to find someone trustworthy, someone to regularly mist Hank's indoor rain forest and occasionally buff to a gloss the teak floors and the gaunt pieces of furniture carved from walnut and mahogany, someone to gaze at the stars through a telescope on the roof and dip into the eclectic Snow-Roper library of books and recordings—Gregorian chants, Pierre Boulez, and the largest collection of West African talking-drum music this side of Adams Morgan. (Not to mention the Callas recordings.) Also, the weirdly landscaped garden out front—my creation—needed a weekly hosing.

I couldn't refuse.

★   ★   ★

From outward appearances, you might be tempted to think of me as a personable gent who delivers loads of pine mulch and moves big rocks, but there is more to the story. I like to think of myself as an amateur psychologist. I plumb the psyches of my clients to uncover their personal vision of paradise—a perfect spot in the garden in which to read the Sunday *New York Times*, say. I am a detective. I study Grandma's garden in the family photo album. "You say you spent summers here?" "Every summer from the time I was four until I was married." I look closer.

I note the crafts that State Department families haul home from postings around the world. If need be, I will hunt up an Indonesian Buddha to complement the *wayang* puppets mounted behind the patio wet bar. Are these folks waterfall people? Do they long for the manicured ambience of a golf course? Would they be game to have their walled patio turned into a set for a Sergio Leone spaghetti western? Were the happiest years of their lives the two they spent at the consulate in Mandalay? Should I give them a New Hampshire woodland complete with burbling brook and the intoxicating scent of ferns? The rocky coast of Norway? The lush forest of the Mbuti? A Zen rock garden?

It was dumb luck in the form of a summer job that got me into the business of reorganizing people's lives via their outdoor space. It turned out that I was good at this line of work. Not that I'm particularly creative—I'm not. But I'm a good observer. And I'm good at deciding if what people say they want is what they need. I give them what they need. At least half my clients are among the newly divorced. They are starting over, and the healing process can't begin until they rip out the goddamn red maple that Harvey doted on, or put in the blessed roses that Maude would never let them have.

I like setting my own hours, and there are days when I even enjoy the theatrical aspects of the job. Basically, it's a con man's game. Image is everything. My van's exterior looks like a million bucks—I spent $1,500 on the paint job. The sides read J. TOWN-

SEND, LANDSCAPE ARCHITECT. Very classy lettering, courtesy of Nina. No telephone number, which lends an air of exclusivity to the enterprise. J. Townsend does not advertise, does not maintain an office, and his phone number changes every time he finds a new place to live. The inside of the van, on the other hand, is a mess—a disaster zone. There are bags of lime, bundles of sphagnum moss, a couple of orphaned cobblestones, a bale of damp, sour-smelling hay. Earlier in the summer a layer of dirt accumulated in the back, seeds sprouted, and Dan began to confuse my mobile terrarium with the great outdoors.

We seem to be back at that stage again.

At Hank and Sylvia's, Nina unloads a number of dirt-encrusted gardening tools from an apple crate and spends the next twenty minutes arranging the still life on a blue plastic tarp. I watch from a couch, peering over a coffee-table-sized book on Stravinsky. Her hair is pulled into a ponytail. She is dressed now in North Vietnamese Army regulation black pajamas and T'ai Chi slippers. Squatting, she brushes dirt into a pile, empties more dirt from a garbage bag. More still; it's so dry it pours like sugar. I am in awe of this woman: her concentration, the way she suddenly retreats into some deep part of herself. A hand axe here, a trowel there, a fork-tailed weeding jimmy standing upright beside a galvanized pail. She lays out the tools and regards the scene with a practiced eye. Perhaps I am witness to the birth of a gardening tool series—a Gardening Tool Period. Perhaps Nina and I will have to buy this house for the effect of September light on blue tarp and teak floor. We might end up living here for the rest of our lives.

I stand at the window beneath the canopy of a monstrous ficus and survey a great earthen mound in the front yard below. The shape of the mound came to Sylvia in a dream, and I was hired to haul in a couple of thousand cubic yards of topsoil to build it. I pleaded for an understated azalea hump, a dogwood knoll, a stand of stately birches, but Hank and Sylvia insisted on constructing what Nina has christened Mount Humpback, planted in jonquils and ivy and crowned with a furze of juniper. It is Sylvia's tribute to Mother Earth. She calls it her worship mound.

"Jack." I turn. The wind at Nina's back has her clothes fluttering like the tail of a kite. *"La Bohème,* please."

My legs go wobbly. I comply.

It is Christmas Eve. Marcello the painter and Rodolfo the poet are in their freezing garret, lamenting their never-ending money woes and the perfidy of women. To warm the room, Rodolfo sets ablaze the manuscript of his latest play. A friend arrives with firewood, wine, and a pocketful of coins. Next on the scene is the landlord looking for the rent, but he is plied with wine and sent packing. Soon everyone except Rodolfo heads off for a night of revelry. He sits down to write. A gentle knock interrupts his work.

Now, the tender Mimi theme. Maria Callas is singing. Nina is painting. I am upstairs on the bed reading *The Origin of Table Manners.*

The wind blows out Mimi's candle. Rodolfo comes to her rescue. Suddenly ill, Mimi faints in his arms. Rodolfo carries her into his room, sprinkles water on her face, and marvels at her beauty. Awake, she starts toward the door but drops her key. The wind blows out her candle a second time. The two of them are down on their hands and knees looking for the key when, lo and behold, the wind extinguishes Rodolfo's candle, too. He takes Mimi's hand in the darkness.

As Rodolfo launches into his great aria about Mimi's ice-cold hand, it occurs to me that Nina could have asked for *Boris Godunov* and painted late into the night. But she didn't. She wanted *La Bohème.* A fire has been smoldering beneath our feet all afternoon. A lunch of bread and salad and St. Pauli Girl, patio theater in Georgetown, bike riding through the concrete canyonland—now La Divina and Puccini.

With Mimi's key hidden in his pocket, Rodolfo sings that he is a poet whose wealth consists only of the richness of his imagination. He tells Mimi that her eyes have stolen his dreams and fantasies, but the loss is nothing now that he has found true love. Quietly he asks for her story.

"Mi chiamano Mimi," she sings. "I do not always go to Mass, but pray often to God. I live alone, all by myself up there, in a small white room: looking down on the roofs and up to heaven, and when the frost is gone, the sun's first rays greet me. Mine is the first kiss of April. I have a rosebud in a vase, and watch each petal unfold. How lovely is the perfume of a flower! But those I make, alas! . . . they have no scent. That is all I have to tell you: I am simply your neighbor, who comes unasked to bother you."

My eyes open in a darkened room as a shadowy figure moves past the foot of the bed and closes the door. Dan knocks it open and collapses beside the bed like a bag of bones. Nina appears beside me, a pale naked ghost, and places a hand over my mouth. Her fingers smell faintly of Varsol. I am instantly aroused. *O uomini! O natura!*

We have entered the no-talking zone. She climbs astride me and leans forward, our bodies still not touching at all. She opens my shirt, kisses my chin, my chest, my face. Callas's Mimi, standing in a flood of moonlight, sings in soaring phrases of her love for Rodolfo as my pants sail against a brocaded screen. "Let me look at you," I say, but Nina covers my eyes with her hands, settling atop me a moment later.

Sex with Nina is heightened by the knowledge that God— irascible old Yahweh—is watching. We taste the forbidden fruit, indulge ourselves in great mouthfuls, certain of our impending expulsion from the Garden. The prospect of eternal damnation powerfully concentrates the mind and other parts of the human anatomy. My world is reduced to a damp brow, flushed cheeks, lips that utter sounds that could honestly be mistaken for fragments of a prayer. I am calmed by the earthy smell of Nina's skin, the downy hair beneath her arms, the tiny mole on her back. She moves hardly at all. In the stillness I am gripped by the sensation that this bed—

and the house and the granite bedrock beneath it—rests upon what amounts to a particle of dust blowing through a wide empty universe.

Nina's eyes remain closed while we clumsily reverse positions. We pause to rest. I kiss her chin. She smiles. I move forward and kiss the tip of her nose. She grimaces, smiles again, bites my cheek. This is sex imitating the stations of the cross. We struggle along, collapse, and continue onward like two battle-weary Crusaders. In time Nina's legs lock around mine, immobilizing me, and I begin to rock. She sighs. Her arms encircle my neck and soon she begins to shudder. I feel an overwhelming sense of sadness when I am gripped by those same small explosions. Quickly, Nina slips from beneath me and disappears out the door.

She returns fully dressed and takes a seat beside me on the bed. My chest rises and falls. She lays a cool hand on my wrist and dabs my face with the corner of the bed sheet. Her gaze climbs the headboard to the teal-striped wallpaper above my head.

"You there?" she asks a moment later.

"Hmmmm."

"Something in one of the languages of Europe, please."

"Hoo, boy."

"Look at me."

I look. A hand grips the front of her long neck, a protective gesture. "Say something," she says.

With my mind trapped somewhere between the joy I felt cavorting like an amazing beast of the jungle and the sorrow of this sickroom scene, I can't think of a thing to say. What's worse, I hear in the heavy silence that hangs between us the first notes of the fate motif—a certain as-yet-unspoken conversation about a certain as-yet-unnamed interloper that is probably going to ruin my memory of this glorious afternoon.

"Did you hear me?"

"I was thinking."

"Oh, Jack," she says, standing. "Let's please save the sad stuff for when we're alone. I couldn't take that. Not now. Why can't we just have enjoyed it and let it go at that?"

Having grown tired of viewing me splayed across the bed like Caligula, she goes to the window and gazes out at the Confederate hills on the other side of the river. At last, she says, "Let's get some air. I'll bet Danny could use a walk."

In hearty endorsement of this suggestion, Dan drags a Frisbee into the room and thrashes the bedpost with it. Then he sits in the doorway and yawns. Finally I am moved to action. Nurse Lawrence averts her eyes as I hunt up my undershorts in the worship mound of clothing banked against the oriental screen. In the old days we would joke around at moments like this, but today we are silent.

Outside, Nina drapes an arm around my shoulders as we walk. It is the embrace of a war buddy. The fires of lust have been extinguished, and with them, the tension that has been buzzing around us all afternoon. For the first time in months, we can talk without fear of provoking an argument. I find this comforting until Nina gets carried away by this spirit of mature discussion and decides to fill me in on what she thinks are the good and bad aspects of our separation. It's apparent that she has been working on this list for some time. Overall, she thinks the decision to split was the right one. She is beginning to find herself—as a woman, an artist, a nearly-lapsed Catholic—but she still misses me; my sense of humor is singled out for particular praise. She admits that she has expected the tempestuous events of the past hour for some time. Had expected them sooner, in fact. Had wanted them. Had actually *dreamed* of them, ladies and gentlemen. I am pleased to report that I did not disappoint.

Now that we are fully dressed and walking with the sun on our backs, issues of human sexuality can be discussed in clinical detail: "What I like about sleeping with you, Jack, is that you let me be myself," says Nina, her head touching mine. "When I'm with you I feel good about who I am. You don't expect things of me. You don't judge me."

Condensation is beginning to collect inside my nylon jacket. I don't like the sound of this ringing praise one bit. As we climb to the playing field at Palisades Park, Dan wheeling and pivoting like a speedy wide-receiver, the question rattling at the front of my brain is this: Since I don't, who does?

Dan fixes on me like a wolf. He's cheating toward the grass, leaning into the field like a sprinter, a signal that he wants the Frisbee thrown. I flick my wrist and throw the disk at the instant he takes off. He runs a long parabola with his body low to the ground, eyes up, waiting for the Frisbee to pass over his head. Across the field, he pushes off his hind legs and snatches the disk from the air at the mouth of a soccer goal post. He thrashes it for a moment, then turns it around in his mouth for an easier carry and comes trotting back, swaggering like a boxing champ. He drops the Frisbee at Nina's feet. She tosses a wounded duck that Dan never sees. He wheels on his back legs, looking, looking. Bad throws disturb his equilibrium almost as much as a trip to the vet. I direct him to the disk and he brings it to me. We're a team: he knows my arm strength and I know his cuts. I can't overthrow him without having the wind at my back; still, he makes every catch into Willie Mays's rundown of Vic Wertz's drive to the center-field warning track.

I let go with a second toss and Dan thunders after it.

"Listen," I say noncommittally. *Very* noncommittally. "So what's new in your life these days?"

Nina suddenly wears a telltale crease of vexation between the eyes. "Marie told you, huh?"

"Well—"

"That woman!"

"Maybe you ought to tell me what you think she said."

"Oh Jack, we're not children."

"No."

"It was bound to happen to one of us."

"Or both," I say. A curveball, the crease vanishes. "So you fell in love and are now planning to live happily ever after."

"I'm just dating."

"As in, um, dating *around?*"

"Not really."

"Not really as in not yet or not planning to?"

"Jack, listen to yourself."

"Are you happy?"

She considers the question. "Happy enough, I suppose."

"Not head over heels?"

"I think I've gotten a little old for that."

"So who's the lucky fellow?"

"I don't really think that matters."

"Then why not say?" She looks away. "Somebody I know?"

"Is this really necessary?"

"Then I do know him."

Losing patience, Dan begins to whack the back of my legs with the Frisbee. I snatch it from his mouth and let go with a toss that takes him beyond the soccer goal.

Nina shades her eyes. "I'm sure Marie already told you, anyway."

"Why would I be standing here making an ass of myself if Marie had already told me?"

"Look, this isn't your business and it isn't her business. It's my business. And I prefer to keep it private. Which is my prerogative. Let's just leave it there, okay?"

"Have you slept with him?"

"No comment." There is a hitch in her voice.

"Yes or no?"

"For God's sake, Jack, knock it off with the third degree."

She storms away, shaking her head. I send Dan after several more Frisbee tosses, but when Nina crosses into the penalty area at the opposite end of the field, his sheep-herding genes suddenly kick in and he chases her down like a stray lamb. She returns to me with fire in her eyes.

"Just exactly what did Marie tell you?" she demands.

"That you've fallen in love with a fancy-pants lawyer."

"That's it?"

"That, and a certain conflict of faith."

"Christ! How do I get through to that woman that I don't want her sticking her nose into my life all the time?"

"You move to Papua, New Guinea, and get an unlisted telephone number."

"Jack, it's over between us, right?"

"That's what we keep telling each other."

"Then why are you trying to make me feel guilty?"

"About what?" I say sweetly.

She takes a seat on a long wooden bench. I sit beside her. For the grandmothers and Salvadoran nannies strolling past, we manage to shroud ourselves in the thinnest veil of civility.

"Back there," I say, "with Rodolfo and Mimi, just what was that about?"

"Oh, Jack, please don't ask me to explain that. I don't know what that was. Lust, I guess. Or monkey-business between two old friends. It seemed to make sense right then. Maybe it was a mistake."

"But this is serious? This is the big time?"

"I don't know."

This is the moment to walk, but I stay put. It is the moment to button my lips, and I decide to, but not before a short sarcastic line slips from the corner of my mouth. "Of all things, a lawyer."

Nina turns on me. "Just what exactly is your problem with lawyers, Jack?"

"How much time do you have?"

"Really, what is it? Are you jealous about the money? Is that it? Is it the money?"

I shrug. "A flea's envy of a tick."

"I *knew* you'd act like this."

"Act like what?"

"Like a jerk."

She has me there. I don't even try to defend myself.

She crosses her arms, haughty Hepburn-style. "I know what's bugging you," she says.

"You do?"

"Yes, I do. And you're not going to like what I have to say."

"Is this free advice or have we entered the realm of the billable hour?"

"We have entered the realm of unfinished business."

"As in unfinished *family* business?"

Her face softens.

"Oh, come on. This doesn't have anything to do with Ray."

She takes my arm and says gently, "You should give it some thought, Jack. I have."

I muse aloud, "Ray died too young, ergo I'm mad at you for sleeping with a lawyer."

"I am NOT sleeping with him."

Heads turn. Strollers glide away from us. The doors to the field house clank shut.

Softly, she says, "Deep down I think you're angry at everyone who makes something of himself in this town. I've always had the feeling that at some level you blame Washington for what happened to Ray."

My brother had talent, but it wasn't a talent for making speeches or twisting arms or anything that could be converted into hard currency or respect in this town. He knew himself. He had a talent for living. People sensed this. They liked to be around him. Bouncers in Georgetown bars, waiters, store clerks, gas station attendants, lifeguards, cops—once a month someone looks twice at my driver's license and asks, "Say, are you Ray Townsend's brother?" To this day.

To Nina, I say, "Maybe I do wish that he had been born

someplace else. And because he wasn't, maybe I lack a certain generosity of spirit toward Washington's high achievers."

"You hate lawyers."

"Some lawyers."

"Look," she says. "Ray's big problem was that he hated following rules. Which might explain why you seem to have focused your anger on the people who make the rules."

This doesn't sound like the Nina of old. The Nina of old would have been content to sketch me in as Gerard in *Andrea Chénier*, defending my impoverished brother while raging about the sloth and avarice of oppressive aristocracy. Focusing anger sounds like sister Liza, but this people-who-make-the-rules business sounds disturbingly like the words of a bona fide rule-maker.

She says, "It makes sense if you think about it."

Sure it does. There are probably a hundred Ray stories to support this thesis. Classic stories: Ray the twelve-year-old loner remaining for three days in a tree house he built high in the branches of a hundred-year-old white oak. Ray the activist organizing a school boycott to commemorate the Sandinista revolution, Ray the rebel, Ray the vandal. Here's a story from the last summer that Ray and I lived under the same roof. This was about ten years ago. A new family had just moved into the house across the street from my parents' place. The couple was too young for Foxhall Road, which even then was overpriced and overcultivated. "Assistant to the President," my father announced one evening as our new neighbor emerged from a chauffeured black Ford. "Think about it, boys."

The implication was that Ray and I could one day travel in the same style if we *applied* ourselves. Right away I saw that Ray was annoyed by Mr. Assistant. The fact that this eager beaver took to waiting outside for the limo every morning, his Yale Law coffee mug steaming, did nothing to endear him to either one of us. "Looks to me to be early thirties," my father said. (You've only got about ten years, Jack!)

Ray said, "With that limo, you wonder why he bothers with the Lincoln." A brand-new aquamarine Mark IV sat in the driveway. "Weekends," my father replied. Ray: "He works weekends." My father: "That so? A lesson there."

A couple of days pass. A tow truck appears in the driveway. Next day, another tow truck; the following week, a new Mark IV, this one algae colored. Ray was a master mechanic, self-taught. His close interest in the saga of car troubles unfolding across the street should have sent up a warning flag, but I wasn't looking for clues.

One Saturday morning I was sipping coffee on the porch, reading the sports page. Ray stood at the screen door. Yet another tow truck was parked across the street. Ray said, "Look at that guy, Jack. What a phony." I looked up in time to see Mr. Assistant throwing rabbit punches at a swarthy kid in greasy striped coveralls. The scene was pathetic. Under any other circumstance, our neighbor wouldn't have given this kid the time of day. Now, though, his weekend plans in jeopardy, he would have done pushups to get his car working. The kid motioned to him to start it up. The engine caught after a moment but it sounded awful and quickly died. Mr. Assistant fired it up again, sending a smoky cloud of exhaust into the garage.

"Better change the wires," Ray muttered. Sure enough, a moment later, the mechanic hooked up a new set of spark-plug wires. No change in the sound of the engine. "Hmmm," Ray mused. "Guess I better have a look at those plugs." The mechanic pulled all of them. "What'd you do to the car?" I asked. Ray grinned. Only somebody who loved Ray as much as I did could have understood that smile. "Me?" he said innocently. "What in heaven's name put such a terrible idea in your head? You haven't seen me anywhere near that car."

Plausible deniability, the quintessential Washington alibi. In this and so many other ways, Ray was years ahead of his time. Crazy as it sounds, every time I see a tow-truck driver monkeying under the hood of a car, I get weepy. And if there's a guy in a yellow tie with a gray suit jacket thrown over his shoulder standing off to the side, regarding the BMW—his emblem of success and fount of testosterone—like it's a turd, I'm liable to break into sobs.

My sister has a different view of Ray. Ellen sees him as a cursed figure. Doomed, like Rigoletto, whose loose tongue and lack of regard for the people around him cast a fatal spell on him. She would never say this of course. The most Ellen will say is that Ray led a tragic life. More like Don Alvaro in *La Forza del Destino,* a victim of bad judgment and a streak of terrible luck.

I've tried to talk with Ellen about Ray, but we never get anywhere. She has repressed all memories of him from about age twelve onward. Not me. The fact is, I miss that kid in more ways than I can explain. Once he said to me, "Jack, you need me. This whole goddamn family needs me. I'm the fuck-up. If you didn't have me around, no one would know whether or not he was on the straight-and-narrow." He was right; events proved that. Every family has a reference point, and Ray was ours—at least he was mine. I hate the thought that he spent his whole life, eighteen years, living defiantly on the edge to show whoever was looking that he had no use for the buttoned-down world and the high-achieving expectations that my parents had set for him. Right up to the end, when he executed a back flip into shallow water at a pool party and broke his neck.

I fling the Frisbee, a lousy toss. Dan stops short and walks it down.

Nina takes my hand in both of hers. "You're too hard on yourself," she whispers. "It wasn't your fault. You weren't responsible."

"Please don't say anything about this being God's will."

"It was an accident. It happened, that's all. Someday it will happen to all of us. If you can accept that, maybe it'll be easier to accept the fact that Ray isn't going to turn up on your doorstep one morning with a football under his arm."

"I hate football."

"You *loved* playing catch with him."

Dan flips the Frisbee onto my foot.

Softly, she says, "Jack, I don't want to fight with you anymore. I want to be friends. I want to stay in touch. What you think matters to me. I don't want to pretend that the years we lived together never happened. They were wonderful. This afternoon was wonderful. I wanted it. I needed to know that we had gotten past the vindictiveness. Both of us needed to know that, I think. But it's over now, isn't it? Isn't that what we decided? Aren't I allowed to try to make it work with Michael?"

Michael? Who the devil do I know named Michael?

"Oh," she says wearily, "you're going to find out one of these days. I've been seeing Michael England."

This is awful news.

Of all people—England! How is a self-respecting fellow like me supposed to react to the news that he's been cuckolded by a guy with a rim-rattling jump shot and no left hand. A clean freak, no less!

"Nina, this is a joke, right?"

"Go to hell," she says, smiling.

An image keeps flashing through my mind: England chugging up the basketball court. He's got the ball; it's three on one. Top of the key, a lousy head fake right, shoulder fake left, England barreling into the lane, up goes the slow-motion layup, up goes the defender—and the ball gets swatted out of bounds.

Nina says, "You've always been hard on Michael, but he's really very sweet."

For the record, no one in my Monday night basketball crowd has *ever* called this guy Michael or Mike or Miguel or anything other than England. As in, "Watch the telegraph on the bounce pass, England!"

I look at Nina. She shrugs, then smiles tentatively. I smile. She laughs. I laugh. "This is all pretty silly," she says. "Crazy stuff," I reply. "And wouldn't you know that just when I think I've got my life figured out, the pot gets stirred up." She rests her head on my shoulder. I put an arm around her. She kisses me and I slip her the tongue, which causes her to pull away, laughing, but she kisses me again and this time the tip of her tongue brushes my lips. There are tears in her eyes.

Blinking away a few tears of my own, I imagine myself carrying Nina home and ravishing her late into the evening. Why, I wonder, must the full force of the love I feel for this woman present itself to me at such a lousy moment. My fingers tightly gripping the weathered wood of an old park bench, I can feel myself being swept away, carried off in the same current which, in earlier times, carried away other relics of Nina's past: a collection of plastic horses, a full deck of Italian prayer cards, artistically flayed blue jeans and tie-dyed T-shirts, an undergraduate craving for cottage cheese and graham crackers.

"So, um, when did this start?"

"Well," she says, "we talked for a while at Golf Night. But Michael waited until several weeks after you left before he called me. It was a month before he asked me out."

That slow first step, so typical of England.

Golf Night is my Monday night basketball group's annual male-bonding (with guest) rite of spring. This year it was held in May at the Potomac estate of Rex Pitesti, Civil War nut and intellectual property lawyer nonpareil. A six-hole course was set up in the rolling hills behind Rex's house. We chipped and putted under rented arc lights, ate barbecued chicken, drank beer, and sat on the back porch late into the evening listening to Rex recount in excruciating detail the events of the fateful second day at Gettysburg.

England came alone. I didn't see much of him the entire evening. In fact, I don't think I said a word to him until after midnight. I had gone out to the driveway to see if the van would start, though I knew it wouldn't. The starter was on the blink and I needed someone to whack it with the end of a baseball bat while

I cranked the engine. So there I was, coming around the corner of Rex's house carrying the aforementioned Louisville Slugger. Suddenly I encounter Nina and England sitting on the edge of the hot tub—rather close together, as I recall. England takes one look at that length of white ash and his jaw drops; I guess he must have thought his days on the planet had come to a crashing end. "Say England, I've got a little engine trouble. Could you give me a hand?"

He flew to my side.

There is more to the story. A week after I took up residence in my McLean country house, I found myself stretching before the Monday night game beside Donald the Fed. As usual, Donald started in on me with his prosecutorial banter: How's the landscaping business? How's Nina? How's the dog? How's the crime rate around Dupont Circle? On and on. This guy stays with a line of questioning like a bloodhound with a scent. It quickly emerged that I was no longer living on 19th Street. Naturally Donald wanted to know if the place was getting fumigated or had burnt down or gone condo or what. "Where are you living?" "Is Nina with you?" "Is your dog with you?" Blah, blah, blah, blah.

Homeless, I said. Dan and I are on the streets.

So there was Donald, shaking his head sadly even as he marched his loosened hamstrings across the gym floor to deliver news to Mr. England about a certain newly unattached *artiste*. Today I scratch your back, someday I'll call on you to scratch mine.

This is an old, old game in Washington. Older than H-O-R-S-E.

WHITE BALL

Come Monday, 7:45 P.M., I am
sprawled on the floor in the hallway outside a junior high school
gymnasium, my rear end pressed to the tiled wall, legs extended
upward. Every muscle in my body cries out in pain as I reach for
my toes. Leaning back to rest, I see an upside-down head framed
above me in the doorway.

England has arrived.

He shoots past me as if hurrying to catch a train. He's dressed
in a blue suit and tasseled black loafers. In this outfit he looks
older—more like a father of a junior-high-schooler late for a PTA
meeting than a gone-to-seed basketball fanatic. England is almost
my height, just under six feet, but stockier, with a sculpted mass of
dark curly hair.

From inside the gym come strains of Michael Jackson. Twenty-odd women in brightly colored tights and sweatbands pivot and kick in time to the music. The aerobics instructor, the woman with the flashiest outfit and the highest kick, calls out, "Twelve more." Then, "Just ten! Higher, Monica!" I climb to my feet and head off to the boys' bathroom, where I find England standing at the mirror, applying deodorant.

"Jack, welcome!"

It feels like he's inviting me into his home.

Too quickly, he says, "Listen, you're just the man I want to see. I've been thinking seriously about redoing my yard. Top to bottom. New lawn, azaleas, a dogwood or two, the works. Of course I'd need help. I can't tell crabgrass from fescue." He pulls a blue tank top over his head and emerges wearing an enormous grin.

"I'm keeping pretty busy these days," I say.

"Oh, I'm not in a hurry. It's just that I want the best. I hear that's you."

Now who would have told him that? "I hear that you're keeping pretty busy these days, too." His ears brighten to the color of raw salmon. "Workwise," I add.

"Oh, that," he says. "Yeah. Busy, busy, busy."

"The sun never sets on the empire of white-collar crime."

"High profile, high risk," he says without a trace of irony.

"Don't work too hard. It seems to me that guys who fill hundreds of thousands of bottles with sugar water and sell it to babies as apple juice ought to spend at least a few years breaking rocks."

"For heaven's sakes, Jack, we're talking about family men. Forget what you read in the *Post*. The whole thing was the result of a misunderstanding. Poor communications." He sprays the insides of his basketball shoes with a talcum-scented aerosol. "A stiff fine, probation, community service—between you and me it's probably warranted. But you can't lock up a man just because he's a lousy manager."

By the time I return to the front hallway, other members of the basketball group have drifted in. There's J. William, the tobacco lobbyist, wearing thigh-length blue Spandex tights under his gym shorts. He is a serious ballplayer, the sort of guy who should have had a tryout with the Albany Patroons to get the dream out of his system. Standing beside J. William is Scottie—"the Helmet," as he's affectionately called.

"Hey, Scott."

"Hey, Jack."

Scottie is a small guy, all gristle and bone. He is still young enough to have some spring in his legs. Cover him and you are sure to end up hurt. He doesn't injure people on purpose. It's just that while the rest of us play basketball with one foot on the brake, so to speak, Scottie darts around the court like a runaway top. He swats at your dribble, attempting a steal, and you end up with a broken finger. Go to block his shot and he'll bury his granitelike head in your solar plexus. I have no idea what Scottie's last name is, nor he mine; still, we are buddies. For some reason, male-bonding activities, like one-night stands, seem to benefit from a measure of anonymity.

Mark "Chaise" Long arrives, followed by bandy-legged Rod Griffith. Then young Max X. Reilly, who claims to have played JV ball at Providence College. I can believe this: there is a decidedly Ernie DiGregorio aspect to the way Max pushes the ball up the court. He's got the same quick release on his layup, and throws deadly accurate no-look bounce passes with both hands. But there the similarity ends. Five or six times a night, Max will uncork the most bizarre-looking slingshot hook—it looks more like a cross-field rugby toss than anything you'd expect to see on a basketball court. Though the shot rarely falls, Max can't seem to purge it from his repertoire, which goes a long way toward explaining why he wrapped up his collegiate career on the Friars bench.

A bouncing ball signals the arrival of Rex Pitesti. Donald the Fed is right beside him.

Rex is the heart and soul of Monday night basketball. He organized the group and found this gym. Rex sees that the school secretary gets a fruit basket each year when our contract is up for renewal. He tips the janitor. He hosts the annual awards banquet. Each Monday he spends most of the afternoon telephoning everyone in the group to make sure we'll have a full-court quorum. For Rex this is a labor of love. Last week he announced that we will all kick in ten bucks for a donation to the school yearbook. He will ask them to run a group photograph in the acknowledgments section. Under Rex's hand, we are fast becoming a Washington institution.

"Bad news, Jack." Rex hands me a photocopied article from the *New England Journal of Medicine*. The article is entitled "Calcium Intake and Nursing Mothers." "This changes everything," he says. "Lacto-ovo is out."

"Rex, I'm not pregnant."

"We've got to get off milk, Jack. The fat's killing us. It's that simple."

"What about cereal?"

"Water," he says grimly.

"Any good news?"

"We're looking at fourteen tonight." He smiles.

Rex's talent is wasted in law. I tell him this repeatedly. He is a born organizer. He should quit the firm and get a syndicate together and buy the Frederick Keys or the Prince William Cannons. In five years' time he'd have major league baseball back at RFK stadium, guaranteed.

The aerobics class, as usual, is running late. J. William and Scottie begin tossing the ball around. Behind-the-back passes, chest passes, overhead throws that kiss the ceiling. Proper male bonding demands an activity—preferably one involving a ball—to shift the focus from the conversation. You break the news about your impending divorce to your best friend at a batting cage, discuss your father's rapidly failing memory with your brother at putt-putt.

Women decry this sort of oblique behavior, Nina among them. "Why can't guys just pour a cup of coffee and get to the point?" she once asked me. Because male friendships can't bear the weight of too much honesty, I replied. This is true. A buddy can be summoned at the last minute to help build a deck. He can be expected to give you a place to stay in a pinch or to stand beside you in a street brawl. He'll store your boat in his garage for years without a second thought. But heaven help the fellow in a men's room who starts carrying on about the lingering pain of his mother's alcoholism to a friend standing at the adjacent urinal.

Scottie's dribbling display brings the Lycraed aerobics coach to the open doorway. She scowls and shuts the door with a clang. This lifts everyone's spirit. It is the hour when men become boys. The transformation has begun. If only we weren't so well groomed! If only we were shod in badly ripped $15 Chucks instead of $150 pump Reeboks. As it is, I feel like Oliver Twist in this group. My clothes do not match. My T-shirt, veteran of a thousand hot-water washings, hangs from my shoulders like gossamer. England, in contrast, wears a burgundy warm-up suit with gold piping and carries a matching Redskins gym bag. Rex wears violet silk shorts that probably cost more than my entire outfit, Air Jordans included.

I suppose it's a question of lifestyle. "There are people who so arrange their lives that they feed themselves only on side dishes" is how my sister delicately put it on the Renoir *Boating Party* card that arrived the other day. She's right on target. I'm the sort of guy who will spend a full day wandering through a wasteland of battered cars looking for a rear-door gasket before I would think to head to the local auto-supply house for a new one. Sure, I save a few bucks—$59 to be exact—but that's not really the point of the exercise. I'm out there because I like junkyards. The scene at Brandywine Auto Parts is more somber than any Civil War battlefield. Standing in the mud beside a van like mine that is squashed like an accordion says something profound to me about the precarious nature of life. And I love haggling over the price of the gasket with three-hundred-pound Junior, who has one hand resting on a red-hot kerosene stove and the other clutching the world's dirtiest telephone.

The exercise music cuts off as a group of Scottish dancers make their entrance. They move down the hall in a mass of tartan. Griffith, Scottie, and J. William are lounging on the floor like Don José's dragoons when the aerobics class departs. These ladies aren't gorgeous, but men who have regressed to age fourteen can't help themselves when it comes to gazing at female bodies clad in skintight outfits. Rex sniffs the air, Don Giovanni-style.

I catch a spicy odor. England is standing beside me. He begins to slap his thighs and massage his calves. He has a forty-foot-long hallway in which to perform these exercises, but for some reason chooses to do them less than a foot from me. Even if he wasn't my rival, I'd still say that there is something fundamentally wrong with this guy.

On the court, tossing up a few practice shots, I watch him out of the corner of my eye. He puts his wallet in the pocket of his dress pants, rolls the pants carefully into a loose cylinder, places this neat package at the bottom of his gym bag, and proceeds to hide the bag beneath the folded-up bleachers. This is Michael, I tell myself. Pay strict attention. This is the fellow Nina wants to try to make it work with. This is the fellow Nina wants to make it with. Recall, Jack: there were men before you and there will be men after you. You are an adult. You are mature.

But other weighty matters press down on me. Vexing questions, such as: am I the last man on the floor to realize that England has spent the past summer trying to steal the love of my life? And more important at this particular moment: how might this terrible news affect my game?

I take Rex aside. "When you're picking teams, please keep in mind that I need to body-slam England tonight."

"Are you under control?"

The look on his face tells me that he knows the whole story. "Barely."

He smiles. "I like that, Jack. Push the envelope. The early bets for player-of-the-game have to be riding on you." He calls out the squads, concluding as always with, "Okay, gentlemen, let's run."

I'm teamed with Max, J. William, Griffith (who has spent the last twenty minutes cinching his groin with tape), and Arne, a tall, lanky Swede with a downy mustache. Arne played varsity ball at Bates or Bowdoin or one of the other Downeast powerhouses, and he spends the warmup period trying to dunk. The other squad has Donald the Fed, Rex, Scottie, Chaise Long, England, and a new guy who Rex plucked from his waiting list. J. William knocks down a twenty-two footer so we start with the ball. Scottie is on the bench. Rex is guarding me. My eyes are on England.

White ball is played to fifteen, win by two; each hoop counts one point. It goes like this: you hurry up and down the court like a herd of buffalo for about seven or eight minutes, trying to run up a 5–3 lead. Soon, the molto agitato period gives way to the andante phase of the game, a leisurely pace with only momentary displays of bravura. Basically, this means we trade baskets for twenty or thirty minutes until the game is over, then head for the water fountain.

There is no trapping defense in the Monday night game, no zone press, no box and one—not even much arm waving. We do not play with the three-point line: we tried this one night but it removed what little incentive there was to go into the paint. This is strictly NBA-style, man-to-man basketball, which in our case means that about a quarter of the buckets come from lagging defenders hanging out at half court.

Five minutes into the first game, it occurs to me that it will take some work to position myself to cover England, a bit of maneuvering. I glance over at the bench and see Jerry the banking regulator lacing up his Avias. I throw up a hand and call Jerry in to battle Rex. A few minutes later Griffith limps off the court and I head in to cover the new guy.

This fellow is younger than the rest of us and eager to make a good impression on Rex in the hopes that he will be invited back next Monday night. Much too eager, it turns out. At one end of the court his hands wave in my face; at the other, his Soloflexed torso slaps against my back. I lean into him and he throws his weight against me. I don't like this at all. With the other guys on the floor, I know when to push and when to hold my ground. With this new fellow, however, the rules of engagement have not yet been established. Young lawyer that he is, he wants to make sure that no one leaves the gym with the impression that he allowed me to push him around. In other words, he's on my back the whole time. This smothering defense is beginning to wear me out. I raise my hand to summon a sub.

My position is small forward, which means that I can't dribble or pass well enough to bring the ball up the court and I get no satisfaction throwing or catching elbows beneath the net. I like to shoot. And frankly, I'm pretty shameless about putting the ball up. Blame it on a lack of formal basketball instruction. Tonight, however, I have been reincarnated as a defensive specialist. I'm ashamed to admit how badly I want to cover England.

At the moment, England is matched up with J. William, and the book on J. William is that he won't sub out of a game short of getting word that his house is on fire. But he does have a habit of hurting himself. Sure enough, with the score tied at nine, J. William suddenly flies out of bounds and catches himself on the bleachers. He stumbles toward the rest of us on the sidelines with his knees locked together. Either he took a shot to the groin or we are looking at a career-threatening Spandex tear. Before his arm goes up, I am out on the court. England loses a bit of color.

Nothing happens, of course. Not right away. England and I chug up and down the court. He tries to cross his dribble and take me inside, but I slap the ball away. At the other end of the floor, I try to get around him on the baseline, but he throws out his pelvis, forcing me out of bounds.

He is smiling. What in the world does this mean?

The score climbs. Soon, we're up 13–12. England brings the ball up the court. He passes to Rex in the paint. Rex tosses up a left-handed hook. It comes off the rim. Donald the Fed picks up the loose ball at the top of the key. He thinks about shooting, but Max swoops in and Donald passes. He gets the ball back. He passes again—this kind of pickup basketball I will never understand. England spins around; I follow him back door, pushing my way through Rex's solid pick. Another Donald the Fed round-trip pass—it must be a fantasy of having played for Dean Smith that makes him behave like this. England leans into me.

"Look," he whispers. "I just hope there aren't any hard feelings."

Sacrebleu! My legs turn to stone. England steps back and takes a bounce pass off his shoelaces. I throw myself in his direction but he's already got the ball over his head. He bends backward at the waist and lets go with a catapault shot. *Swish.* 13–13.

I am unmanned and humiliated. I must shoot my way clear of this embarrassment. I take the inbound pass and dribble the length of the floor and clang one in from the top of the key. 14–13. My fortunes are changing. Neurons are firing, endorphins are being released, adrenaline is flooding my bloodstream. My body is fast filling with chemicals that seem to put me on top of my game. A voice inside me says to relax and put the ball up. It will fall.

This is a form of macho juvenile insanity, of course. Just because I wish to be transformed into Michael Jordan, it does not follow that I *will* be transformed into Michael Jordan. But my game has picked up, no question about it. And the here-for-business look on my face has shaken England's confidence. His next shot, uncontested, is a brick. The ball comes back to him and I go up with him and swat his second shot out of bounds. The inbound pass goes to

England, but he passes off. He is seriously rattled. An errant shot hangs on the rim; Arne grabs the rebound and heads downcourt. I want the ball. Everyone on my team wants the ball. The only glory in pickup basketball is banging in the winning shot. Arne knows this as well as any of us. He pulls up and unloads a twenty-footer.

But this is my story, after all: Arne's shot catches the rim and comes off to the left, a long rebound. I hold England inside, go up by myself and, with the left hand, tap it home off glass. That's the ballgame. England pats me on the back.

"Nice shot, Jack."

"Thanks, man."

He follows me out of the gym. I sense that he is bird-dogging me and I am consumed with scrotal unease. Out of earshot of the rest of the crew, he leans toward me and says, "Listen, do you think we could talk sometime?"

This I'd welcome like an IRS audit.

"Sure," I say. "Whenever."

He thinks. He doesn't know how much of my time to book. Suddenly I sense that this is a spur-of-the-moment request. Michael England, meticulous planner that he is, has not thought through this gambit. He isn't exactly sure what he wants to say to me, isn't sure whether we'd be better off taking a walk together on the canal towpath or meeting over a couple of plates of pasta and a bottle of Chianti.

He says, "Maybe I could get you over to my place. Talk about the yard work, too. That way we'd kill two birds with one stone. How about if I give you a call? Do you have a card?"

"What's this *about*, England?"

"Aw, heck. Nothing really. I'll look you up."

"I'm not in the book."

Mention of my homeless status makes England wince. I bend to take a sip of water.

"I tell you, Jack. All I really want to say is that I hope the other stuff doesn't affect hoops."

"The other stuff?" I hear myself say as I begin to slow dance with the water fountain.

"Look, forget it," he says.

Before we get a chance to play out one of the wonderful operatic duel scenes from, say, *Ernani* or *Eugene Onegin,* he is gone. He had me on the ropes and he walked away. This guy has no sense of timing, no feeling for the flow of the game. Oh England, I want to say, naif of Short Hills, of course this will not affect hoops. Nothing is allowed to affect hoops. Hoops is all that remains for me. Castrato that I have become, I must prove myself on the hardwood floor. Since I cannot bring myself to fight you, I must learn to score on you at will.

In game two I settle down. First time England gets his hands on the ball, he tries to gear up the fast break. I steal his dribble and drive for an uncontested layup. Next time down the court, I swish a fifteen-foot jumper. My confidence is sky-high. The mere sight of England's sculpted head hurrying back on defense gives me the courage to go up with the left hand. Everything is falling.

But then he screws me up. Instead of giving me the Jack Nicholson shrug to say, "Tonight's your night on the court, big guy, but where are you headed after the show goes dark?" his expression goes hangdog. Plainly, he's feeling sorry for both of us. He stops chasing down rebounds, which is very unEnglandlike. He starts lagging on defense and I start throwing up bricks. Basketball is a contact sport; without England on my hip, my little jump hook can't find the rim, much less the net. After three or four ugly misses, I stop seeing the ball.

The game grows ragged. At one point, five minutes pass between baskets. Arne gets a hot hand, so he gets the ball every time we come down the court. By the time the session is finished, after we have chugged through games three and four and the clock strikes ten, I am grateful to be able to walk off the court with my ankles intact.

We gather at J. William's red Porsche as J. William hunches over a cooler and starts opening beers. Rex arrives last, wearing a Del State T-shirt. The talk around the cooler touches on Redskins football, billing receipts, Kathy Ireland, and balloon mortgages. I have nothing to add. I lounge on the sidewalk, sipping a Dos Equis, and entertain Rex with a story I read in the *Post* the other day. It was a feature piece in the Sunday magazine about a guy who had been a sniper in Vietnam. A helicopter would drop him miles behind enemy lines and he would crawl through the jungle to a preselected spot overlooking a North Vietnamese camp. There he'd assemble his rifle and shoot the NVA colonel he was ordered to shoot. Then he had to lie motionless in a shallow trench for two or three days while enemy soldiers beat the bushes looking for him; when they finally gave up, he would crawl home. That was his job; he missed the excitement.

Rex loves this stuff. I collect stories for him about the Civil War, Vietnam, and, especially, medical oddities. At work he has two Rolodexes: one for business associates and friends, the other devoted entirely to the medical profession. Off the top of his head, he could tell you the name of the best internist in Portland, Maine; or the most experienced allergist in Atlanta, Georgia. In the trunk of his Saab, beside the spare tire and jack, you will find a portable heart monitor, blood-pressure cuff, and more splints, soft casts, instant heat packs, ace bandages, and adhesive tape than you'd probably find in all the pharmacies of Managua.

"Gentlemen," he calls out, "the dues through the end of the year come to twenty dollars."

A cascade of bills rains down on Rex.

England is not drinking. In fact, not only is England not drinking, he is conducting his toilette on the sidewalk. His shirt is off and he's wiping himself down with a hand towel. Next, he tears open a musk-scented Wash'n Dri and begins to rub his body vigorously with it. He is utterly absorbed. The shirt he dons is brand-new, still braced in cardboard and wrapped in plastic. He coifs his hair in J. William's side mirror. The rest of us are already into our second beers by the time he starts across the parking lot.

"Hey, England," someone yells. "Where you off to in such a hurry?"

"Brief due tomorrow," he mutters.

"Pair of briefs," Scottie calls.

There is much good-natured, male-bonded laughter at this remark, but I am quietly fuming. In another era, I would already have challenged England with the white glove. At this moment my man Ruiz would be arranging the duel with England's second. The score would be settled quickly. But instead of sipping cognac and cleaning duelling pistols while awaiting our dawn showdown on a bluff overlooking the Potomac, England will probably take Nina to Nora's for apple pie and a glass of Chablis, and I'll park myself on Hank and Sylvia's rooftop patio, sipping Gatorade and reading the chapter on Maya warfare and captive sacrifice in *The Blood of Kings*.

England swings past us in a brand-new BMW. The music is loud—Screaming Blue Messiahs, I think, which doesn't fit this guy at all. I would have guessed Crosby, Stills, Nash & Young. It consoles me slightly to realize that when Nina rides in that car, she will insist that England shut down the sound system. She has no patience for loud music in cars, unless the music happens to be, say, *Tosca,* with Kathleen Battle. Still, I can imagine Nina getting a thrill out of riding in England's BMW. I can see her hair blowing out the window as they head off to dinner at the Old Ebbit Grill.

"Jack," I hear Rex say, "you were starting to tell me about a guy in Lansing who came down with elephantiasis."

I am a rational human being. Moreover, I am an adult. My assets exceed my liabilities. Most of the time my two feet are firmly planted on the ground. My future is as bright as I want to make it. All it will take is desire and discipline and a little willpower. Ellen is right: it's time for me to get on with my life. I must break myself of the habit of taking a mental bead on the red taillights of the enemy BMW as it disappears into the night. Does this inclination indicate arrested development or has my obsession for Nina led me back to adolescence? Perhaps circumstance is to blame. It's ten o'clock on a Monday night and I find myself loitering outside a junior high school in sweats and high-tops, a beer bottle in hand, talking about LURPs and sappers and deadly bacteria and the inexorable northward migration of the killer bees.

THE HOLY
LAND
OF AMERICA

At home the red light on my answering machine is blinking. The message is straightforward: "Jack, Liza. Give me a call."

I am elated.

Nina's sister Liza, younger by two years, is recognized by one and all to have the levelest head in the family. She is finishing a Ph.D. in family therapy at Catholic University and works in the psychiatric ward at Holy Trinity Hospital. Neurotics and madmen telephone her home at all hours of the day and night. So what's one more, I think, punching in her number.

"Liza, Jack."

"We should talk," she says.

"Agreed."

"What does your day look like tomorrow?"

I pat my pockets and rifle through the sheaf of papers on the telephone table. My scheduling envelope is nowhere to be found.

"Wide open," I say.

"Lunch then?"

"Perfect."

"Can you make it over to Catholic?"

"Sure."

"Might be a nice day for a picnic," she says.

I can hear her husband's voice in the background. He is saying something about a monastery.

"Did you get that, Jack?"

"Bruce wants to check me into a monastery?"

Bruce Howe—"Father Bruce" to Marie—is a defrocked priest, a sociologist–slash–community activist, and a man who has somehow managed to spend forty-odd years on this planet without developing a discernible sense of humor. In this last trait, he and Liza are perfectly matched.

"He suggested we meet at the Franciscan Monastery."

"Will they let me in?"

"Of course."

"Will they let me out?"

"How about twelve-thirty?"

"Done." And before she can hang up: "Liza, one last question."

"What's that?"

"The sign of the cross: it's forehead, solar plexus, left shoulder, then right?"

"That's it."

"Even for lefties?"

"Goodnight, Jack."

★ ★ ★

The day is glorious, a cerulean blue sky filled with cherubic clouds worthy of Fra Angelico. I am new to this section of northeast Washington. A group of black men are hanging out on Quincy Street in front of the Suds 'n Subs. Climbing a long steep hill in low gear, I pass trellised brick houses converted into shrines and foreign student housing. "Come let us adore Poor Clare's Perpetual Adoration Chapel. Open to public," announces a sign in front of one. A placard on a neatly trimmed lawn reads, "Pro-Life: Where would you be without it?" I park in an open lot alongside a bus marked "D'Amico Tours."

The church is a tawny building, as squat and solid as an astronomical observatory, set behind an imposing wrought-iron fence. Child of the material culture that I am, I skirt the main door and head toward a wheelchair ramp to the right of the church, the entrance to a gift shop. A white-goateed friar stands at the doorway, hands locked behind his back. I nod, but he is too deep in contemplation to return the greeting. Inside the shop, I am the only customer. A round-bellied monk patrols the narrow aisle behind a long glass cabinet. I move slowly, overwhelmed by the extraordinary collection of Catholic geegaws spread across a table at the center of the room. Locked display cases contain the more valuable artifacts. I can feel Brother Aloysius's eyes on the back of my head the whole time.

"Help you with anything today?" he asks.

"Just browsing, thanks."

Is that likely? Do people actually arrive here uncertain about whether they want to pick up a Hail Mary kitchen plaque, a rosary egg, a set of Young Martyrs light-switch plates and holy water dispensers, a car statuette of Jesus, a vial of Saint Anthony's Blessed Oil, or a "Journey of Jesus in Palestine" wall map? Are the Saint Christopher medals piled up in a clear plastic bucket like Thin Mints considered impulse items?

I disappear into the adjoining room, which turns out to be a small museum, and spend a few moments trying to collect my thoughts as I look over what must be the most extensive collection of Holy Week clappers, incense thuribles, and offertory water spoons this side of the Atlantic. Ahead is a group of auditorium chairs, empty now. A sign indicates that this is the gathering spot for the hourly guided tour of the subterranean catacombs. I guess it must not be enough to have a beautiful church anymore. Pilgrims won't get off the Beltway for stained glass and Gregorian chants. Tour bus operators want something more than shaved crowns and clipped gardens.

So the Franciscans have built an exact replica of Rome's catacombs. They have put together a mini-museum with gold on silk chasubles behind glass, high-tech offertory candles (drop a coin through a slot in the top of the sealed container and the candle lights automatically; a timer cuts it off), a Cardinal Mindszenty cabinet, and, set up in grudging ecumenical spirit in an unused corner of the room, a glass-fronted Jewish cabinet. It contains a shofar, a seder tray, the fragment of a leatherbound 1825 Torah, and a piece of matzoh. The matzoh looks very, very old.

Another door leads me back to the gift shop, and I find myself facing a rack of books with such arresting titles as *An Armchair Retreat, The Joy of Full Surrender,* and *The Incorruptibles.* This last one turns out to be the definitive account of all the saints whose bodies did not decompose after death. I wish Nina were here. She could explain this stuff to me. Marie used to send us books like these; no doubt she bought them here. I recall a guide booklet to confession that advertised itself as "suitable for all adults, including converts" that somehow found its way into the straw basket in our bathroom filled with J. Crew catalogues, ancient issues of *Sports Illustrated,* and a host of revisionist Catholic newsletters sent courtesy of Liza.

"Beautiful day outside," says Brother Aloysius.

"Magnificent," I reply.

"A blessing, wouldn't you say?"

Here we go. This is how the Inquisition began.

"Jack!"

Liza is silhouetted in the doorway. I am saved—that is, rescued. My guide has arrived. It turns out that she is on a first-name basis with Brother Aloysius, whom she calls Al. I stand beside her at the counter while she buys a packet of mustard seeds from Jerusalem. Outside I ask her *why* she bought a packet of mustard seeds from Jerusalem.

"These?" she asks. "Oh, these are for Mother."

"Marie wanted you to get her mustard seeds from Jerusalem? Whatever for?"

"I haven't the foggiest," she says, slipping the packet into her Guatemalan bag.

Liza has short brown hair and large oval glasses. She is a solid woman. Her legs could support a body twice her size. Still, she walks with a light step. There is something regal in her bearing—the erect way she holds her head, I think. I've never seen Liza flustered, never heard her raise her voice. She takes my arm and guides me toward the entrance to the gardens. We stop at a mosaic, the Patroness of the Americas. The design has a huge Virgin Mary standing on the back of a small Indian child.

"It's odd," says Liza. I think she's talking about the symbolism of this depiction of the Patroness until she continues: "I had a dream the other night. I was walking in a garden. It was overgrown, kind of spooky. I was looking for you, Jack."

"Someone to trim the trees. Sounds logical."

"Nooo," she says. "A garden, Jack. *The* Garden. Don't you get it?"

We pass a marker for the twelfth station of the cross. "Jesus Dies on the Cross," the inscription reads. And beneath it, "Pray for Mary Rose McMichael." I note the cruciform topiary. A bed of impatiens spelling out the word "pax" needs tending; at first glance I think the word is "pox."

"So what does it mean that you were looking for me in the Garden?"

"Well, look where I found you," she says, touching her head to my shoulder.

In the sunlight, the smell of boxwoods is overpowering. It is a smell that evokes my childhood, the smell of a particular day when Ray rolled over two beautiful boxwoods while he was backing out of my parents' driveway. They released the most intoxicating scent, though I doubt Ray appreciated it. He was facing the prospect of spending the rest of the summer earning the money to replace them. My mother insisted on mature plants, which even in those days cost a small fortune. I made the mistake of suggesting to her that the desire to plant ought to be connected to the joy of watching a shrub or tree grow. She replied sharply that at her time in life she found greater pleasure keeping the things around her just as they are. I suppose that exchange marked the beginning of our estrangement. Coincidentally, it also marked the beginning of my career as a man of the soil: that same night, I slipped into a neighbor's garden and retrieved a couple of boxwoods that were being choked to death at the center of a magnificent stand. Ray and I wrapped the roots in burlap, fixed price tags to branches, and backed my VW convertible into the driveway with these two beautiful plants sticking out of the back seat.

Station number ten: "Jesus Is Stripped of His Garments."

Liza and I are in the shade of a towering sweet bay magnolia. Periwinkle covers one side of the paved walk, English ivy the other. It's tasteful; I like this place.

Liza says, "Talk to me, Jack. That's what I'm here for."

Should I free associate? Should I flog myself with a handful of willow whips and carry on about my poor relations with my mother? Should I mention the bizarre dream I had last night in which I spent the better part of a day trying to dislodge a fat man from the driver's seat of the van? Maybe I should make up something to get the conversation rolling. Liza wants to help me. I want to help her help me. The trouble is, I don't know where to begin. Station number eight: "Jesus Exhorts the Pious Women."

"I sense that you are undergoing a spiritual crisis," she tells a chickadee perched on the Francis X. and Mary Walsh memorial bench.

"Did Nina put you up to this?"

"Jack," she says scoldingly. "I thought you knew me better than that."

"Marie?"

"I won't dignify that with a response." Her eyebrows lower. "Do you want to talk about Nina?"

This isn't nosiness. Liza is here in a quasi-professional capacity. Furthermore, she is as reliable as a priest in the confessional. Nothing I say will leave this garden.

"My heart is too full of Nina to talk about her," I say with Byronic flourish, prompted in part, I suppose, by the inscription on the second station: "Jesus Takes Up the Cross."

Liza steers me toward a green bench set at the base of a stand of cedar. She takes a seat and peers at me over the tops of her glasses.

"Is what you are feeling love or is it cathexis?" she asks.

What I am feeling is what the poets write about. Ask them, I want to tell her. But I don't. You have to choose your words carefully with Liza. She listens with an intensity that I, as a speaker, find exhausting. And I'm no match for her when it comes to the intellectualization of emotion.

"It's love," I say.

"Love," she says, turning over in her mind the various definitions of the word as she pulls a smashed, foil-wrapped sandwich from her bag. "You joining me?"

I shake my head.

"You're welcome to my little box of Ritz crackers."

"Angst takes away my appetite."

"Why right now, Jack?"

"Because she's got the hots for a jackass lawyer, in case you hadn't heard."

"So it's jealousy?"

Sure. Add spite, vengeance, and fury to the list as well.

"That's probably part of it," I say.

Liza swallows. Her face wears a sad, soft expression. "Has it occurred to you that you might be having a problem with ego boundaries?"

"Ego boundaries?"

"Maybe you're having some difficulty separating where you end and Nina begins. It happens to couples. All the time. It could be that the separation is her way of trying to get those boundaries reset in their proper place. She might need to spend some time alone discovering who she really is."

"Alone?"

"Away from you."

"So where does England fit into this theory?"

"Companionship." Her voice rises on the last syllable, turning the statement into a question.

"I get the feeling that she's looking for a little more than companionship."

"Good heavens, Jack. Companionship doesn't rule out intimacy. It may complicate the work she has ahead of her, but so what? Life is complicated."

I get a sudden urge to pick up a stone and hurl it into the woods. Liza wouldn't understand the impulse but she would nod sagely nonetheless and pick a sliver of tuna fish from the corner of her lip. I keep my hands in my pockets.

"So your advice is to hold tight," I say.

"I'm not here to advise," she replies. "I'm just trying to help you sort out your feelings so that you can understand them."

"I know exactly how I feel. I feel like charging up a hill John Wayne–style."

"Bullheadedness doesn't qualify as a positive strategy, Jack."

I could argue with this statement. Fourth and one on the goal line, seconds left in the ball game, down by six—if that's not a moment that calls for bullheadedness, there never was one. How about arguing a parking ticket with a D.C. traffic court judge? Convincing Nina of the value of our relationship fits neatly beside these examples. As I see it, the situation is pretty straightforward. Nina is confused. Confusion calls for clarification, clarification requires intimate conversation, and before that can happen, England must take a walk. The strategy makes perfect sense to me as I describe it to Liza.

"And where do you end up?" she asks.

"Maybe I get Nina back."

She shakes her head.

"It's simple enough, isn't it?"

"Sounds a little too simple, if you ask me. What if the premise is wrong?"

"It isn't."

"How can you be sure of that, Jack?"

"Infallible intuition."

Liza folds the sheet of aluminum foil into a neat little square. "You're talking about a guess. Guesses just don't count."

She is dead wrong. Intuition is the voice of the godhead inside us. It is the manifestation of grace. Without intuition we are plodding, dull creatures. I would like to explain this to Liza, but reconstructed Catholic that she is, she would never buy it. She is too deeply entrenched in the process of integrating religion and modern science. Her Catholicism is a stripped-down, supremely rational dogma. Religion as metaphor. No Jesus *literally* walking on water, no water *actually* becoming wine, no Red Sea parting, no Lazarus rising from the dead. Heaven, she once told me, should *not* be seen as a never-ending succession of days on an extraterrestrial, PGA-quality golf course. Rather, it is the eternal life in Christ. Another word for this, she explained, is bliss. Bliss is ephemeral—it comes and goes in a nanosecond. Thus, she believes, entrance into the eternal life in Christ begins with the acceptance of the ephemeral nature of life. Here she is talking about coming to grips with death.

To be honest, I prefer the golf-course imagery.

Liza stands. She walks to the entrance of a replica of the Lourdes Grotto. Three clumps of ivy, like huge, thick Rastafarian dreadlocks, hang down over the mouth of the man-made cave. The cave itself is finished with cement and looks as if it has been patched a hundred times over the years. Set behind a wrought-iron railing, it resembles a zoo habitat. In fact, the layout of this garden reminds me of the bear-and-otter section at the National Zoo. Over to my left should be the gray seal pool; up that hill, antelope mountain.

I don't understand the point of this place. It sounds cynical to write the whole thing off as just another Disneyesque fund-raising stunt, but what other explanation is there? Can replicas be invested with holiness? Maybe it's the sheer number of replicas that has me reeling. The Lourdes Grotto, the Tomb of Mary, the Grotto of Gethsemane, Rome's catacombs, the Holy Sepulcher of Jesus— they're all here. Right down to the nondescript "Jewish Tomb," tucked away on a dead-end path, as easily overlooked as the lesser panda cage at the zoo.

Liza crosses her arms. "You know what I think, Jack?"

I knew that if I waited her out, she'd tell me what to do.

"You've got to slow down. Stop running. Face up to your fear of being alone. Max Picard says that the flight from oneself is the flight from God. Think about that."

"Who is Max Picard?"

"Swiss philosopher."

I am deeply skeptical of the wisdom of the Swiss.

My hands digging to the depths of the pockets in my khaki trousers, I tell Liza that I am not running from myself. I'm running toward Nina. On this subject, I can hear the voice of God as clearly as if He were to send me a sign by setting my pants on fire. What He's saying is that Nina Lawrence is the woman for me.

"Jack, do you really believe in God?"

"Of course I believe in God."

"I just don't get it," she says.

"I'm on a Holy Crusade."

"Aren't crusades a little passé?"

Imagine asking such a question, standing here!

I say, "You know, Marie's behind me on this. She knighted me and gave me my sword."

Liza smiles wanly. "Joanie and Nina have Mother turning herself inside out. She's invested so much of her psyche raising those two girls, and from where she sits everything about them seems to have turned out wrong. Mother can't separate herself from them. She can't accept the loss of control. It's a bad situation, for everyone involved. Terribly unhealthy."

"So what's the latest word from Mohican Hills?" I ask.

Liza sighs, indicating that the news will be rich and contentious.

"Anna is trying out for JV cheerleaders, which Joanie thinks is as reprehensible as selling herself on a street corner. Dad is looking at property, which means the family will be moving next year, which has Mom in a fury. Joey is applying to law school. And then there's Patrick."

"Serious?"

"Very serious." Serious signifies matters of health; very serious, matters of faith. "Lately he has been talking about the priesthood."

"What does Marie have to say about that?"

"Not a word. I think she's afraid God would strike her dead if she expressed her reservations. But she did ask Bruce to talk to him."

"And?"

"He wouldn't."

"He *wouldn't*?"

"Not without Patrick initiating the discussion. Bruce told Mother that it was Patrick's business. It is."

I can sense the throbbing heart that is rocking the foundation of Richter's château. No wonder he wants to move.

I miss that family, the whole crazy lot. I miss the wonderful and bizarre conversations around their dinner table that regularly touched on the power of novenas, aspects of martyrdom, the authenticity of the Shroud of Turin, the efficacy of Saint Christopher medals in light of his Vatican demotion, the travel plans of the Pope. My last supper there, Marie held forth for an hour on the proper way to bury a statue of Saint Joseph to speed the sale of real estate. During Lent, their house smelled to me of catacombs: some combination of ashes, candle wax, Gallo Hearty Burgundy, and (I liked to imagine) a smear of the sacred ointment hidden in the secret compartment of the huge crucifix hanging in the front hallway. Nina accepts the ways of her family as a matter of course, but at their table I always feel like an anthropologist who has wheedled an entrée into a secret brotherhood of hashish smokers.

We are climbing.

"So what exactly did Nina tell you?" I ask.

"She said she didn't know which was more difficult, seeing you or not seeing you."

"So she just decided to split the difference?"

"I don't think that's how she would put it."

"The question in my mind is, why rush right into another relationship?"

"Oh, come on, Jack. Why do any of us do the crazy things we do? Is she looking for security? Trying to avoid being alone? Perhaps she just wants to open herself up to the world a little bit. Who knows?"

"So you think it's healthy."

"Maybe yes, maybe no. Nina will have to figure that out for herself." Liza stops. "It's none of my business, Jack, but it sounds to me like you're too focused on her. What about you? What's going on in your life these days?

The question sounds off the cuff, but Liza is not an off-the-cuff kind of gal. This is gratis therapy, the five-minute hour.

"Lately," I say, "I've been thinking a lot about Ray."

"Talk," she says.

I shrug. "He was my brother. I could count on him. Maybe I'm looking for people I can count on right now."

"You feel betrayed by Nina?"

"I feel betrayed by both of them."

"I take it you still haven't resolved your feelings about Ray's death."

"It happened. I accept it. I don't really have any choice."

"Grudging acceptance won't take you where you need to go."

"Right now it's the best I can do."

"Have you thought about seeing someone?"

"Of course not."

"Well," she says quietly, "do."

The thought of paying a stranger to analyze my dearest memories seems almost a betrayal. I recall a cold January day, the wind whipping up bits of snow that sting my face like slivers of glass as I walk through the gates of a cemetery. I am looking for Ray's stone but soon give up as the snow really starts coming down. I stand for what seems an hour at the grave of a stranger—"Amelia Hardaway 1907–1925 Safe at Last," her stone says—and feel the loss of Ray more keenly than I have ever felt before. Beyond the gate, hidden in the bushes like a getaway car, sits Nina's blue Citroën. She rolls down the window and says, "Come sit with me, Jack." I don't know how she found me. I have known her for less than a month, but it feels like we've been together for years. We sit there for an hour with the engine running, watching the church-yard fill up with snow. I tell her about the last time I saw Ray, as he was slipping out my window on a night he was supposed to be grounded. The roof was slick and I whispered, "Be careful," and he said, "No way, José. Not until the day you catch me wearing

---

81

my pants hiked up to my chest." He blew me a kiss, grabbed a tree limb, and stepped into the darkness.

"Listen to this," I say to Liza. "Nina thinks I blame Washington for Ray's death. It's true. I do. I know that Ray could have pulled that stunt in any other city in the world, but he didn't. He did it here. Deep down, he hated what this town represents. He never stopped rebelling against it. I understand how he felt. I know that Washington didn't kill him. But the mentality of this place didn't give him anything to live for, either. I also know that a day will come when I'll feel more resolved about his death than I do at this moment. And on that day, I'll hate the bullshit side of this town just as much as I do right now."

"Is there a lesson there?"

"Don't do backflips into the shallow end of swimming pools?"

"That's not fair, Jack."

"Don't you see—he was *right*. He had this place pegged. That's my whole problem. That, and the fact that Ray understood me a thousand times better than I understood him."

"Let me hear you explain it."

"First, I have a question for you."

Her eyes drop to the ground. She's worried that I'm going to ask her about her sex life or the absence of children in her home or something equally embarrassing. We can talk about my problems until the cows come in, but the first hint that our discussion has swung toward the personal affairs of Liza Lawrence-Howe and she grows visibly uncomfortable.

"Is this affair serious?"

"Nina's?"

"No, yours."

Still an old-fashioned Catholic girl at heart, she blushes.

"You want my opinion?" she says.

I nod.

She drops her chin as she considers the question. "Off the record, I'd say short term, yes. Long term, probably not."

"Footnotes, please."

"Well, she obviously likes the guy. It seems that the relationship is mutually supportive. I'd guess there's a dynamic at work that Nina finds interesting."

"Meaning she wants to sleep with him."

"I didn't say that."

"She does. I'm sure of it."

Liza, the consummate professional, wears an inscrutable expression as she considers the comment. "How do you feel about that possibility?"

"Frankly, it seems a little daring."

She looks surprised. "No sense of betrayal?"

"I want to throttle the two of them. Of course I won't. I'll probably just butt my head on a tree stump. Wait it out. Once the deed is done, the show will be over between the two of them."

"How can you be sure?"

"A little bird told me. A little bird with the wingspan of the Holy Spirit."

"For your sake, Jack, I hope you're not disappointed."

"Surely you don't think they're going to tie the knot?"

She chooses her words as carefully as a State Department spokesperson. "I would tend to think that the dynamic that's holding this relationship together now won't hold it together forever."

I wait.

"As I see it, it's a question of values," she adds.

"The mixed marriage issue?"

"More of a mixed attitude-toward-life issue."

I want to kiss her.

In the Rosary Portico, she says, "Jack, tell me something. How do you feel about Michael England?"

"You mean personally?"

She nods.

I shrug.

"You don't dislike him?"

"Of course not."

"Then what exactly does he represent to you?"

"He's a threat."

"A threat?"

"Liza, we're talking about a guy who my girlfriend wants to screw. It bugs me."

"Is this a restatement of the ego boundary issue?"

"Put yourself in my position. How would you feel if Bruce went for that nun he works with?"

"Sister Regina?"

"She's small. Albanian, I think."

"Number one, the premise is ridiculous. Number two, my reaction would depend on the circumstances."

"These are the circumstances: I saw Nina four days ago. We had lunch and rode bikes and then went to my place and listened to *La Bohème* and slept together."

"And how did that make you feel?"

"Like I wanted to do it again. That day, the next day, the day after that."

"Is that realistic, Jack?"

"Depends on the circumstances, no?"

"Let me put it another way: What can the two of you hope to gain if you do sleep together right now? And what might you lose?"

While she begins to wax philosophical, I recall the comingled smell of Carmex and Varsol, among other intoxicating scents. And I wonder about Liza. About her private life. She shows me so little of who she is. Do she and Father Bruce ever cut loose? I mean *really* cut loose? Do they ever howl like alley cats? I can't imagine such a scene, but then it's probably the mild-mannered folks who work themselves into the most outrageous positions behind closed doors. That's just a guess, a hope, really.

Liza takes my arm. "Jack," she says softly. "It may not be over forever, but it's over for now. If you don't accept that, Nina will end up losing respect for you. Maybe you can find a way to sleep with her every now and then. But if you do, you'll poison the relationship. One day she'll walk out your door, or you'll walk out hers, and you'll both realize that you're never going to see each other again. I've seen it happen. It would be a tragedy. For all of us.

"Call me sometime," she says, brushing a lock from the middle of her forehead. "Come have dinner with Bruce and me one of these days."

O Liza! If only I could find a woman as sensible as you!

Standing alone outside the gates of the Holy Land of America, I resolve to take this advice to heart. From now on, each minute of the day will be lived with a view toward spiritual health and self-actualization. I start to eat mounds of vegetables and fruits, and my bowels respond with gratitude. I sit quietly in a darkened room each morning and evening for fifteen minutes, breathing rhythmically, making an effort to empty my mind. It helps. My life begins to seem richer, less complicated. I run into an old friend who has devised a way to run a router and lathe from his Mac, and we bat around the idea of starting a high-quality, mass-produced furniture company. Soon we rent space in a medical-supply warehouse in Silver Spring. We design a futon sofa prototype that really looks like a couch and is actually comfortable to sit and sleep on. I cart it around to shops in Georgetown. Orders follow. On weekends we cut and assemble.

Thursday evenings I practice T'ai Chi.

Everyone notices my change in attitude. Ellen, in particular, is impressed. But she is not convinced. When I drop the hint that I would not object to her applying her considerable talents as a matchmaker on my behalf, she becomes frankly skeptical. She wants assurances that I won't backslide. We exchange postcards.

Her Homer woodcutter quotes Schiller: "Jealousy is the great exaggerator." My Cooperstown Roberto Clemente carries on its back a line from the Book of Revelations: "Behold, I stand at the door, and knock." We negotiate by telephone. She agrees to find me a suitable dinner companion as long as I promise to study Miss Manners's guide to etiquette. I will have to submit to a quiz.

"Can't I just promise to be polite?"

"The last time we tried this your napkin never even made it into your lap."

"I guess that means I need to find someone who's not so hung up on civilized behavior."

"You've just been through that," says Ellen. "Look what happened."

I could debate the logic of this remark, but to do so would risk alienating myself from a woman who seems to be acquainted with most of the unattached women in Washington. Reluctantly, I agree to tackle Miss Manners.

"Hon, I'm so proud of you," she says. There is a pause, the shuffle of papers and scratch of a pen. "Thursday this week or Friday next?"

I experience a sudden need to buy time. "Friday next."

"Back in a moment." She puts me on hold. A minute later: "No good. How about next Saturday?"

I consult my envelope: a Dunbar–DeMatha scrimmage. "Saturday won't work."

"Well, we're off to Montego Bay for a week on Monday. What about next Thursday?"

"Fine." I am beginning to feel like the principal in one of Evan's unfriendly takeover bids.

Ellen's voice disappears and returns. "Thursday it is. Seven P.M."

"Um, can I ask who you've got on the other line?"

"Haven't you ever heard of a surprise?"

"I hate surprises."

"You'll like this one."

"How about a name?"

"Nope."

"A description?"

"Guess," she says.

"Tall, dark, Mediterranean. Someone like Carmen?"

She laughs, then hangs up on me.

DEADLINES
MUST BE MET

Ellen's house at dusk is a vision. The floodlights I installed last spring lend an air of majesty to the whisper white clapboard and cornflower blue trim. A massive repointed brick chimney rises like a portal to the heavens. The trees are neatly pruned, their leaves packed into a pumpkin-face plastic bag sitting at the curb. The lawn, bordered by beds of marigolds and a walkway of shiny black flagstones, has the surface of a putting green. Ellen's attention to detail—the alabaster white porch furniture and matching birdbath, two silver Volvos (sedan and station wagon) aligned in the pebbled driveway, tomorrow's mail clothespinned to the letterbox beside the door, the solemn, descending chime set off by the doorbell—suggests order and respite, a plot of land existing outside the law of entropy.

Mrs. Stubbs answers the door. She gives me her finest look of bemusement. "Lordy, now look at what the wind is a blowin' in. You are late a course, and the children have been a waitin' and a callin' for their Uncle Jaack. Won't nobody ailse do for them right now, dearheart. Come in now. Come in." Dan shoots past us and races up the stairs.

Evan sits at a computer in the small office off the foyer. His hands are locked over his head, eyes glued to the amber screen, red suspenders seemingly attached to his ears. Without turning, he calls out, "Got one for you, Jackson. Instaform at twenty-eight and a third."

"I picked it up last week at twenty-two."

"You dog."

The kitchen, a sea of black and white and chrome, smells richly of lemon and rice. Four hunks of salmon marinate in a shallow pan. I lean toward the counter and pick out a sprig of dill.

"Lordy, child. Next t'ing you will be eating out of the seas like the Japanese folk." Mrs. Stubbs moves me toward the table with a sweep of her broad arm. "I don't onderstand how anyone can eat somet'ing that is still moving on the plate. Only a barbairian would do somet'ing like that, Jack."

Mrs. Stubbs has a passion: animal welfare. She is inconsistent in her defense of this cause, standing there in a dress cinched at the waist with the skin of a lizard, feet encased in cowhide, finishing off a bologna sandwich. But her conviction that no animal should be brutalized is heartfelt and unequivocal. More times than I can remember, she has reminded me that "In the Bible, Jaysus tells us to watch over the birds and the fishies. He don't say anyt'ing about these nasty experiments. Nothing at tall."

Tonight the topic is whales. She whisks a salad dressing as she talks, the red polka dots on the hem of her dress bouncing like a dozen little balls. "There are some people complaining about the moaney they are spending in Alaska. But honestly, Jack, I say use the moaney to save those poor creatures. It tis better than spending it on bombs now, wouldn't you say?"

That it tis.

My gaze falls on a newspaper lying open on the kitchen table. An ad for the Central Union Mission reads: "Please help us at Thanksgiving: $13.90 feeds 10, $27.80 feeds 20, $55.60 feeds 40, $139 feeds 100." Below it is another advertisement with this head-line, "Want to feel good? Try repeating to yourself, I drive a Jaguar."

"So where are the little ones?" I ask.

Mrs. Stubbs frowns at a faceless wall clock. " 'Bout now they should be finishing their bath. I told them you were a coming, so I expect that they are a hurrying."

"And this friend of Ellen's who's coming to dinner, what do you know about her?"

"A fine young lady with a good, good mind. So don't be popping off too much tonight, Jack."

"Sounds a little too serious."

"Kate's not one for larking about if that tis what you are asking."

"But she does have a sense of humor?"

"She'll be laughing when it tis time to be laughing," Mrs. Stubbs says sternly.

"Will I like her?"

"I am shurrly not a mind reader, Jack Townsend."

"Well, if she's a friend of Ellen's she can't be anything like Nina."

This comment earns me the darkest of glares. Mrs. Stubbs has me cast as Pinkerton in *Madama Butterfly,* the sort of brute who would see to it that both his house and his sweetheart could be disposed of with one month's notice. There is something perverse in my soul that enjoys this regular scolding.

"Now don't you start carrying on like a lost lamb after all you have done to that poor woman."

"It was *her* decision."

"Lordy, Jack! Did she see a ring? Did she see some serious intentions from you, child? The answer is no and no. Don't be sitting there expecting wailing and lamentations from me. I've got no crocodile tears for you."

"It was Nina who refused to get married."

"Did she now? And did you get down on one knee, dearheart?"

"We talked."

"So it twas a discussion and not a question!"

"It was a conversation."

"Tell me why it tis that the young men today, they don't onderstand the first thing about courting a lady. You want to lairn somet'ing about romance, dearheart, then you'll be shure to start listn'n to your sister."

On cue, Ellen arrives. She is wearing a paisley print skirt and a pale green silk shirt and has her reddish hair pulled back in a French braid. She offers me a lightly powdered cheek.

"So tell me about Kate."

"You're such a snoop," she says. "Kate is a wonderful, attractive, sensible woman whom I have wanted you to meet for ages." She leans on the word "sensible," an obvious swipe at Nina. "You're going to like her, Jack. I know the two of you, and I just know you'll find that you have a bundle of things in common."

Right. Like we both have always dreamed of building miniature doll houses and attending stock car races.

"Does Kate have a last name?"

"Baldwin."

"Kate Baldwin," I say. "Kate Baldwin sounds like a lawyer."

"SEC," says Ellen. "She's really more of an administrator."

I groan.

"Dearheart, everybody in this town is a lawyer. Round here the law is the honey that draws the bees."

"Not you, Mrs. Stubbs. And not me."

"Then we are the only exceptions."

"Kate's a real down-to-earth person," Ellen says. "She loves bookstores. She loves ethnic food. She loves conversation. Just don't jump to any silly conclusions until you've met her."

The telephone sounds but Evan grabs it before the end of the first ring.

Ellen studies my clothes. She approves of the nicely starched white oxford shirt but is not happy about the faded corduroys. And the penny loafers are strictly déclassé. I can see in the recesses of her eyes the ghost of a thought: she wants to send me to Evan's closet for pleated sharkskin pants and Italian lounge slippers. But she quickly drops the idea. There's my ego to consider and the obviousness of such a ploy—no self-respecting woman would fall for a thirty-two-year-old man who has been dressed by his older sister.

"Uuuncle Jaaack!" comes a cry from the heavens.

At the top of the stairs, I snort like a dragon. Small voices squeal. I open and close a few doors, breathing fire all the while, stepping carefully through a minefield of sturdy wooden toys. *"So where are those little children!"* I snarl at the door to Willie's room. *"We're in heeere!!!"*

Willie and Sondra have separate bedrooms, but most nights they sleep together in Willie's double bed. Everything in his room is purple: pillows, stuffed animals, rug, walls, light fixtures, pebbles in the fish tank. Only the milky, translucent fish have escaped the decorator's brush. The kids are lying on top of a purple bedspread. Both wear faded pajamas with purple feet.

"Bugsy died," Willie announces solemnly.

"Poor Bugsy," I say.

"He got sucked into the pump."

He points at the aerator. I regard the tank. A bug-eyed fish swims past the light, showing me a tracery of blood vessels and bones.

"So who's this?" I ask.

"Bugsy II. And you know what?"

"What?"

"Yesterday we found a dead raccoon in the yard."

"It had babies," Sondra adds.

"It had *rabies*," corrects Willie. "An' Uncle Jack, you know what?"

"What?"

"It was right next to my bicycle so we had to wash it with Clorox."

Willie is five and Sondra is three. He is a young version of his father, lean and angular with short, curly brown hair and green eyes. Sondra, a dirty blonde, has lately developed a wide-eyed, slightly startled gaze that suggests to me the first flower of genius. It's my guess that her métier will be performance art. Even now I can imagine her smearing chocolate on her naked body and dancing frenetically in the plaza at Lincoln Center.

Aside from Dan, these kids are the only beings in the world who kick and scream with delight at the prospect of going for a ride in my van. Strapped in like astronauts (I welded steel braces to the floor to rig up their carseats), they howl in concert to a tape I made for them: "Cowboy needs a horse, needs a horse, needs a horse, if he's gonna keep ridin'. . . ." The best part of this monotonous song is a long, drawn-out sigh, which I imagine is supposed to suggest a worn-out cowpoke settling down by the campfire after a long day in the saddle. But any precocious three-year-old can tell you what this sigh is really about: "It's doo-doo, Uncle Jack! It's doo-doo, isn't it!"

Lying on the bed, Sondra develops an impish expression.

"What is it?" I ask.

Smiling widely, she flings her face into a pillow. Willie follows suit. Soon they stand and dance around the bed, arms akimbo, Pee Wee Herman style. Dan thumps his way out from beneath the bed and begins to bark. I grab a child in each arm.

"Uncle Jack, do you know what Sondra was going to tell you?"

"No, what?"

More giggles. The children exchange glances, throw their heads to the side in Pee Wee grimaces. Then Sondra leans toward me, her body bending as only a supple three-year-old body can bend. "Stereo's all fucked up," she whispers. This brings another round of laughter and Pee Wee dancing, more barking from Dan.

I read books to them, *The Polar Express* and *Truck Song*, with Willie chanting the words a fraction of a second behind me:

> . . . . *past the farms and fields of wheat*
> *through the rain so cool and sweet*
> *windshield wipers keeping time*
> *lower gear to make the climb*
>
> *up mountain roads*
> *'round hairpin curves*
> *with eagle eyes*
> *and steely nerves*
>
> *tractors pull*
> *trailers full*
> *deadlines must be met*
> *journey's end*
> *around the bend*
> *gonna get there yet*
>
> *off the freeway*
> *into town*
> *shifting*
> *shifting*
> *shifting*
> *down . . .*

Next it's story time. This is a new activity for us, one Willie and I discovered the other day while I was driving him to Sidwell

Friends School for his weekly tennis lesson. It works this way: I set up a little scene, and he weaves it into a story. Whenever he starts to flag, I throw out a new detail or two, and he pushes the narrative forward. What I love most is the dreamy expression that comes to his face while he talks. He becomes a little white shaman, retrieving ancient stories from the collective unconscious.

"There's a little duckling on the towpath," I say. "And he can't get across."

"Why?"

"You tell me."

"Because of all the bikers," says Willie.

"So what happens?"

"The duck decides to build a bridge," he says.

"But isn't he too small to build a bridge by himself?"

"Well, Uncle Jack, he asks the bikers to help."

"And what's the duckling's name?"

"Dumpster!"

"Dumpster Duckling?"

"You see, he can't get across the towpath. And he has to, to get to the river. But the bikes are just coming too fast. They come very close to him. And Mr. Bookman's scared—"

"Who's Mr. Bookman?"

"Mr. Bookman's the duck," he says impatiently. "That's his other name."

"So he's scared—"

"—but he doesn't want to cry and he doesn't want to interrupt his father, who's at work, so he calls out, 'Please, bikers, *stop!*' And one does."

Sondra is rapt.

"And the biker says, 'How come you want me to stop, duck?' "

"What's the biker's name?"

Willie puts a hand to his chin, as if trying to recall. "His name is Bikehead."

"First or last name?"

"Both."

"Bikehead T. Bikehead?"

This brings yips of laughter from both of them.

"So Bikehead stops," I say.

"That's right." Willie goes dreamy again. "He stops his big red bicycle and he locks it to a tree so that no one will steal it. And he talks to the duck. And the duck tells him that he can't cross the towpath because he's going to get run over. He needs a bridge over the towpath to get from the canal to the river. And he also needs a bridge across the river."

"Why?"

"To take books to the children in Virginia."

"Oh."

"So Bikehead asks, 'Is that all, duck?' 'That's all,' says Mr. Bookman. So Bikehead stops the bikers. . . ."

"How?"

"He has a whistle, Uncle Jack. A big silver whistle that he blows and everyone stops. And then everyone locks their bikes to the trees and begins to build the bridge. Somebody gets wood and somebody gets a saw and somebody gets a hammer and some nails. And since everyone is helping, before too long the bridge is finished. And now the duck and all of his friends can get to the river to swim and see their mothers, and Mr. Bookman can take books to the children in Virginia." He shrugs. Just another case of cooperative behavior paying off in spades. What could be simpler?

Ellen is standing in the open doorway. She is beaming.

"Kate's here," she whispers. Then louder: "Are you two ready for bed?"

Foot banging and cries to the negative. Ellen slips a tape into the VCR on Willie's desk. Dan throws himself under the bed, grumbling. Lately he has developed an aversion to the snow sound of VCRs. Soon the black-bearded Raffi begins to croon in Spanish.

" 'Night, kids."

" 'Night, Uncle Bikehead!" says Willie.

" 'Night, Uncle Doo-doo!" says Sondra.

In the hall Ellen stops me and gives me a once over, front and back. She touches up my hair with her fingertips and says, "I should tell you that Kate's Jason is smart as a whip."

She knows my weakness for children.

"So Kate's divorced?"

"Hon, these days just about everyone in the world is divorced. You can't hold that against her. The thing is, Kate's *happily* divorced. She's the most well-adjusted single mother I know. And she's not a bit desperate. Why the other day, she and I had lunch, and I asked her what it was she wanted most in a man. And do you know what she said? Before a good father or the right income level or proper grooming or anything?"

I feel strapped to a carseat bolted to the floor of a dirty van. "What's that?"

"A sense of humor." Long pause. "That's you."

"I think I just lost my sense of humor."

"Well, then Kate's the woman to help you find it again." She moves us toward the stairway. "Now I know I shouldn't tell you what to say, but please try not to get too personal. Remember, this is just a get-acquainted night."

"What you're saying is that even if we really hit it off, I'm not supposed to spend the night at her place."

"Hush."

Ellen descends the steps ahead of me. Evan is standing in the doorway of the study, stretching in such a way as to suggest that he is trying to break free from some invisible bond that tethers him to the room. He gives me a broad wink and mouths, "Kick ass." This makes me nervous. Kate is standing at the entrance to the kitchen, a shoulder to the doorway. "Well," says Ellen. Kate turns quickly. She is fine-boned, brown-haired, blue-eyed. Her face is narrow, her expression forthright. She is svelte: one clean line from the top of her head to the tips of her shoes. She is wearing a scoop-necked navy blue jersey and calf-length gunmetal blue pants crisscrossed by zippers.

"Jack, this is Kate Baldwin. Kate, my little brother, Jack."

Kate has a gentle smile that trails off on the right side of her face, a faintly ironic expression that seems to recognize the absurd nature of our situation. She is Bacall restrained, not a trace of shyness as she takes my hand. The grip is firm.

Right then a thought creeps forward: I know this woman. I have seen her somewhere. Her smell—of all things!—is familiar. Cocoa butter and Agree shampoo. My olfactory archive tells me more: the last time I encountered Kate she was humming a Joni Mitchell song. Was it at Glen Echo? The lobby of the Biograph? Food seems to somehow enter into the equation, but I can't for the life of me come up with the cuisine. The admonitions of Miss Manners still ringing in my ears, I breathe not a word of this to Kate.

"Ellen tells me that you're an opera nut," she says.

Quando rapita in estasi! She approves!

Evan says, "Jack listens to opera the way the rest of us listen to the news."

"It *is* the news," I say earnestly.

Before I have a chance to explain, Ellen shepherds us into the living room. Kate and I are seated on either side of a platter of thinly sliced French bread encircling a slouching wedge of warm brie.

Evan stays on his feet, bobbing like a light heavyweight as he collects drink orders. Ellen starts fiddling with the dimmer switch to get the mood just right. Mrs. Stubbs can be heard in the kitchen, talking to the salmon. Kate is sitting absolutely straight, her knees and ankles together. I am the only one eating.

"So," says Ellen. "Finally I persuade you two to meet!"

"Here we are," Kate says. Her glance leaves me feeling as though she and I are in cahoots, two crooks about to pull off a scam.

Evan returns with three glasses of white wine and a Scotch

and water. He winks broadly as he presents the Scotch to me. He thinks I asked for the Scotch to make a statement. ("He works as a landscaper *and* he drinks Johnnie Walker.") Perhaps he's right. Exactly what does Scotch and water signify?

In a brilliant conversational ploy, Evan asks if anyone has seen the news that the FAA is ordering the replacement of 7200 rivets in 291 Boeing 737s. Somehow I missed that story. But I nod, feigning interest, and thank God that somebody has taken the time to study this morning's *Washington Post*. Soon we are roaming down page A1. Kate tells us that the guy who claims to have sold dope to Dan Quayle, a federal prisoner named Brett Kimberlin, was scheduled to hold a news conference just before the 1988 election, but instead found himself locked up in solitary confinement (this was the first time in our nation's history that the director of the Bureau of Prisons personally ordered an inmate into solitary confinement) and kept on ice until six days after the election. The reason for the order: fear that Kimberlin's drug allegations might have prompted retaliation by Quayle's supporters in prison.

"Quayle's supporters in prison?" Kate asks. "Did he have *one?* I mean, let's not forget that this was a guy who spent his Vietnam years xeroxing for the National Guard."

I like Kate. I like the edge to her voice, the slightly cynical way she purses her lips. She is an ally. Though dressed for success, there is something in her manner that announces to me that I am in the presence of a woman who does not take herself or anyone else too seriously. In Washington, a woman like this is as rare as a two-dollar bill. I want to kiss her fingertips, but she has them curled tightly in her lap, which gets me wondering if I might have misread her completely.

When Evan again begins to disparage the work of the FAA and the regulatory community in general, having apparently forgotten that securities regulation is what the guest of honor does for a living, Ellen gears up for an interception. She's wearing the sort of glassy expression you see on the face of a kid who is preparing to cut into a swinging jump rope. In midsentence she dispatches Evan for more ice. Kate and I exchange smiles. Ellen launches into her own conversational gambit, a list of the many interests Kate and I share: a love of quirky bookstores, certain sections of the Sunday *New York Times* (the wedding announcements are a particular favorite of mine), cheap ethnic restaurants in Silver Spring and Arlington, the National Arboretum, the miniature version of Rome's Spanish Steps between California and R Streets, a Chagall mural in someone's backyard in Georgetown.

Kate seems embarrassed by the degree to which Ellen is making a fuss over the two of us and she begins spreading brie on ovals of bread as though setting up for a White House reception. I am falling for her, for the cant of her head and the slight indentation at the tip of her nose. I know this unequivocally when Evan starts pressing her about the new regulations at the SEC and Kate sends a wink my way before replying sternly to Evan. "I should warn you that I'm under orders to report all contacts with anyone asking for information about the new regs. The names go into the IRS code-blue data base."

He nearly exhales a gob of brie. The dinner chime sounds.

The truth is that I would give anything to be allowed to spend this evening alone with Kate. Lifting a flaky forkful of perfectly broiled salmon, I have a sudden desire to be eating a messy plate of Thai food in a richly smelling restaurant that has at least two young kids writing out their homework assignments at the bar. I want to be drinking Singha from a jam jar. I want a big plate of *pad thai,* heavy on the noodles, shrimp, and peanuts, on the table between us. I want to be sitting three feet away from her, our elbows glued to the sticky Formica, our knees touching, our heads nearly colliding when our taste buds call simultaneously for *haw mok.* To my mind, that's the only sort of setting where two people can hope to get acquainted in one evening. Certainly not here, listening to Evan relate the news that some rich guy paid $4,400 for two love letters that young Ronald Reagan ("I'd like to be tossing off a short one with you, too") wrote to a gossip columnist.

A discussion about the trend in interest rates makes me want to dive headfirst into the arugula. But Ellen's sharp glance tells me to buck up. She wants me to show more enthusiasm. I think. How about: "Let's talk about the divorce rate." Or: "Raise an arm if you have alcoholism or drug abuse in your genes." Instead, I am forced to smile politely as Evan beats to death the subject of just exactly how a capital-gains tax cut will stimulate this sluggish economy.

With Mrs. Stubbs resting a hand on my shoulder as she fills my glass with wine, I become consumed by a thought: *I need to get out of this town.* My preoccupation with Washington—the scent of power and greed that hangs over the city like swamp gas—and the miserable effect it had on Ray is misplaced. It's me I'm really worried about. It's me who's dying a slow death on the Potomac. I violate Ellen's rules of engagement and ask Kate if she has ever given any thought to moving away from Washington.

"Almost every day," she sighs. "I actually can't think of a thing about this town that I'd miss besides the museums and the weather in the spring and fall."

Ellen claps her hands. "Why Jack himself was making noises last week about moving to Oklahoma. That's how desperate he is."

"Oil and gas," Evan says warily. "I don't see a rebound out there for some time."

"Why Oklahoma?" Kate asks me.

"Because Jack likes to be contrairry," calls Mrs. Stubbs from the doorway to the kitchen.

I say, "I saw an ad for twenty acres of land. The price was right."

Evan: "That's it?"

"That, and it was near a town that I couldn't find on the map."

He smiles. His teeth are like piano keys. "I get it," he says. "A tax write-off."

Ellen asks Kate, "Would you ever consider moving outside the Beltway?"

"My dream is five hundred head of cattle in Wyoming," she replies. "Of course, I'd have to marry a veterinarian."

"Why Jack just loves animals. You know, he doesn't go anywhere without that crazy dog of his."

Dan, who has bullied his way through a thicket of legs to lie beneath the dining room table, climbs to his feet, and bullies his way back out. He sounds like an old man ascending the steps.

The telephone rings at intervals, stirring Evan's head from its position over his plate of salmon and pignoli-studded rice. On the second ring an answering machine kicks in. The volume is turned loud enough for us to hear Evan's message—not the words, but the tone of his voice. He sounds like a man locked in a closet, speaking very deliberately. Each time the machine beeps, Evan's ears perk up like a spaniel's.

A butter dish makes its way around the table and I catch Kate's eye. She gives me a wink that seems to say, *"Let's get the hell out of here!"* I'm ready. If she wanted to rob a bank right now, I'd volunteer to drive the getaway car without a moment's hesitation.

Her hands are small, the nails elegantly manicured. They remain in her lap until a lock of hair falls into her face and she rakes it to the side. There is a tiny mole next to her eyebrow. I can imagine how she looked as a child.

Mrs. Stubbs is circling the table with a pot of coffee, spreading the scent of almonds in her wake. In a moment of silence Kate says, "Tell me something, Jack. Have you been in therapy?"

Evan's chewing slows to a halt. He gives me a wide-eyed look suggesting he'd like to help me out, but can't think of a thing to say. Ellen starts an inventory of dessert forks and coffee spoons.

I have never been in therapy. The thought of spending days or months or years delving into my own conflicted past fills me with the sort of existential dread that I imagine an astronaut might feel, drifting helplessly in space.

"No," I reply. "Why do you ask?"

"Curiosity," she says.

"And you, have you been in therapy?"

She nods slowly. It is a portentous nod. "I couldn't have gotten myself together after the divorce without it."

"How long have you been divorced?" From the corner of my eye, I see that Ellen's face wears the wild expression of a woman who has been treading water for days in the open sea.

"Separated for four years, divorced for two."

"Do you have children?"

"A boy. Jason."

I dab the corner of my mouth with a napkin, keenly aware of what feels like a taut strand of piano wire stretched between Kate and me. My neck is clammy; my whiskers seem to have grown during the course of the meal.

"I like kids," I say.

Kate laughs. She looks to Ellen. "You did tell me that, didn't you?"

Ellen seems slightly embarrassed. "Willie and Sondra think the world of Jack, don't they, darling?"

"Jack's an awfully good uncle," says Evan.

Forget about trying to analyze *why* people fall for each other. Forget attempting to chart *how* this happens. Were I to tally up Kate's appealing qualities—the throaty laugh, the flecks of gold in her blue eyes, the spirit of independence, the off-beat sense of humor—the sum doesn't begin to explain the happy queasy feeling in the pit of my stomach. But the attraction is real. What else would explain my sudden loss of appetite or the boyish enthusiasm I bring to a conversation about the long-term impact of the Reagan-Bush years?

Our political round table cuts to a commercial when Mrs. Stubbs arrives with a tray of desserts. We have Black Forest cake, almond-apple torte, chocolate-covered strawberries, and pecan pralines. Kate takes the strawberries.

"Dearheart," says Mrs. Stubbs. "So tell me about what kind of shampoo you are a using right now."

"Well, different kinds," she says warily. "I switch off."

"The reason why I am asking is to make shure you know the good ones and the bad ones. A course there is no reason to be using the shampoos that they are still squirting into the eyes of those poor little rabbits. Now what has a little rabbit ever done to desairve somet'ing like that?"

The doorbell sounds.

"Lordy," Mrs. Stubbs exclaims. "At this time of night, a darbell is nothing but trouble."

We sit in waiting-room silence. From the foyer comes Mrs. Stubbs's voice, then another woman's voice—quiet, insistent—then Mrs. Stubbs again. "I don't think so, young laidy. Not tin the middle of dinner."

It's Nina! I am convinced of it.

I imagine her in the other room, shaking the cool night from her wool cape, preparing to play the famous mad scene from *Lucia*. Soon will come the trills and the coloratura passages. She will float through the doorway, a weird smile frozen on her face to indicate that she is bereft of all reason. When Nina spies Kate, the fury lodged in her Calabrian soul will unleash itself. Plates will fly, candlesticks will be chopped in two, the tablecloth will be set afire. Mrs. Stubbs will growl; Ellen will shriek; Evan will flee; Kate will not flinch. I will cry out for restraint, and Nina will shout back that I am a *fine* one to be talking about restraint. The two of us will make a terrible scene and then escape out the front door with our arms locked around each other. It will be magnificent!

Who finally appears in the doorway is not Nina, but a short, stocky woman wearing biking tights and a black beret. Scanning our faces, she fixes her gaze on Evan. "Mr. Evan Barton?"

A praline lodges in his throat. His face turns ashen. "Yes," he croaks. "What's this about?"

"Sorry to interrupt your dinner, Mr. Barton, but I'm here to serve you with a summons and a complaint."

THE HARDBALL DIMENSION

What would Miss Manners recommend at such a moment?

Should we simply pick up the conversation where we left off? We were beginning a discussion of the relative merits of different private schools, as I recall. Or do we continue to police the invisible crumbs scattered around our plates while Evan pores over the summons. Soon he has papers spread across his end of the table. Knowing Evan, he is looking for an opening, trying to figure out which card to play. He's probably already plotting his revenge. He has a microcassette recorder pressed to his bosom, which he whispers into at intervals. "Talk to Mary about travel receipts. Wayne, get me overhead costs. Sally, put together the on-line charges."

Then he grins. Charging forward to snatch victory from the jaws of defeat is what gets this man out of bed in the morning. There is no shame in this for Evan, not as there is for Ellen, who has spent the last fifteen minutes in the kitchen.

Kate looks to me for help.

"I get it now," Evan mutters. "Franklin and Adamson are behind this. This has their fingerprints all over it. It's the old power play. Those sons of bitches." He smiles again.

From the other room, Ellen says brightly, "Could we talk about this later, hon?"

"Are the kids asleep?" I ask.

Evan stops shuffling papers. He looks at me. Given the suspicion in his gaze, you would think I had just asked for his latest tax return.

"What did you say, Jack?"

"I asked about the kids. Your children. Are they asleep?"

"Will and Sondra?" He looks at his watch, then at the kitchen door, then at me. "It's after ten," he says blankly. And I say, "Maybe I should take a look."

Kate is right behind me as we climb the stairs. We step over a huge fire truck blocking the hallway.

"What in God's name was that all about?" she asks.

"A learning disability. Evan shorts out if he tries to concentrate on matters of law and family at the same time."

"It was spooky."

"Another few seconds of that and I would have asked you to say something in Latin."

"I don't speak Latin."

"Neither does he. But it would've snapped him back to the present."

"I'm not sure anything would take his mind off the summons. Honestly, I thought he was having a heart attack when she handed it to him. He was actually vibrating in his chair."

"That was excitement. The knowledge that the full power

and authority of the United States judicial system is on his tail gets his juices flowing."

"Poor guy."

"Poor guy who probably bilked his clients out of *millions.*"

"Why did Ellen offer that woman a cup of coffee?"

"She couldn't help herself. She defaults to the hostess mode."

"Poor Ellen."

"Poor Ellen is right."

Willie's room is flooded by static and gray light. He is lying on his back. A Matchbox truck rises and falls on his belly. Sondra's head is at his feet. She is asleep on her stomach, her little bottom sticking up in the air, an outstretched hand still gripping the arm of her Dolly Lama. I turn off the VCR and gently rearrange them before throwing the comforter over the bed.

" 'Night, Uncle Jack," Willie whispers.

" 'Night, kid."

"Drive safely."

"I will. And you be careful on your bike tomorrow. No wheelies."

"What's a wheelie?"

"Forget it, Guillermo."

"That's not my name."

"It's your name in Spanish."

"That doesn't mean you have to call me that."

"Get used to it, chum. Pretty soon that's what everybody in the country will be calling you."

"Not my mom."

"You've got that right."

"Uncle Jack?"

"Yeah?"

"What's a process server?"

"So where have you been sitting?"

"At the top of the steps. I couldn't sleep."

"Then why was the VCR on?"

"I just turned it on so that you would think I was sleeping."

"Then why didn't you pretend that you *were* sleeping?"

"I had a question to ask you."

"A process server is someone who brings important papers to your house."

"Like a mailman?"

I gaze up at the stars through the skylight. "Yeah, sort of."

"Then why is my dad so mad?"

"Sometimes you get mail you don't like."

"You mean like invoices?"

Where do these words come from? "That's right."

"Is the process server the one who wants to take my dad's shirt?"

"I wouldn't worry about that, *compañero*. He's got plenty of shirts."

"But it's *his,* Uncle Jack."

"Your dad's a smart cookie. He'll hold on to his shirt." I kiss his forehead. "Now you get some sleep."

Kate is standing in the doorway. Her eyes are shining. I have wooed her with my bedside manner.

In the hallway she whispers, "Now what do we do?"

"We tie bedsheets together, descend to the garden, and escape on horseback."

First Ellen's voice floats up the stairs. "Well, if it's not serious, hon, then why did they bother to serve the papers in the middle of the night?" Then Evan's: "Christ! How many times do I have to explain to you that this is just a good old-fashioned power play. Happens all the time. CalumNet's lawyers write to say that they think our charges are too high. I write back saying welcome to Washington, D.C. It would have died right there if Franklin hadn't gotten it into his head that he could prime CalumNet's pump and slip me the shiv at the same time. It's classic. I'd be the first one to give him a round of applause if it wasn't me who was getting stuck."

"But Joel's your partner."

"I took the firm into the big pond, and Franklin discovered that he couldn't swim in deep water. He's turned Adamson. These are guys who look at their percentage like it's some kind of retirement. *I'm* the one who's beating the bushes for new clients. *I'm* the one who has to keep an eye on the bottom line. For that I get a lousy third. It's not right, not with the work I've put in. So I spread the overhead around a little bit. And start value billing. Big deal. That's business. If CalumNet doesn't like our work or doesn't want to pay our fees, they can go somewhere else. That's business, too."

"But it's all legal, right?"

"Darlin', this isn't about legal and illegal. This is about knocking heads. This is the hardball dimension. Say, did I leave the recorder at the table?"

"Ev, can't you at least wait until Jack and Kate leave?"

He chuckles. "You wait, you're prey," he says softly. "You move, you become a predator."

Kate and I are sitting on the top step. Her head is resting against the banister; over the top of it, I can see down into the foyer. Evan is pacing with a cordless phone pressed to his ear. At certain angles he looks as though he has an antenna sticking out of his head. Ellen stands beside the closet, a whitened fist pressed to her lips.

"I don't need to talk to him, Sam. Just tell him to meet me at the Westin at seven. Tell him it's time to circle the wagons. There's trouble in Dodge City."

Kate whispers, "It makes me want to cry. This is all so sad."

"The mass of men lead lives of quiet litigation."

"He might be innocent, you know."

"He might."

"I guess he probably isn't. Completely, that is."

"From the look of things, the odds of that seem rather long."

Quietly Ellen says, "Ev, please!"

The antennaed head disappears into the study.

It makes me sad to realize that Kate Baldwin and I, budding paramours of three hours and seventeen minutes, are closer to one another at this moment than Evan and Ellen Barton, duly wed spouses of thirteen years. If the papers had been served on me, I hope I would have said, "Aw, shit," and thrown the unopened envelope into the kitchen drawer filled with tape, glue, staples, tax receipts, three kinds of hammers, and a shoe box crammed full of unpaid bills. The intrusion would have angered and embarrassed me, but I would have mugged it up for my guests—and for myself. No frosty silence, no cordless phones, no dry chuckles or weird aphorisms about life in a world of carnivores.

"Why do I feel like I'm in junior high school?" Kate says. "Look at us."

"We've finished our homework and we're trying to fall asleep but our parents start arguing downstairs so we came out here to listen?"

"That's it."

"Only my parents never argued."

"What'd they do?"

"They had serious discussions."

"That sounds awful."

"It was. The main reason I got into therapy was to learn to express my anger."

"Did it work?"

"So far I can only get irritated." She says this without a trace of irony. "What about you, Jack? What was it like for you growing up?"

"The first commandment at the Townsend house was 'Thou shalt disappear at the first sign of distress.' "

"What were you supposed to do with your anger?"

"Convert the negative energy into work. Tidy up a spice rack, mow the lawn, wax the car, rearrange snow tires in the garage."

"How did you come to grips with that?"

"I guess I developed strong attractions for people who have no self-control whatsoever."

"Nina," she says knowingly.

"Ellen warned you, huh?"

"She may be your sister, but she's also my friend."

"What did she say?"

"A secret," Kate whispers. "The question I have for you, Mr. Jack Townsend, is this: am I talking to a man who is on the rebound?"

"I honestly don't know."

"Which means yes."

"Probably."

"I can handle that," she says. "As long as everything between us is up front. No surprises. I want to know what's on your mind."

"Honey, I'm not sure you want to know what's on my mind right now."

Kate smiles slyly. She is pleased that we are moving a little too fast. She is not put off by the subject of sex. She can talk about it. She likes it. I can see in her eyes a matter-of-factness that unnerves me a bit. Frankly, I'm not used to this. Nina wasn't keen on verbal foreplay. Our lust was born in silence and darkness for the most part, give or take a little Puccini.

"I've got a good feeling about you, Jack Townsend. You're a sweet man. I haven't run across many of those lately. Not in this town."

"I'm not to be trusted."

"At least you *know* that. Which puts you miles ahead of the pack. Lately I've gotten stuck with guys who seem to think the way to impress a lady is to sprinkle a French phrase or two into the middle of a dinner conversation. Or bore you to tears with their hobbies. Last week a guy asked me back to his place to watch his swing videos."

"Um, how were they?"

"Sweaty. The worst part was that he would stop the VCR

and beg me to practice some of the moves with him. 'Larry, I don't swing' just didn't get through to this guy. The other day he called and asked me to join him at a weekend swing camp in the Catskills. Honestly, I felt like I was riding the wrong train in a Woody Allen movie."

I find the tough-gal demeanor alluring. Now Kate's arm is around my neck. She's fingering my shirt pocket. I take her hand. The size of my hand in relation to hers makes me feel like a giant. Her expression grows serious.

"I need to ask you something," she says.

"Fire away."

"What is the exact nature of your problem with women?"

"Is this another version of 'Mr. Townsend, would you please tell the jury exactly when you stopped beating your wife?' "

"Sort of. But there's no reason to take it personally. All men have problems with women."

"They do?"

"Judith and I have been talking about this for months."

"Who's Judith?"

"My therapist."

Suddenly it's two against one and I'm speaking for the record. "Can I have some time to think about it?"

"Nope. I need your first reaction. That's important."

"My problem with women." I give the subject some thought, but nothing that I would care to reveal comes to mind. "Did you ask Ellen?"

Kate nods gravely.

"What did she say?"

"No comment."

This line of inquiry seems about as fair as a rigged election. But two can play the same game. I adopt a pensive expression and sit there quietly until Kate looks at her watch.

"I'm already late for the sitter," she says. "Let's have it."

"I'll call you in an hour with my answer."

A shake of the head. "Jason's a light sleeper. Wednesday night to Saturday afternoon he's with me. Saturday night to Wednesday morning he's with Tobias. Until Thanksgiving, that is. Thanksgiving through Memorial Day we switch."

It sounds so much like a train schedule I feel the urge to pull out my wallet and make a note of the custody arrangement on the back of an automatic teller receipt. I'm not exactly sure why she's telling me this, but I'd be willing to bet that neither the francophile nor the swingmaster ever got young Jason's sleeping schedule.

"Now let's see. That means you're solo on Saturday, Sunday, Monday, and Tuesday nights?"

"Whoa, boy," Kate says.

"Sorry. It's been such a long time since I laid down the ground rules in a romantic relationship. I hope I didn't offend you."

"Shut up and kiss me goodnight, you fool."

This is different. This is chaste and juicy all at once. Kate kisses with her eyes open. The flecks in her irises are gold and wheat-colored. She smells of the beach. We retreat to each side of the railing, out of breath.

After a moment she says, "So you ducked my question altogether. That's very interesting."

"I'm still thinking."

"You ducked it, Jack. Plain and simple."

"What does that mean?"

"For one thing, it means you're a Wasp at heart."

"Guilty," I say.

"Could be just the tip of the iceberg."

"No doubt."

"I'll have to watch you like a hawk."

"Does that mean I get to see you again?"

"It's required."

"How about tomorrow?"

"Tomorrow Jace has his Suzuki lesson from six to seven."

"How about seven-thirty?"

She thinks. "You come to my place for dinner. Homemade pizza. We talk. You go home before Jace goes to bed. And we take it from there."

"I love pizza," I say.

She mashes her nose against my arm. "You're a romantic jerk. Admit it, Jack."

"Well, there you are!" calls Ellen, climbing the steps. "I won't say another word except that I'm glad I didn't have to go any farther to find the two of you. It's nice to see that the evening has been a success for someone."

"How is Evan?" Kate asks.

Ellen's gaze lifts into the darkened hallway behind us. "Oh, he's fine," she says brightly. "A little embarrassed is all. Thank God for E-mail or poor ol' Ev wouldn't sleep a wink tonight."

Poor ol' Ev. The fact that I am related by marriage to poor ol' court-summoned Ev does not mean he gets my sympathy over this. This is payback time. This is trouble Evan richly deserves. The image of a process server in Lycra tights and beret interrupting the dinner of a wealthy man who has been bilking his clients for the last five years says something profound about the possibility of justice in America.

Kate stands. "Ellen, the dinner was delicious and, until a few moments ago, my dinner partner was a perfect gentleman. I can't thank you enough."

At the front door, she has kisses for both of us. Mine is a discreet peck on the cheek.

Ellen and I remain on the porch while Kate plods through a sea of golden pebbles to a Honda Accord parked at the end of the driveway. The engine catches instantly, so quickly it startles me. I am reminded of Nina's old Citroën, whose engine routinely cranked for thirty seconds before it caught. Often it wouldn't start at all. Taking the subway out to Takoma Park to fire up Elvira (named for the character in *Don Giovanni* who is animated by revenge) was always a fifty-fifty gamble. And having to travel with a special packet of Citroën-starting tools made me feel like a cat burglar. Even Nina, who by nature abhors poking around beneath the hood of a car, could prime the carburetor with gasoline, roll start Donna Elvira in either direction, and, with her eyes closed, locate the wire that regularly jiggled loose from the starter. But it always seemed to be something new that broke on that damn car. Bent over the engine with a succession of tow-truck drivers, I learned as much as I ever want to know about ignition assemblies, air-to-gas ratios, clogged carburetor jets, and loose alternator belts. As soon as one thing was fixed, something else would conk out. Still, Nina won't part with La Donna. She likes the color, a midnight blue.

I hate to bring up Nina's car at a moment like this, but the difference between the make of hers and Kate's automobile seems, well, striking. I always thought that I hated that Citroën, but now I'm not sure. This Honda seems unnaturally quiet and efficient. With a toot of the horn, Kate is gone.

"Well," says Ellen, "I am glad to see that you aren't the crazy old fool I thought you had become."

"Are you okay?"

She looks out at the street. "Now don't you start acting like a worrywart," she says.

"It can't be easy."

"It'll be fine. Ev's already got the best lawyer in town. He'll take care of everything."

I take her to mean that Evan has already put the house in his brother's name so the courts can't seize it and, as we speak, has begun to lay down a gloriously thick paper trail.

"El, I was asking about you."

"Oh, don't worry about me," she says. "Stick around and you'd see that tonight's like any old night around here."

"Ellen—"

"Honey, this is boring."

"I think it might be important."

"A lawyer gets involved with the law. That's his business. Mine happens to be good at what he does. One of the best. Which means he gets more involved than most."

"You're not worried at all?"

"And just what am I supposed to be worried about?"

"Those charges sound pretty serious."

"Enough!" she says sharply. She is forcing herself to smile. "Not another single word until you tell me everything that you and Kate talked about. I was right about her, wasn't I?"

"She's interesting," I say.

"More than that. That woman is quality. In a lifetime you don't meet many like Kate."

"That's true," I say.

Ellen frowns. She is troubled by the note of hesitancy in my voice. "Whatever you do, hon, don't start in on her right away with any of your crazy ideas. Better to keep it low key for a little while. Let her get to know you. And don't you dare make any comments about the way she's raising Jason or what she eats or reads or how she lives her life."

"You're suggesting I play a role?"

"I'm suggesting that you mind your manners."

"I've got to be honest with her, El. We have an agreement."

"Just don't be honest to a fault. Show her that you can sit on the porch and read the Sunday paper and talk about the things in the world that are *important*, not just the creepy stories on page A32."

Why should I hide from Kate that I have a minor passion for wire service reports about people who stuff their pet cats and put them on the mantelpiece or eat a hundred salamis to get into the *Guinness Book of World Records*?

"If it's not going to work, it would be best for both of us to find out right away."

Ellen kisses her fingers and touches them to my cheek. "Just act like a regular guy for a little while. That's all."

What exactly does she mean? Is Ellen suggesting I pack away my angst like old clothes in a footlocker? Is that what women in Washington want these days—a guy who doesn't pop off too much, who knows how to put on a happy face, whose thoughts are so simple and linear he *always* makes sense?

WHEN TO SURRENDER

This is what I know about Kate Baldwin:

She was born and raised in Pelham, New York, the eldest of three girls, all currently unmarried, aged twenty-nine, thirty-two, and thirty-four. Her father is a CPA and her mother publishes a magazine that is targeted at big spenders in the art-auction market. Kate attended Episcopal preschool, day school, and prep school, then Bryn Mawr College and the University of Pennsylvania Law School. She spent three years on Wall Street and put her ex-husband through law school. After Jason was born, she decided to quit the rat race and took a job at the SEC. She intends to stay there until Jason graduates from high school. At age 46 she will retire from the federal government, sell the house she owns free and clear (thanks to an inheritance from her grandmother), and move out of town. Her dream, it turns out, is not Wyoming and five hundred head of cattle, but an energy-efficient bungalow on Cape Cod with a view of the ocean. There she plans to open a small business: a bed and breakfast, a nursery, a craft gallery, something like that. Could be anything, she tells me, anything but a law office.

Romantic jerk that I am, I begin dreaming of low sandy swales and tidal creeks and cranberry bogs. One could do worse than spend one's declining years on a temperate coast loading bags of rich black soil into late-model station wagons. One could also do worse than spend one's inclining years in a cozy home at the District line in Friendship Heights.

Kate's brick row house, built in the 1940s, is an end unit with a screened porch facing a small yard. A tall Norway spruce stands next to the porch, and an ungainly hackberry grows in a far corner. By Kate's standards the place is a mess. Perhaps yard work was Tobias's job. Still, I can't help but wonder why she hasn't taken the gardening chores under her own wing. An hour a week is all it would take, half an hour for a time-and-motion phenomenon like Kate.

I've never met anyone who could put fifteen minutes to greater advantage. In the kitchen Kate will make yogurt cheese or rinse alfalfa sprouts while she's talking on the telephone. Her current reading *(West with the Night)* hangs on the arm of a rocker in the living room. Her quilting projects and rug-braiding paraphernalia emerge from and disappear into a Shaker blanket chest that doubles as a living-room coffee table. The storm doors and shutters in need of a new coat of paint move like barbershop customers from their hinges to the saw horses set up on the upstairs porch. Every night Kate scrapes and sands while listening to the first segment of "All Things Considered." "It's a good transition," she said. "The only way I seem to get out the frustrations of the office is by working with my hands."

Her house is as neat as a pin.

It amazes me that she has no real awareness of her efficiency. The way she tackles household chores seems second nature, almost relaxed. She doesn't lose herself in the work. The instant Jason needs her, the crocheting needles get jabbed into a ball of yarn and Kate drops to one knee. If one of the twice-weekly phone conversations with Tobias grows serious, she'll throw a kitchen towel over the glob of bread dough she's kneading and take a seat at the dining-room table.

It is during date number two that I get a rundown on her marriage. The photo in Jason's bedroom shows Tobias to be one of those stocky, square-jawed, brushy-mustached, plaid flannel-and-moccasin types. A real underachiever: pre-med Phi Beta Kappa at Stanford, law degree from Columbia, Ph.D. in chemical engineering from MIT. Kate tells me that he is a nice guy but very controlling. He once wrote a software program to plot the nutritional content of their meals. He used to type up his weekend plans, which proved to be even more scheduling than Kate could stand. Also, he is undersexed.

We are eating sushi when she tells me this. I have just consumed a length of raw eel.

"Undersexed?"

Kate leans forward. "Tobe just wasn't interested, Jack. For years I thought it was me. I have self-image problems as it is, so naturally I started punishing myself. It's a wonder I didn't end up with an eating disorder."

"Did you ever talk about it?"

"Sex is not an issue you discuss with Tobias. I think it goes way back with him. His mother is very controlling, too."

She trolls a piece of tuna through the soy sauce. I put a dollop of *wasabi* on my tongue and inhale.

"He hates to let go," she says. "He won't let anyone see him in a vulnerable position."

"Surely he must have learned to trust you."

"We were married for eight years, Jack. In all that time he never once left the bathroom door unlocked."

Kate has a theory that all male behavior is motivated by sex. Now I realize that this sort of statement, made by a woman whose bookshelves contain six linear feet of feminist literature, is likely to be dismissed out of hand by some guys. But she might have a point. It does seem to me that we (perhaps I should just speak for myself here) do have a rather large section of the brain devoted to the subject, cordoned off from the more mundane functions in much the same way that the X-rated tapes are kept on high shelves at the local video store.

"So how does Tobias fit into this scheme?" I have to ask.

"He got short-circuited. He won't admit it, but he's operating against all the healthy urges."

This talk of healthy urges, coming as it does before any healthy urges have been acted upon, makes an impression on me. Liza might describe the attraction as an example of the rebound-opposite phenomenon. Marie would accuse me of grabbing for the brass ring. Joanie would say I was acting like a horny bastard. No doubt they all have a point, though I refuse to let myself get swallowed up in too much psychological speculation.

That's not to say that I don't sometimes wonder about the significance of Kate's overgrown lawn, the dun-colored grasses woven into the chain-link fence, the layer of leaves mulching on the ground. Am I expected to pitch in here? Has Kate set this territory aside for the next man who comes into her life? Is this a test? Or could it be that at some deep level she still considers the yard Tobias's domain?

It is a Saturday evening at the end of October, two weeks and two days since I met Kate. I am standing at her front door holding a fistful of marigolds which I ripped from a Foggy Bottom flower bed just three hours earlier. Jason answers my knock. Dressed in gray tweed and loafers, he is gearing up to make the journey downtown.

"G'day mate," I say in my best Australian accent.

"Hullo, Mr. Townsend."

Either Jason got someone's lousy sense-of-humor gene or the divorce has tamped down his personality a little bit. Maybe it's the clothes. It must be difficult to clown around when you're always dressed like an Oxford don.

"One of these days you and I ought to get out to the Capital Center for a Georgetown basketball game," I say.

"I don't really know if I would like basketball."

"Maybe we ought to just take a chance."

"You'll have to ask my mom."

He climbs the stairs slowly, at each step moving his hand to a higher grip on the railing.

Kate's in the kitchen, back to the wall, ear to the telephone. She salutes me with a can of beer, takes a sip, and then pours the rest into a pot of chili. I snack on a plate of toasted cashews under the watchful gaze of a huge gray squirrel parked outside on the window ledge. Kate motions with a hand; I crack the window and, like the cashier at a self-service gas station, push a couple of nuts toward the squirrel's waiting paw.

Hanging up, she says, "Well that was some news this morning."

"And to think we saw this nasty business begin to unfold."

"Wish I hadn't, if you want to know the truth."

Today Evan made the front page of the *Washington Post* Metro section. Now the world knows that he has been sued for legal malpractice and indicted for fraud. According to the article, CalumNet's officials assumed that they were paying poor ol' Ev by the hour. None of them could recall agreeing to allow him to bill the corporation at his "premium" rates. Evan's partner, Joel Franklin, was quoted at the end of the piece saying that he was "shocked, dismayed, and completely in the dark" about all the financial details of the case. "Evan Barton was the rainmaker," he said. "He took the lead on the CalumNet work and we didn't question him. If we're guilty of anything, it's of putting too much trust in a friend."

"How's he taking it?" Kate asks.

"He's going to countersue."

"God, he's irrepressible."

"He's a crook."

She ladles cornbread batter into a pan. "Ellen must be a mess."

"When the *Post* called last night for his response to the article, she packed up the kids and drove to Philly. They left at midnight."

"That poor woman."

"Five counts of mail fraud, a suit for more than two million dollars in overcharges."

"It's probably an exaggeration."

"Fine. Say he only helped himself to a half million. That's five hundred thousand-dollar bills."

"It would seem that he has a serious problem."

"To put it mildly."

"Don't be too hard on him, Jack."

"Darlin', with the wrong judge you can do time for stealing polyester suits from Sears."

"He got greedy. He saw a lot of money switching hands and thought he deserved a bigger piece of the pie. He's not the first lawyer who got caught with his hand in his client's pocket. And he won't be the last." When we both hear Jason clomping around upstairs, she says, "Enough about that, cowboy," and gives me a long, greedy kiss on the lips. I swoon.

"So who am I meeting tonight?" I ask.

Kate's dining-room table, a wide oak board with enough scars and burns to suggest that it dates back to the time of the Conquistadors, is dressed with seven orange and green Mexican placemats and seven orange and green candles. The wine glasses are handsome, misshapen pieces of blown glass. The napkin rings are welded hunks of barbed wire. Each plate has a colorful, impressionistic sketch of a rooster. Kate has begun to describe tonight's dinner guests—so far I've heard about the bookstore owner and his mosaicist wife—when the doorbell sounds. Three quick rings. Jason arrives at the bottom of the steps with his traveling gear, which includes a miniature suitbag.

"Excuse me for a moment," she says.

I can't resist taking a peek. Tobias remains on the porch, Kate stays in the doorway. They peck one another on the cheek. I can't hear the conversation. The only thing I can see is Kate's back, rigid as a board.

The front door shuts. She leans into it, resting her forehead on the wood.

"Advil," she says. "Bring me Advil."

"You want to talk?"

"We don't have that kind of time, Mr. Townsend."

"Is it always like this?"

"Only when Tobe decides he's going to be sweet to me."

"Which means what?"

She turns. She is holding a rose.

"I realize that this is none of my business, but if you don't want his flowers maybe you should tell him that next time. Say it straight out."

"He would act wounded."

"Forever?"

"When Tobias acts wounded, I am transported back to the end of our marriage, which was four months of the most polite backbiting you could imagine. One round of that was more than enough. I couldn't take it again. So I take his flowers and kiss my little boy good-bye and chew ibuprofen."

It turns out that tonight's meal is a regular event. Kate gets together once a month with this group of friends for a potluck supper. "Our moveable feast," she calls it. Ted and Alma, the bookstore owner and the mosaicist, bring a salad covered with orange slices. Rolf the chemist and Karin the zoo-habitat designer bring apple pie. Sandra, a wildflower photographer–cum–real estate agent brings decaffeinated Colombian coffee. I bring marigolds and an appetite.

We begin with a round of Quaker hand-holding. Then Karin reads a selection from Kahlil Gibran, something about thirsty camels and walking with a sharp stone in your shoe. Ted listens with his eyes closed. Rolf worries an earlobe. Afterward Kate opens two bottles of wine and starts them around the table in different directions. Here we are, seven adults sipping Chianti, soon deeply ensconced in a discussion about the sexual stirrings of children and the dilemma a parent faces when a young son reports that the seven-year-old girl next door told him to "lie still and play the girl while I lie on top of you." "Is this normal?" Alma wants to know. I honestly can't say. Kate regards my empty bowl with what seems to me a look of disapproval and asks if I want more. I do—her vegetarian chili is delicious—but the reproving glance causes me to shake my head.

Rolf is reporting on a strange baby-sitter. "So I said to Helmut, 'Show Daddy how he washed you, darling.' "

Karin turns to me and says, "I suppose to someone who doesn't have children this must sound really obsessive."

"Actually, it brings back memories of my own childhood."

Her eyes widen. "Was it traumatic?"

"Oh, gosh."

Kate stands and carries a stack of dishes to the kitchen.

Karin says, "Did you suffer? I hope it's not too personal to ask. I'm really just interested in how you got through it. As a parent, you understand."

Everyone is sitting forward, assaulting me with expressions of concern. Did I suffer as a child? Of course I suffered. Suffering is in the *nature* of childhood, isn't it?

"I wasn't tortured or anything," I say. "But I hear that with help kids can even get over that."

"Let's get back to your experience, Jack. That is, if you don't mind sharing it with us."

"You know, it really wasn't so bad being locked in a closet. Once you settle in, it becomes sort of peaceful."

Kate returns from the kitchen and her gaze sweeps the table. She doesn't see me, which means I'm in big trouble. I'd much rather get a wicked glare than be ignored. I curse myself for lacking the poise and wit to gracefully deflect this conversation from my corner. I've never been good at moments like this. Ten eyes stay fixed on me.

Kate hands me a wine bottle as she takes a seat. "So did you talk to your neighbor about her daughter, Alma?" she asks.

Five hands reach for dessert forks.

The guests have gone home, the candles are extinguished, the dishes washed, dried, and put away. I am sitting on the dhurrie rug, my back to the blanket chest, watching Kate, who is polishing the dining-room table with furious little circular strokes.

"You were making fun of them," she says.

"You think I wasn't telling the truth?"

"Alright Jack, who locked you in a closet?"

"Okay, it was my grandmother who used to get locked in a closet. The thing is, I heard that story so many times when I was a kid I started believing that it had happened to me."

"You're backpedaling."

"Ellen and I had an evil baby-sitter."

"Jack."

"Well, she seemed real to us at the time. I'm sure a good psychologist could find something in that. I did grow up in a weird family."

"We *all* grew up in weird families," she says sharply. And then, quietly: "Just do me a favor and be more aware of what's behind what you say. Tonight I sensed aggression. There was no call for it."

Something is in the air. Act I of this evening needs to conclude with a disagreement for much the same reason that a tea kettle needs a hole in its spout. Early this morning, when Kate called to let me know what time I was expected, she asked me to spend the night. "That is, if you'd like to," she said. "No pressure, of course." Maybe not for her, but the realization that I will soon find myself naked in this woman's bed has been with me all evening.

I can't say for certain what's going through Kate's mind right now, but I can guess. She doesn't want our progressing to what she calls "the physical side of things" to become a crucible. She tells me that taking this step should be natural. I agree. What seems unnatural to me, though, is the way this affair has progressed. In lieu of indulging in any old-fashioned fun, we have spent the last weeks talking about sex. Frankly, we've talked the subject to death. I've heard everything. I know all about Kate's inactive sex life since the divorce, about her inability to have an orgasm during intercourse and her recently conquered inhibitions about masturbation. I have heard about the various affairs in the SEC's enforcement division and the saga of the fellow in the next office who used to spend lunch hours composing sex fantasies on his word processor—it turns out he's in the same league as Poindexter and North when it comes to deleting computer files.

As much as I enjoy these stories, by the time Kate and I are ready to make our big splash together, I can't rid my mind of all the talk. I can't relax. Something essential seems to be missing. The mystery, say. The sense of wonder. There doesn't seem to be a single piece of forbidden fruit left on our plate. I know that Kate has a box of *Consumer Reports'* top-rated condoms in the drawer of her bedstand. I know that we will be performing with the lights on. "If I can't *see*," she confided, "then I just don't get turned on."

I am lying in Kate's bed, perusing an article in *Cosmopolitan* entitled "12 Ways to Please Your Lover and 14 Ways to Leave Him." The bedside lamps are turned on, as is the overhead light, the hall light, and a naked bulb in the closet. Even the Yogi Bear night-light beside Kate's dresser throws off a lumen or two. There is a bluish glow coming from the bathroom across the hall. Kate is humming as she finishes brushing her teeth. I hear the toilet flush. She calls out, "Jack, you want a glass of ice water?"

"Please."

A body flashes past the doorway and descends the steps.

She reappears holding two glasses, dressed only in a pair of white socks. I'm not entirely comfortable with this modern style of romancing. I prefer darkness at a moment like this. Hands seem infinitely better suited to the task of discovering the wondrous treasures of the human body than two eyes assisted by five hundred watts of Sylvania soft whites. Looking at Kate *in puris naturalibus,* I see everything and nothing. I'm left with the impression that she has all the right parts in all the right places. Her breasts are smaller and her legs longer than I would have imagined. The hair on her head looks shorter. She has a mole beside her navel to match the one near her eyebrow.

Dan, behind her in the hallway, wears an admonishing expression. He clomps down the steps as if dragging a body behind him.

"Well," I say finally.

"Let me see *you,*" she says.

The sheet is removed and shy Jack vanishes from the scene. Kate is playful. My boorish behavior at the dinner table is forgotten beneath the klieg lights. Her skin is soft, soft. Kate is a smiler. Everything I do seems to please her. She whispers instructions. I follow orders like a well-trained Cub Scout. Yes. Yes! *Yes! YES!*

Now it's my turn. First she, um, *assists* me with the condom, a bold stroke. There's the usual amount of kissing and probing of forbidden flesh. In time she climbs atop me and we frolic and sigh, and then we reverse and scoot up toward a mountain of pillows.

"You're so virile," she whispers.

I close my eyes and try to chase this word "virile" from my consciousness. Something rum about the sound of it. I try to recall the theme from *Chariots of Fire,* the *1812 Overture,* Handel's "Hallelujah Chorus." I seek to connect myself to the rhythm of the ocean. Soon I find that I'm no longer bothered by the bright light above my head; soon I pay no mind to the pale rump over my shoulder that is rising and falling like the proverbial moon.

During the wrestling phase, Kate falls silent. Our bodies glisten. I finish like a wobbly-legged triathlete, throwing myself at the tape. Kate is lying beside me, saying, "Um, um, um." Her eyes close at last. She wants to be held, and she communicates this without saying a word. I can feel her pulse in my lips, which are pressed to her temple.

It occurs to me that the gentlemanly thing to do would be to rouse myself and offer to fetch Kate another glass of water or a piece of pie or a warm washcloth—*something*. But I'm so tired. My legs have turned into boughs of oak, my arms dead branches. Sleep is coming upon me with the speed of a thoroughbred. Kate rolls against me. Her arm encircles my waist; the other rests against my back, a hand cupping my shoulder.

"Jack, are you awake?"

"Mmm."

"So you're one of those," she says.

My mind has shut down. I am orgasm-drugged, sunk beyond all measure of brain-wave activity, aware only of the scent of warm skin and Opium, and I drift off to sleep thinking that these are the finest aromas on earth.

Sunday morning I awake in an empty house. "Went for a run," says a note scrawled in magic marker on the bulletin board in the hallway. "Help yourself to coffee and whatever. Back at 10."

The clock on the stove says 8:05. I stumble around the kitchen, avoiding the sleek, metallic gadgets strewn here and there that roast, mill, crush, powder, and prepare coffee—it would seem one could do almost everything with a coffee bean in this kitchen except grow it—and pour myself a cup of instant.

Dan is outside reclining in the sun, his head held up like a noble lion's. His eyes open and close like window shades. Sitting on the porch sofa, I too can feel the weight of my eyelids. The air on this October morning is warm and damp, but the chill of winter penetrates the soles of my bare feet.

So, Kate's Sunday morning routine includes a two-hour run. I give some thought to the fact that marathons are run in little more than two hours. Major league baseball games sometimes finish in two hours. Where does this woman get her energy?

I spot her a long way off, jogging up 41st Street. She has a rabbity gait and does not seem to be enjoying herself. She stops at a tree and stretches out her legs. Dan stands at the fence, watching her. I sip my third cup of coffee, hidden from Kate's view by the Norway spruce.

"So where is he, Danny-boy? Is that tired old man still sleeping?"

Dan trots toward the house. He stands at the base of the porch steps and begins to bark at me.

"You there, Jack?"

"Caught," I say.

Kate climbs the fence and starts across the lawn, walking stiff-legged. From a backpack she produces the *New York Times* and I suddenly recall where I first saw her: it was at the Georgetown Bagelry. The stiff gait and the silver nylon jacket and the black tights and pink Nikes are all familiar to me. I was toasted sesame with cream cheese and Kate was oat bran with veggie spread on the side. She was fussy about how the bagel should be prepared—heated but not toasted, I recall—and always took a good ten minutes at the counter. I remember hurrying to beat her through the front door so as not to get caught behind her in line.

"So what's in the news?"

"Bank scandal, stock scandal, drug scandal, sex scandal," she says, sitting beside me.

She isn't sweating exactly, just radiating a sweet-smelling dew. She leans against my arm and kisses the side of my face. I can smell the fresh bagels in her pack. I know that there is a block of cream cheese in the butter compartment of the refrigerator. I flip through the newspaper and settle into the sofa, fully prepared to dedicate myself to a quiet Sunday morning whisking eggs and slicing melon.

Kate says, "You've been on my mind, cowboy. I sure hope you're not one of those fellows who slurps down his coffee and rides off into the sunrise."

"No, ma'am!"

"You're free this morning?"

"Free as a bird."

"That's wonderful." She looks at her watch. "We should leave in about twenty minutes."

"Um, where are we going?"

"Wess," she says.

"Wes who?"

"Not a person. Sort of a gathering," she explains.

"Please tell me right now that you don't belong to some weird religious cult."

"I don't belong to some weird religious cult."

"But we're going to church, aren't we?"

"We're not going to church."

Remember, this is a lawyer speaking to me. "Are we going to some kind of pseudo-church for people who want to go to church but can't handle normal church?"

"We're going to a platform."

"Sounds dangerous."

"Not in the least. It's a meeting of like-minded, liberal-thinking folks like ourselves."

"The fact is, I'm really very conservative. You should hear me on the subject of reducing the capital-gains tax or balancing the budget or getting criminals off the street."

"You'll enjoy it, Jack."

"I don't have the right clothes."

"The dress is casual."

"No matter what I say, I'm not going to be allowed to slide out of this, am I?"

She shakes her head slowly.

"This is one of those get-togethers where everybody sits on fold-out metal chairs in a small auditorium and someone tells us how we should live our lives, isn't it?"

"The chairs are plastic and they're really quite comfortable."

"It sounds a lot like church."

"But it's not about God, Jack. It's not about slavishly following the dictates of a group of old men with ideas that come from the Middle Ages. It's about introspection. It's about enhancing the quality of our relationships. And caring. It's about educating ourselves to create a more ethical culture within this society. It's about community. It's really thought-provoking. Uplifting. Lots of food for thought, I promise."

Food for thought just doesn't cut it with a man who has spent the past two hours dreaming about scrambled eggs and crispy bacon.

Wess, it turns out, is spelled WES, and it stands for the Washington Ethical Society. It *is* like church, the Unitarian variety, except here you get the coffee and sweet rolls before the service. Kate was right: the dress in the auditorium is decidedly casual. Blue jeans are the favored apparel for men, *huipiles* for women. A number of people wear name tags. Kate and I take our seats as a hammered dulcimer plunks out a mournful tune. I am uneasy. There's too much conversation in this undersized auditorium. And no murmuring. I can't get comfortable in a church with no murmuring. The churches I like best are the big dirty cathedrals with cold marble floors and grotesque statuary and air that smells a hundred years old.

The Senior Leader, the featured speaker, is a guy named Stu. He is wearing a cream-colored suit and has a Joe Theismann bouffant hairstyle and blue, blue eyes. This week's talk, the "platform," is entitled "When to Surrender." Kate sits forward, her head held high as Stu warms up by talking about the spiritual journey of life, the evolution of our spirit, and the notion that each of us builds her or his spirituality over time. This sounds all wrong. If you ask me, each of us is born with a great reserve of spirituality, which we bury as we grow older. The task isn't to create spirituality but to recover it—to get back to some true sense of ourselves.

Kate is nodding. Something about the way she bites her lower lip brings to mind an image from last night. I snap shut my eyes and listen to Stu.

Learning to surrender, he says, means letting go so that we can learn from others. Yes! Of course, this can lead to dependency, which is destructive. But, he reminds us, it is just as destructive never to give up control. Surrendering to our spiritual needs means taking time to listen to ourselves. Stu announces that we will now take a few moments to listen to our own thoughts and feelings.

I peek. Kate's eyes are shut so tight you'd think she was counting off to one hundred for a game of hide-and-seek.

My own thoughts inexplicably drift toward the Orioles. I'm worried about their future. I can't help wondering whether next year will be a sorry repeat of the last. Instruct the front office to get rid of the high-dollar free agents and restock from the minors, I tell God, but He probably isn't listening, given that His name hasn't come up once in here. By the way, it's the New Testament God I'm addressing, the God you're supposed to talk to. I envision Him as Don Fernando in *Fidelio,* someone you can summon to pull you out of a tight spot with a few blasts on a trumpet. If anyone's in a tight spot these days, it's the Baltimore Orioles.

"Okay," says Stu, "come back to the room."

Kate leans toward me and whispers. "What do you think?"

"I can go along with everything but the music."

She smiles.

"Did you see the program?"

The smile grows. She is actively biting her lip.

"Putting Mick Jagger and Keith Richards to hammered dulcimer would have to be considered a sacrilege."

Stu announces that there are times when we must surrender to authority, as a student must surrender to the will of his teacher—or a musician must surrender his tie-dyed T-shirt and dulcimer for sequined tights and an electric guitar, I'd like to add. There are times we must surrender to loved ones, times we must surrender to spiritual ideals in order to come to some conclusions about what it means to live the good life. The dulcimer comes alive with a mournful version of "Mixed Emotions" as men and women begin to circle the congregation passing around straw baskets. I toss a couple of bucks into one and head for the door.

FLORIDA
IN WINTER

At Thanksgiving Kate and I are still together. In a moment of madness, she invites me to accompany Jason and her to Pelham for turkey with the Baldwin clan and I, equally mad, accept. Thus we set off on a blustery morning in Kate's Honda, as snug as any nuclear family. I feel uneasy driving these two across the industrial wastelands of New Jersey. The toll takers on I-95 seem to regard me with vague suspicion. Even Jason senses the absurdity of my presence. Crossing the George Washington Bridge, he fills a stretch of silence with this thought: "Mom, do you think Grandma will have enough turkey for Mr. Townsend?"

Dinner is a quiet affair of tight smiles and rapid mastication.

Kate's people are as parsimonious with conversation as they are with food. The whole point of Thanksgiving, that quintessentially American day of worship at the altar of overconsumption, seems lost on these folks. Even their napkins are undersized.

I will remember my silverware clinking against Royal Doulton china, wondering why I alone seem incapable of eating without making a racket. I will remember the food, the smallest Thanksgiving portions and the driest turkey I have ever encountered. Also, the bird is kept in the kitchen, so each request I make for another helping requires most of the family to swing into action. "Jack wants more turkey, Luce. Would you mind terribly?" "No, but let me come out and get his plate." "Carol will bring it in, won't you, Carol?" "There doesn't seem to be much meat left, Mother." "No meat? Why that's nonsense!" Fifteen minutes later: "Here you go, Jack. I trust this will hold you."

"Um, is there any more dressing?"

My heart goes out to Jason. Imagine being a kid and having to spend your holidays in such surroundings. No Pee Wee Herman videos, no sliding down the gleaming wooden banister. There isn't a toy in the whole house as far as I can tell. Just the smell of mothballs and Lemon Pledge, and the hourly death knell of a grandfather clock.

At one point, Arthur the CPA, says, "John, Katharine tells us that you are in the private sector."

"As a matter of fact, I am."

"And in Washington, D.C. Bravo."

We return to showing each other the tops of our heads. I feel bloated with gas. My clothes have become too tight, especially in the crotch and neck. It's all I can do to stop myself from standing up and rearranging myself. For starters, I'd like to take off the damn tie that Kate insisted I wear, open my shirt collar, and breathe again. A man who does not wear ties regularly does not own shirts with collars that fit his neck. I gaze at my dinner companions and wonder why I have yet to feel a sense of outrage at being treated like a visiting Neanderthal. Perhaps this is an orchestrated scheme to drive me away. Jason describes my van to Grandma Helen, and she is plainly horrified. "And Mr. Townsend has dirt in it, and shovels, and there's a place in the back where you can look down and see the road!"

"A business vehicle. . . . Wouldn't that be tax deductible?" Helen asks.

Arthur nods, chewing. He frees a brussel sprout from the tines of his fork. "Deductible doesn't mean affordable," he says quietly.

Lucy begins clearing plates. Carol makes a big show of brushing the crumbs from my placemat into her hand. Kate gazes at the candle flame. The expression on her face is unreadable. I haven't been able to catch her eye all afternoon. Jason, too, seems resigned to the staid Pelham rules. He doesn't try to climb into Kate's lap after dinner. She doesn't brush his hair while she talks to him. She doesn't caress him at all in this house; she squeezes him like a sponge. To keep myself occupied, I pay attention to details. I note that Helen polishes the dining-room table after dinner as if she were waxing a car. She picks up her needlework in the living room and begins to stitch before she sits down on the sofa. When she concentrates, her nose crinkles as though she has just caught a whiff of something unpleasant. I respond to the onset of depression by eating three slices of pecan pie.

On the drive home, we pull into the Vince Lombardi rest stop at the entrance to the New Jersey Turnpike. Jason and I study the collection of trophies in a glass case. I let him pee standing up on the rim of the toilet. This is terribly daring and he laughs the whole time, ruining his aim. In the parking lot, he runs toward the car, trips, and hits the deck. Kate rushes to his side, but he comes up laughing.

Back on the road, she whispers, "What a fiasco. What a mistake."

In the rearview mirror, I see that Jason is asleep, trussed up in his seat belt harness like a parachutist caught in a tree.

"It's always been stuffy at home," she says. "But I had no idea that it was *that* stuffy. Tobias used to complain about the Pelham trips, but I wrote it off as in-law competition. Visiting his folks was no day at the beach." Ten miles of guardrail slide past the window. "Why couldn't I see that for myself?" she asks.

I can't think of a thing to say.

A moment later she adds, "Jason was not enjoying himself."

"He was a little quiet."

"A little!"

Farther down the road she takes my hand and squeezes it.

At Baltimore, we exit the highway toward Towson, where Tobias's parents live. Poor Jason has another Thanksgiving meal to consume, another set of relatives to behave for. I despair to think how much this kid's life resembles the life of a politician: the hectic schedule over which he has no control, the competing interests to balance, the constituencies to please, the votes to garner, the cameras popping in his face at odd moments, the certain knowledge that every move he makes is bound to disappoint someone.

Kate directs me past a line of bleak storefronts. She counts traffic lights and notes landmarks: a Dunkin' Donuts, a Goodwill van parked beside a tire store, a sewing shop called Taylors—"She carries *everything*," Kate says quietly. At a Methodist church, we turn into a quiet neighborhood of small houses set back on well-trimmed lawns. We stop in front of a rambler with four small Japanese red maples lined up in the front yard. The crowns of the maples are perfectly rounded, aggressively spherical.

Jason is roused and unbuckled. He stands on the sidewalk beside his gear, the side of his face sleep-puffy, his hair mashed to the back of his head. Kate leads him to the door. She shakes hands with her former in-laws, then chats earnestly with Tobias, who listens with his head sunk against his chest, arms crossed. Occasionally he nods. At the end he kisses her on the cheek and sends a friendly wave in my direction.

As we climb the ramp onto the highway, Kate drops her seat

to the horizontal position and closes her eyes. It is dusk. A vee of snow geese passes overhead. I can see the lights of the harbor; I can see the halogen lights of the highway south of the city.

"He wanted to meet you," she says, eyes still closed.

"You should have brought him over."

"Oh, please."

"He seems like an awfully nice guy for an ex-husband."

"As nice as nice can be. Tobe's been a nice guy so long he doesn't know how to be anything else."

"Maybe that's who he is."

"I must sound like a shrew," she says.

"You sound tired."

"I'm exhausted."

"Um, could I trouble you for *yet another* helping of turkey?"

This brings a smile to her face. "The funny thing is, as much as Tobe complained about my family, he really fit in there. I didn't realize just how well he fit in until today."

After a moment she continues, "He can still make me angry, which drives me crazy. Judith thinks I still love him. Maybe I do. Only more like a brother. A stepbrother, say. Sometimes I think that's how it has always been. It's as if I haven't gotten over the fact that we were forced to share a room for seven years. And I miss sharing the room, too. Isn't that weird?"

It makes perfect sense to me. It explains why—listening to Kate's end of their phone conversations, watching them from a parked car—I have the sense that at some greatly reduced level they are *still* married.

"He left me," she says suddenly. "No one knows that except Judith. And now you." She returns the seat to the upright position. "You can't imagine what a big deal it is for me to tell you this. We told everyone else that the decision to split was mutual. That was our agreement. Tobias didn't want to be the villain, and I didn't want to be the victim." She fingers a well-folded chewing gum wrapper. "What happened was that Tobias decided that he still loved me but couldn't live with me anymore. I guess I must have felt the same way about him, but I wasn't far enough along in therapy to realize that. I was holding on to a lot of baggage, determined to have the perfect marriage and the perfect family, etcetera, etcetera. I mean, we hadn't slept together for seven or eight months and there I was, pretending that everything was fine." She shakes her head. "Working with Judith has given me perspective. I don't feel so victimized anymore. That is, I recognize the feeling as it comes on and try to overcome it."

Kate is living proof that therapy works. No doubt I could learn a thousand things from this woman.

"Jack," she says, "you can't possibly understand how good this relationship has been for me. Our relationship, I mean."

I am sinking into a black spell. Too much dry turkey and too many hours on this bleak roadway. Kate, who seems to have good instincts for my moods, does not press. We listen to WHFS and roll down the windows and crank up the heat. Trucks as big as super-tankers sail past us into the night. Suddenly we are partners again. We talk about the effects of travel, how it makes you feel alive, makes you wonder why you live most of life like a sleepwalker.

"There are days when I am desperate to get out of Washington," Kate says. "I drive to Great Falls. Just drive there and listen to the water."

"And that works?"

"No, but pretty soon it starts to get dark and I have to go home."

The cars on the Beltway sprint past us like greyhounds.

Kate says, "The pressure builds and builds and then one fine day you know that you've got to get on an airplane and go somewhere else." A moment later: "Go anywhere." And then: "Jack, a woman in my office got stuck with some tickets to Orlando. I picked them up for a song. Next week, Jace and I are going to Disney World. I couldn't talk you into coming with us, could I?" I would go almost anywhere with Kate and Jason: Great Bear Lake,

Patagonia, Vladivostock, the Mississippi Delta. But Florida in winter—

"Just think about it," she says.

At Kate's house we eat cereal. I dole out Cheerios, Wheaties, Rice Krispies in equal amounts into a soup tureen, topping it off with a scattering of old Lucky Charms. Kate eats Total. We sit on the porch under a tartan blanket, clicking spoons against bowls. It becomes a game, drowning out conversation. Afterwards we walk toward Fort Reno Park, guided by the blinking red light of a radio tower. We pass a field on Chesapeake Street where I used to play soccer when I was in high school. I was a goalie. Ray used to come watch me play here. He'd sit behind the goal post and we'd talk most of the game. During corner kicks he'd let me know if an opposing player was trying to slide in behind my back. "Left," he'd call. "Two steps." Or: "On your butt, Juan." Strange to think that I haven't said a word to Kate about Ray.

On the walk home, she says, "Jack, today's been wonderful. I didn't expect this at all. Thank you."

The light goes from red to green, and for a moment we stand there, lost in our own thoughts. I have to wonder what Bogart or Hammett would do in this situation. Would they know right off that there wasn't enough zip in this romance, or would they shrug off the absence of zip in the face of other qualities—peacefulness, companionship, maturity (on Kate's part). Somehow this list seems short and incomplete, but I can't decide what's missing. Or what's essential.

This issue dogs me the following week. It's with me when I awake, and when I am tossing frosty tennis balls for Dan on the frozen tundra of the Palisades. It's with me while I cruise 19th Street, studying the lights in Nina's apartment, scanning the parked cars for England's BMW with the 1LAW license plates. The issue is with me the night Kate calls from Florida, giddy with Jason's exultance at finding himself in a grown-up world filled with toys.

"I wish you were here," she says. Strange to say, I wish I was there, too.

The Thai Room on Connecticut Avenue is not my favorite restaurant, not even my favorite Thai restaurant, though once it was. The food is good, but lately the portions seem to be shrinking. Kate and I are sitting in a booth next to the front door, and every time it opens, a blast of arctic air slams into the back of my neck. Worse still, we are in a perfect position to get a long look at each person who comes into the place. This plays havoc with an already fragmented conversation that so far has touched on romantic relationships, Kate's trip to Florida, the effect of divorce on children, and *Gorillas in the Mist,* the movie about Dian Fossey's struggle to save the mountain gorillas of Rwanda. I have just gobbled down one of those tiny green peppers that explodes in your throat and makes you talk like Marlon Brando in *The Godfather.*

"Eat some rice," Kate says.

I gesture. I have no rice.

Bless her heart, this tanned angel goes to the kitchen for steamed rice. Such a contrast to Nina, who would have uttered an ejaculation to Saint Blaise, the patron saint of throat ailments, and left my fate in God's hands. Three bowls of rice and the heat is still there, but lessening. It feels like most of the nerve endings in my throat have been burned away. My appetite is gone. The waiter arrives with Kate's Singha and my Dewar's on the rocks.

She says, "Jack, I'm surprised." I bring the glass to my lips. "I mean, *Dewar's.*" She smiles.

It does such a good job anesthetizing my throat, I order another.

"I suppose there are a lot of things about you that I still don't know," she says.

I say, "My grandparents were married almost fifty years. Just before my grandmother died, I asked her why my grandfather hated talking about his childhood, and she shrugged and said, 'He's still such a mystery to me.' "

"Are you trying to tell me you think the tendency to be secretive is genetic?"

"I'm just telling a story."

Kate is slow with a menu. Her technique is to eliminate selections one by one. "I just don't think I can handle basil or ginger tonight," or "Last time I was here the mussels were small and sandy." She wants to know exactly how long the steamed fish is steamed. She wants the texture of the curry described. Myself, I stick to *pad thai* and don't bother opening the menu. I'd be the first to admit that this approach lacks creativity, but it makes life so much simpler. It's a habit Nina and I share. She'll find a dish she likes and stand by it like an old friend. Not Kate. For her, ordering the same dish twice at a restaurant indicates a lack of spirit.

She requires two, three, four visits from the waiter. Even then, she has a change of heart and goes off to the kitchen to switch the order from pork with salted mustard greens to beef with oyster sauce. When she returns, I accuse her of displaying a little Dian Fossey–inspired macho will. She likes the comparison.

"You'd have to be tough as nails to survive eighteen years out there," she says. "Could you have done it? If you were on a mission to save gorillas or stamp out smallpox or something?"

"I don't know."

"You could have," she says. "If it was the right cause and they let you bring Dan along, you'd be gone tomorrow." I study my placemat, a neat diagram of the Beltway with the exits marked. "You have a real streak of solitude," she adds. "You don't need people in the same way most people need people."

"Could be an act," I say.

She looks at her hands, spread flat on the table. "Tell me something, Jack. How close did you and Nina come to getting married?"

"Close," I say.

It was T minus three months when we called it off. Nina and I had gone to a seedy office on New York Avenue to look at videos of different bands that we could hire for the reception. Afterward, we walked. It was the middle of February, windy and cold, and we spent most of the time dodging the frozen slush flying off the wheels of passing Metro buses. We had coffee at a dive carryout. Neither of us said a word until the check came. We fought over it—$1.15 and we fought over it. "What are we doing?" I said. And she said, "This feels like someone else's story." Outside, we took turns boot-skating on the icy pavement. Then we went to the Biograph and watched a Fassbinder double feature. Later I asked Nina when she realized that we weren't going to go through with the wedding and she said, "The moment that guy started leaning on us to put down a deposit on Gerry Purvis & the Originals. If you're ready for Gerry Purvis & the Originals, then you're ready to get married."

The meal arrives. I set to work on my noodles with gusto. Kate spins her plate, studying the terrain.

"So what happened?" she asks. "I mean what *really* happened?"

I shrug. Despite two Scotches, I have the presence of mind not to expose these old wounds. "I don't know. I guess we got to the end of the ball of string."

Kate looks unconvinced. "Something happens to your face when you talk about her. Your skin droops." This comment illustrates why I don't want to get started talking about Nina. "I think you have something left for her," she says. "A spark inside you that hasn't gone out. Maybe it won't ever go out."

Wonderful. I can just see myself as a stooped old codger, a latter-day Dr. Zhivago searching for Nina's face at every crowded Metro platform.

Kate leans back. Her head is canted with professional reserve. "Could be it's the price one pays for intensity, no? The down side? As far as I'm concerned, the one thing that recommends second marriages is that you go into them with your eyes wide open. I can't imagine falling head over heels for anyone ever again. I wouldn't let it happen."

Tugging free a shrimp from its chitinous tail, I consider what she has said. It makes no sense to me.

"Tell me something," she says. "How would you feel if Nina walked through the door right now?"

A blast of cold air hits the back of my neck and a young man in a tan overcoat passes the table carrying a large stuffed bear.

"I'd be surprised," I say.

"Just surprised?"

"Well, alarmed."

"Why alarmed?"

"I guess the sight of her would stir up some old feelings."

She takes my hand. "I have a favor to ask, and it's not something you have to answer right away. It's a suggestion—let's call it a proposition, okay?"

I say okay, without a shred of conviction.

"Would you be willing to meet with Judith and me? Sit in on a session or two? On me, of course." The thought of sitting in on one of Kate's therapy sessions sends a chill into my toes. "I think it might help both of us sort some things out."

"What kind of things?"

"Our goals, for example."

"Do we really need Judith for that?"

"Look, Jack, I come with some baggage—I guess you know that by now. When I sense myself starting to think about us getting serious, I freeze up. My nightmare is reliving all the bad relationships I've had in my life. I don't want that. One of my big problems with Tobias was that our goals were synchronized."

I can feel the wind in my face as we plummet suddenly toward that region of unexplored feelings, that range of untrammeled emotions that I and most of my gender would prefer to set aside for all time like a plot of wilderness donated to the Nature Conservancy.

"Tobe and I wanted the same things. We competed all the time. We didn't give each other much support—none in fact. It was exhausting. Terribly unhealthy."

"We're safe on that score, I think."

"That's just one example. I'd also like to explore our partnership expectations."

"Partnership expectations?"

"And our respective childhoods."

"All this in two sessions?"

"Ninety-minute sessions," she says. "It would help us isolate talking points."

The scar tissue above my right testicle starts to ache. O Kate, sweet Kate, why can't we stick to lychee and rambutan? Why must we seek to learn the truth about ourselves and each other? It would be a mistake. The news will not be good, I promise. Right now I should tell her that I will submit to written interrogatories, video testimony perhaps, but nothing more. I can't imagine sitting with Kate and this stranger, both of them nodding pleasantly as I bare my soul about my childhood, Ray, my relationship with Nina. Dr. Judith would probably ask me about my mother. She'd encourage us to talk about our sex life and I'd end up spilling my guts.

"Can't we just have a long talk by ourselves and pretend that Judith is with us?"

"This is important to me, Jack."

"I'd say yes but I don't have any confidence that I'd show up for the appointment."

Kate smiles. She thinks I'm kidding.

A group of five middle-aged women take a table near us. Ex-nuns, I think. I can't say what the tip-off is at first. The air of sensibleness suggested by a ring of sturdy walking shoes, the do-it-yourself hairstyles, the reserve you see in teachers—in anyone, I suppose, who spends the better part of the day being watched. Still,

I'm missing the definitive clue. If Nina were here, she would pick it up in a glance. A few moments eavesdropping and she would be able to pin down the diocese that each of the women had grown up in.

The fact is, Kate has me pegged. Nina is still with me in a big way. I think about her all the time. I dream about her. Lately this obsession seems to be getting worse. Kate and I were at Kramerbooks last Friday evening, drinking coffee and splitting a slice of Kahlua walnut pie. She was filling me in on the latest word in child rearing, some foreign doctor's recommendation that young children sleep in their parents' bed to promote a sense of security and self-esteem. Kate was intrigued by the idea, which sounds to me like a scheme fraught with sleeplessness and parental resentment. As she weighed the pros and cons of the arrangement, my gaze drifted over her shoulder. I scanned the shoppers. Suddenly there was Nina—her head, anyway—perched atop a pyramid of *The Road Less Traveled* on the pop psychology table. We stared at each other for a good ten seconds. Her expression went from stony to furious. I glanced at Kate, who was now considering the issue of nudity, then glanced back at Nina. She was gone.

According to the liturgical calendar Marie gave me as a birthday present last January, today, the eighth of December, is the Feast of the Immaculate Conception. At 7:15 in the morning, I don Hank's tan mackintosh and head over to the Church of the Little Flower. Marie's green Toronado is parked beneath a basketball hoop in the church parking lot.

Inside, I take a seat in the last pew and scan the backs of the heads at the front of the church, looking for the Lawrence clan. I've attended church with them here, and I know where they like to sit. But I can't find them—rather, I find them but don't recognize them. My gaze sweeps past them half a dozen times before Richter turns his head, showing me his gray heron's crest. Just four Lawrences today: Richter, Marie, Patrick, and Anna. It wasn't many years ago that this family made a splash when they arrived at Mass, ten in all, charging through the vestibule like a well-drilled football team. How odd it must seem to Marie to arrive now in a simple gang of four. She is on her knees; her head is resting against the pew in front of her.

Frankly, I don't understand why the Catholic Church loses so many members. After eighteen years of training, I, for one, would make a point of staying with the program. I would find some renegade priest who still said Mass in Latin and would hold on to his communion rail with both hands. I would be one of those Catholics who could be counted on to send ten dollars to a post-office box in Paramus, New Jersey, for the complete and un-abridged nine-hundred-page edition of Brother Michael of the Holy Trinity's "The Third Secret of Fatima." With my weakness for mysticism, I'd probably end up a Rosicrucian.

I envy true believers. Marie tells me that faith comes through hard work, but I don't buy that for a second. I don't think it's something you can pick up in your thirties. Look at Richter: thirty-four years a convert to the Catholic Church and he still looks lost in here. Faith seems to me more like a tennis serve: if you don't get the practice in while you're young, you never lose the hitch in your motion. This is something I learned from Nina, who could differentiate the church-bred from the converted across an apse. The clue was in the eyes, she explained, the windows to the soul. A soul laved with holy water over the course of twenty or thirty years looks different from one that has been recently dry cleaned.

Growing up in the Catholic Church, Nina had the sense that with enough prayer, anything was possible. She would gaze up at the crucifix during Mass in the hopes that she might see the cruci-fied Christ bleed or cry out or transform Himself into a dove. The focus was always outside herself, on the pagan baby she was collect-ing pennies to buy or the weekly sketch of the Gospel that Sister Margaret Mary required each Monday morning of third grade.

Back in those days, you could still find a Latin Mass. Everything about the Church seemed mysterious and sacred, Nina said. She never had expectations of complete understanding; she was gratified just to get the gist of things. Often she got the story wrong. For the longest time she thought the Good Samaritan was a medical specialist of some kind: the Good Veterinarian, the Good Surgeon, the Good Obstetrician. She was comforted by the generic nature of the hero of this story. To root his character in place—who knew where Samaria was?—and call him the Good Mexican, say, or the Good Pole would raise all sorts of vexing questions about the other folks of those nations, if finding one good man in the lot was such a rare occurrence that you had to write a story about it. Leave it to Luke to bury his anti-Semitism in a well-known parable about the importance of mercy.

Ruminating about good and bad Samaritans brings to mind the thought that it will soon be time for my weekly conversation with another exiled child of Samaria, one whose family made transit stops at Odessa, Berlin, the Lower East Side of Manhattan, and Short Hills, New Jersey. It's more than a little depressing to think that the only news I get about Nina these days comes in burps and grunts while I'm stretching out to play basketball.

Monday night I have no enthusiasm for the game. I briefly consider phoning Rex to tell him that I've come down with a tricky virus. As fearful as he is of contagion, he would certainly excuse me. But he would be so disappointed. And he would probably start calling day and night to monitor my condition. He'd start keeping temperature charts on his Mac and book an appointment for me at the CDC. It's easier just to go.

An hour into the match and I have been running the court like a hobbled horse. I have a single basket, one miserable tip-in. Rebounds I can count on one hand. Between games I tank up on water and head for the boy's bathroom. Half-squatting at the low trough, I hear the door behind me swing open. It's England.

"Hey, Jack."

He ducks into the stall beside me. The ceramic wall is built to screen twelve-year-olds, which means I can see the sculpted mass of England's head rising above the partition like an osprey nest. His head turns and I see forehead.

"Long time," he says.

I redouble my efforts to concentrate on the task at hand.

"Look," he calls above the cascade, "I really admire your maturity through all of this." The hair on the back of my neck stands up. "I mean, you're a pretty easygoing guy and I knew from the very beginning that you'd say, 'Well that's life,' but the fact is, most guys couldn't keep up the friendship we have." His eyes appear above the stall, then disappear. "And any problems between us would affect the whole group."

My stream suddenly quits, though my bladder is still full. I count to ten in my head and it starts up again.

"I should tell you," says England, "that I was prepared to drop out before it came to that. I talked it over with Rex. You can ask him. He recommended taking it one game at a time. The point is, my fate was in your hands"—those damn eyes pop up again—"and you handled everything like a man."

Our streams die simultaneously and the conversation suddenly seems too intimate.

I say, "I take it things with Nina have gotten pretty serious."

The crown of his head drops out of sight. His waistband snaps. He laughs. When he appears at the entrance to the stall, even in this dim light, I can see that he is blushing. "Well, I wouldn't say that, Jack. What I mean is, I guess you'd really have to ask her."

This romance has been good for him. Just look at the changes on the court. It wasn't so long ago that England would fake left and go right every time. Or telegraph a dreadful bounce pass that always got booted. Now he's working on his left hand. In the first game he threw up a soft, ugly, left-handed hook that rolled around the rim and fell through. There's a bounce in his step. He seems lighter on his feet. I haven't swatted his jump shot in over a month. And he's always smiling.

"I guess you can imagine the torment Nina's been going through this last month," he says.

We are standing at the mirror. England is leaning into it, his eye popped open as he adjusts a contact lens.

"She's been, um, sick or something?"

He laughs. "That's rich, Jack. That's good. Sick with worry, I guess you'd say. With the show coming up, I mean."

This is the first news I've had about a show.

"She was nervous about inviting you. I mean, she wanted to, and I encouraged her to, but she didn't know if the invitation would seem insulting or something. She didn't want it to be taken wrong. And then there were the six canvases to finish up"—he makes it sound like she's painting a house!—"I sure haven't seen much of her these past weeks."

Pobrecito!

"We hope you're planning to come," he adds.

We!

"Between you and me, Jack, I think she has an awful lot of talent."

I need a prop: fingernail clippers, Chapstick, a comb to touch up my hair. "Say, what's the date on the opening again?"

"This Friday at seven."

"The Chase, right?"

"Oh, no, no, no. She's showing at the Emilan Gallery in Bethesda. Nice space, upscale clientele. Serious collectors. It's a real break. The women who run the place really like Nina's work. The sister of the managing partner at my firm has an interest in the gallery. She made the introduction. It's so rare to have something like that work out," he says.

Nina has a show opening in four days and she hasn't breathed a word about it to me. I didn't even make the guest list. Not so much as a brief apologetic note on the back of an artsy postcard.

155

Maybe she doesn't want me there because she's afraid of hurting my feelings. Maybe she thinks Jack Townsend can't handle a demotion to friend of the exhibitor.

I can picture the whole scene: England, the impresario, will have seen that the gallery is packed to the track lights with pinstripes and alligator hide. Three-quarters of the basketball crew will be there. My entrance, like Ernani's from the secret panel in Elvira's bedroom, will add a touch of drama to the cocktail chatter. In deference to commerce, I will smile pleasantly and congratulate Nina as the red "sold" dots hit the labels beside her paintings.

No.

It would be a mistake to go. It would be ungentlemanly, ill-mannered, positively boorish. One thing Nina does not need on Friday is to have her old flame arrive on the scene unexpectedly. My presence would turn the opening into a circus. No, Friday night I'll put up my feet and click through the cable channels looking for professional wrestling or a movie starring Burt Reynolds and a souped-up GTO. My absence will give Nina space. It's the right thing to do. The only thing.

THE SANDBOX

Emilan Gallery is tucked away like a kiva at the base of a thirty-story bank building in the heart of new Bethesda, a sterile canyonland of white concrete and red brick that overlays a town I used to love. The artfully designed lighting that skirts this building conveys a sense that the architect's plans were rendered so precisely you would probably find blue pencil marks at the edge of the curb. I miss the human scale of old Bethesda, the smelly dumpsters and shaggy willows and warrens of alleys and ten-car parking lots. A couple hurries past in the cold.

Ahead, at the doorway to the gallery, stands a slight woman with dark hair that hangs to her shoulders in thick ringlets. She is wearing a leopard-print dress and has gold bracelets extending on both arms from elbows to wrists. Her fingernails are black, the gloss matching her stiletto heels. She smokes a cigarette like a guy screwing up his nerve to rob a gas station. Beyond her, through the plate glass, I see some familiar faces: Joanie Lawrence, Rex Pitesti, Donald the Fed bent over a cheese platter like a medical examiner.

Kate takes my arm. "Run it by me one more time why we're doing this."

"To support the arts in Washington."

"Couldn't we have just sent a check?"

"You getting cold feet?"

"Of course."

"I thought you said you wanted to go."

"As a fly on the wall. I'm sure Nina has enough on her mind without having to deal with me."

"It's been six months. She already has a new boyfriend."

"It's still an ambush, you creep. Swear to me you won't try to put us together." Near the door Kate stops me. "One final question. Were you actually invited?"

"In a manner of speaking."

The dark-haired woman at the door carefully steps on her cigarette and cups the crushed butt in her left hand. She throws out her right. "Emily Zarcoff," she says. Her voice is Marlboro husky. "Welcome. Please sign the registration book and help yourself to the wine and hors d'oeuvres. We have four exhibitors in the 'Young Washington Artists' show: two painters, a ceramicist, and a fiber artist." I nod absently and start past her, but she steps into my path and says, "Sorry, I didn't get your name."

"Flood," I say.

"Flood." It would seem she is running through the guest list in her head.

"I could have sworn England said—"

"Mr. Flood!" Her eyes sparkle. "Please be sure to let me know if you see anything that interests you. We have more work in the back. At group shows like this one we run out of space, I'm afraid."

I smile. Kate smiles. Ms. Zarcoff smiles.

It turns out that Emilan Gallery is named for the aforementioned Emily and petite blonde Anya, who flits around the place like a hummingbird. Their shop is L-shaped with a short flight of steps leading to a narrow upstairs gallery and a small balcony overlooking the front door. This is where Nina is standing, her back to me and the rest of the world, when Kate and I arrive. She looks uncharacteristically stiff. Joanie stands beside her, facing us, her eyebrows knit and lips pursed as she studies Kate. I catch her eye. Her head shakes slowly. When Kate turns toward the main part of the room, she mouths, *"You dog!"* Then she grins.

In all, there are some thirty people scattered throughout the front room. Kate has migrated to the far end and is engaged in a spirited conversation with a short, stocky fellow with two gold earrings in his left ear. England, who was parked on a couch like a long-distance commuter when we arrived, puts down the catalogue he's been studying and joins them. Joey Lawrence is standing in front of one of Nina's paintings, exploring the furthermost reaches of his pants pockets.

Joanie sidles up to me at the wine table and whispers theatrically: " 'He stood still, dragging at his moustache with a lean, weak hand. "I don't think you would have cared for its *dénouement*," he said with sudden grimness.' "

From Kate Chopin to Edith Wharton in the space of months!

"I'm way out of line, aren't I?"

"Depends on the motivation," she says.

"Moral support?"

"Oh bullshit, Jack. Still it's great to see you."

"Fill me in."

"Joey you see, Barb and Zalman promise to arrive momentarily, Marie will float in on Dad's arm during the waning minutes of the fête. Liza and Bruce are no-shows—"

"Another retreat?"

She shakes her head. "It seems the season of Advent coincides precisely with the high season of clinical depression."

"And Richey, Jr.?"

"Touch and go. He's hard at work trying to ensure that his Colombian client's laundered drug profits can remain protected in one of our federally insured banks."

"What's the news from the other camp?"

"Mr. England saw to it that six of my talented sister's paintings were purchased before the curtain went up. He bought two himself."

England has left Kate and is making his way toward us with a wide smile pasted to his face.

"Have I missed something, Joans? I mean, is there something to fall in love with beneath that thousand-dollar head of hair?"

"He's a nice boy, Jack."

"Sure he's a nice boy. The city is full of nice boys. What I want to know is where Nina and this nice boy are headed."

"Beats me."

"I'm asking for the benefit of your experience. You've been close yourself, what, a half-dozen times?"

"Four is not a half dozen."

"What do you think, Joans?"

"I think she will grow weary of that boy one of these days. But maybe that's wishful thinking. Maybe I'm biased." She kisses my cheek.

"Jack!" England calls out. He claps me on the back like we're old buddies who haven't seen each other for years. "Isn't this something!" He leans in: "I know it's crass to compare, but Nina's work really shows up well here. Talentwise, those other three can't touch her. It's a fine venue, don't you think?" He takes my arm, steering me away from Joan, who curls her lip at him for my benefit, and whispers, "This I did not expect. This is classy, Jack.

Class A. I respect you for it I admire you. Thanks a hell of a lot. I mean that."

I haven't a clue as to why he has interpreted my crashing this party as somehow prompted by magnanimity. Nina, in contrast, knows me better than to trust the vacant expression on my face, which may explain why she hasn't descended from the upper gallery.

England continues to rock happily on the balls of his feet. "And listen: I just want to add that I think Kate is an impressive and attractive young woman. I'd have to say that you really landed on your feet." Across the room, I catch Kate's glance. Her eyes close very slowly. "She seems awfully bright," England says. "She had some interesting and provocative things to say about Nina's work. A singular point of view."

What modicum of social grace I possess suddenly flies out the front door. I want to be left alone. I want England to stop talking to me. I want him to cut cheese or pour wine or work the front door with Ms. Zarcoff. I want him to leave.

"Kate didn't tell you much about herself," I say.

England looks puzzled.

"What's she's been through, I mean."

His eyes widen. "Not a word."

"I try to get her out whenever I can. I never feel like I'm doing enough, of course."

"You mean she's not your girlfriend?"

"Sister-in-law. That is, she *was.*"

He winces. "My God, Jack. What happened?"

"Not now," I say, turning away from him.

I melt into the crowd feeling angry and guilty and more certain than ever that my presence here is a big, big mistake.

Everywhere I turn I am confronted by Nina's paintings. *Lovely Saint Rita,* a triptych; *The Lottery; Yo-yos; A Visit in the Country; Palisades*—all are new to me. This is some of the best work she has done. *Palisades* is a view of an unmade bed in afternoon light. The teal-striped wallpaper behind the headboard shows the faint outline of a crucifix. Gazing at it, I feel like a sinner. I feel as though I'm in church. *The Lottery* is the scene of a hand taking two tickets from a countertop. *A Visit in the Country* shows a trowel buried to the hilt in a pile of dirt—the leaves of Hank's ficus fill one corner of the painting.

I make my way over to Kate and she fills me in on the story of the earringed gentleman, who, it turns out, is a podiatrist who also owns a sushi bar near the zoo. I shoot the breeze for a moment with a couple of basketball chums, but we are awkward together without having a ball to bounce between us. Only Rex seems perfectly at ease. He is studying the sculpture of a torso—more precisely, the sculpture's ceramic buttocks. I stand beside him.

"They're perfect," he says. "You never see that. Nudes are rarely true to life."

Joan spears a wedge of pineapple and whispers, "Cut the suspense, Jack, and get your butt up those stairs."

"Just tell me one thing. Is she hiding out?"

"She is riddled with guilt about not inviting you, so don't give her any crap about it, okay?"

"What should I say?"

"Tell her that her paintings look great and that she looks great and it's wonderful to see her."

"I think that might be a bad idea, Joans."

"Ask her something then." She pokes a finger into my back and marches me, Wyatt Earp–style, to the foot of the steps. "Ask her to marry you, for God's sake."

"And what if she accepts?"

"Christ, Jack, you really are hopeless."

At this moment Barb arrives. Zalman is behind her, a white silk scarf dancing on the lapels of his shiny black suit. The easy way he inhabits dress clothes gives you the impression you are looking at a movie star. Barb kisses my cheek, which brings to Joan's face an expression of shock. This is the first kiss I have ever received from Barbara Lawrence-Kolb.

She scowls at Joan. "I'm allowed to kiss Jack. I'm allowed to miss him." She whispers to me, "Without you, it's just me and Zalman and a houseful of damn Catholics."

"I heard that the new fella is one of yours."

"He's *meshugga*. He smiles too much. And beneath that veneer, I'd bet, is a classic case of terminal maleness."

"So what's the latest on Jerusalem? Are we finally looking at international status?"

"Not a chance." She grins. Another first: I have teased Barb without drawing her ire.

This gives me confidence as I climb the steps. Nina is standing at the far end of the narrow gallery, flanked by ruby-throated Anya and bulky England. Nina whispers to him, dispatching him. He gives me a big horse grin before shambling down the steps. I stop to look at one of Nina's smaller paintings entitled *The Sandbox*. In it, a young girl sits at the edge of a sandbox with her back to the viewer. There are clumps of dirt in the sand. Looking closely, I see a veritable garden growing at the girl's feet. The detail is exquisite. Like all of Nina's best work, the painting is beautiful and haunting. I catch her eye, but she glances away.

"You'll bring down more wine?" Anya calls.

"Couple of minutes," Nina says. "One or two?"

"Whatever." Anya disappears.

Nina is wearing black stirrup pants, a black and gold batik shirt. I smile at her. She gives me a shrug and tries to smile, but the effort seems as though it might cause her face to crack.

"Whoever painted this," I say, "is possessed of genius."

"Knock it off, Jack. I'm strung as tight as a piano."

"It's awfully good."

She won't look at it.

"You know it's good."

"I like it all right," she says. "So let's stop talking about it."

"Who bought it?"

"Donald Royal."

Donald the Fed? In the shock-and-disbelief index, this news has to rank up there with Marie's donating center court seats to the Georgetown-Villanova NCAA basketball final, which she won in a radio contest, to Little Flower's fund-raising auction. "He picked this one out himself?"

Nina smiles. "He said that he wanted to buy the best painting I had in the show and asked me to choose it. I chose this one."

"The BMW seven series. How could you do it?"

She rubs thumb and forefinger together. "In case you forgot, that's the point of this whole thing."

"England arranges for the space and sees to it that almost everything in the show is bought before the doors open. Is that what this is about?"

"It's about freedom, Jack. It's about buying time. If those last two sell, then I'm quitting the Geographic and painting for a solid year."

"You're kidding!"

"I'm not kidding."

"That's fantastic."

"You really think so?"

"Who's been begging you to quit for the last three years?"

"Michael thinks I ought to try to get my hours cut back."

"Well, I guess that tells you something about the difference between him and me."

"It bugged me when he said that. But that was Marie's reaction, too. Their intentions are good."

"Neville Chamberlain had good intentions. Lyndon Johnson had good intentions. Rigoletto and Boris Godunov both could make a strong case for their good intentions."

"Look," she says. "I'm sorry I didn't invite you. With my nerves on edge and all, I just wasn't sure that I could handle your being here. I was worried about a scene."

"Between us?"

She smiles. She is standing beside me at the railing, looking down at the mob below. The tenor of so many wine-sharpened conversations fills the room with a palpable sense of desperation. Nobody is looking at paintings now. Richey, Jr., so fresh from K Street he's still belted into a fur-lined overcoat, stands with England, Scottie the Helmet, Arne, and Rick Long. They are as thick as thieves in the corner. Kate and Joan converse beside a huge goblet filled with business cards.

Nina studies Kate. After a moment she says, "I'm impressed, Jack. She looks like the real thing. Where'd you meet her?"

"I picked her up at a bar in Georgetown."

"You're a liar."

"Ellen introduced us."

"I would have expected Ellen to find you someone with more sensible shoes," she says.

From this vantage point, Kate's iridescent high heels look as though they were recently doused with gasoline.

"Kate's really very nice," I say.

"Is it serious?"

"Some days I think so."

"Does Miss Kate have a last name?"

"Baldwin."

"Kate Baldwin," says Nina. "Kate Baldwin sounds like a lawyer."

"SEC. More of an administrator."

"Jack!" She stifles a laugh. Her hand grazes my side as she leans toward me, her breath in my ear. "You scab," she whispers. "Don't you *ever* let me hear you running down lawyers again."

"Not all lawyers," I say.

She looks Kate over again. "So, on the days when it seems serious, just, uh, how serious does it seem?"

"You mean, am I sleeping with her?"

"I didn't ask that."

"But you've got to be curious."

"For your information, that's the last thing in the world I want to know."

"We're both grown-ups," I say. "It's no big deal."

"Jack, I can assure you that I have no interest in the gory details of your private life. If you'll excuse me, I need to get some wine."

She heads toward the storage closet. I follow.

"At least admit that the thought crossed your mind."

"Not even remotely."

She slips past a louvered panel. Again, I follow, pulling the panel shut behind me. The closet is long, with deep wooden racks lining both sides of a narrow aisle. The ceiling is an inch above my head. Cardboard boxes filled with paper plates, napkins, and bottles of Almaden Mountain Chablis rest on the floor. A twenty-five-watt bulb hanging in the center of the room fills the corners with jagged shadows.

"The truth is, I've slept with her," I say.

"Jack, I'm just not interested." Nina squats. A satiny thigh brushes against my leg.

"In fact," I continue, "I don't think it was really such a hot idea. It was fun—don't get me wrong—but it seems to have short-circuited something. You know how that goes."

"I haven't a clue."

She seems to be regarding an Almaden label with the same degree of concentration that Evan brings to the stock-market tables. Her hair hangs in a thick braid to the middle of her back. She is wearing spiral gold earrings that I don't recognize.

"I may be going to see Kate's psychologist."

At once she turns. "What in God's name happened?"

Who but Nina or her mother would first assume that a visit to a psychologist must be court-ordered?

"Nothing happened. It's Kate's idea. A suggestion. Sort of a secular pre-Cana rite, as I understand it. A couple talks to a professional to find out if they are compatible."

"A complete stranger?"

"Father Mike was a complete stranger, too."

"Not to me."

"Well, Kate's been seeing Judith for years."

"Her name is Judith?" It's clear Nina thinks that anyone familiar with the stories of the Old Testament would be nuts even to consider offering his head to a woman named Judith. "Just what's the point here?" she wants to know.

"Goal reconciliation."

"Goal reconciliation?"

"You know, tally up the pluses and minuses and see how we come out."

"Are you going to do it?"

"I don't know. I suppose so. Would you?"

"No psychologists for me, thank you very much."

"Is there another round of pre-Cana in the works?"

"No comment."

"So it's that serious!"

"I didn't say that. It's just that it's my business, and I don't really want to talk about it right now."

"Is it the talking about sex that makes you nervous or my standing over you in a dimly lit closet or both?"

"I haven't said a word about sex."

"Would you please satisfy my dirty mind. Yes or no?"

"I hope this Kate woman realizes that she is running around with a pervert," she says.

"Please to answer the question."

"I forgot the question."

"It relates to you and England performing certain unmentionable acts."

"That is *none* of your business."

"He's a little shy, isn't he?"

"Jack."

"Is he a virgin?"

"I haven't a clue."

"So you haven't slept with him!"

"You are hounding me," she sings softly.

"But with the best intentions. I am prompted by *concerns.*"

"Such as?"

"Such as, that England will be all over you like flypaper if you sleep with him. Trust me on this. I've played basketball with this guy for two years. We're matched up together almost every Monday night. I know all his moves. You sleep with him and he'll start bird-dogging you. Pretty soon he'll be begging you to marry him. Talk about being hounded! I'm an amateur compared to this guy. England spent three years *training* to be persuasive. He once convinced three Supreme Court justices of the merits of segregation. Think about trying to stand up to that kind of pressure."

"Please let me know when you're finished."

"If he's a virgin, the scenario will be a thousand times worse."

"Am I in any danger?"

"Come on, Nina. Spill it. You had him pegged the day you two met—yes or no?"

"No comment."

"Then let's do it like Woodward and Bernstein: one bottle of Almaden means yes, two means no."

"I am not interested in playing Watergate, Jack."

"Just admit one thing: fooling around in here is more fun than hanging around out there."

"It's a heck of a lot easier, if that's what you mean." She leans back against my leg. "Jack, now do you understand why I didn't invite you?"

"What does it tell us? By any measure, we shouldn't care anymore. Not after six months."

"Five months and twenty-two days." She looks up at me with an expression of warmth and regret that takes my breath away.

I smile. I touch the side of her face with my fingertips.

"Nina, are you in there?"

England's bulky shadow is resting on the louvers. I don't know how long he has been standing there, but I'm sure that on the basketball court he would have been whistled for a three-second lane violation.

"Yes, Michael."

"Need a hand with anything? Uh, Anya sent me up for more wine."

Standing, Nina cups my mouth. Her wild, furious, conspiratorial eyes demand silence. I work to contain the rumble building in my rib cage.

"No, thank you, Michael." She cracks open the door. "Jack and I just got carried away with one of our crazy family discussions."

England chuckles nervously. It is gratifying to see that this man does possess an imagination.

"Jack," says Nina. "My advice is to follow your heart."

"You really think so?"

She nods sagely.

"Sometimes that takes courage," I say.

"Then be courageous." She starts out, carrying a bottle of wine.

"Nina."

She turns. I'm holding another bottle.

"Do you need two?"

"No," she says hotly.

England, playing doorman, ushers me out and closes the louvered doors behind me. It bugs me, his proprietary air. "One painting left," he says. "I'd venture to say that we're looking at a clean sweep."

The moment calls for a suave gesture, like the scene in *Lucia* when Edgardo shows up after Lucia's marriage contract to Arturo has been signed. Instead of throttling his rival, he sings of restraint.

I am not equal to the challenge.

From the balcony I spot Rex, still communing with that buttocks sculpture. I hope he has bought it; if not, I'll have to buy it for him. Rex hasn't a stick of furniture in the living room of his Potomac mansion—it's just bare walls and an oak floor covered with a Persian rug. Imagine those buttocks, track-lit on a white marble pedestal at the center of that room! Rex catches my eye and gives me an apologetic shrug. I'm not sure whether he's feeling sorry for me or feeling chagrined by the fact that he can't seem to tear himself away from the sculpture. I shake my head and he gives me a winning smile.

Nina is downstairs, standing at the center of a group; England is beside her. Her wine glass is full. Her shoulder rests against England's shoulder; I can see in her body language the bad news marching past me like a float in the Macy's Thanksgiving Day parade. Tonight's the night—I feel it in my bones.

Sola, perduta, abbandonata!

As if at a funeral, friends approach me one by one. First Barb: "I should be closing ranks with a fellow believer, Jack, but this match looks like bad news all the way around. This kid desperately needs a year on a kibbutz." Then Joan: "They're going to burn a hole in the rug any minute." Finally Kate: "So what, exactly, possessed you to do this to yourself?"

"Nina and I can't avoid each other forever," I say.

"Sure you can." She takes my arm. "Jack, I think you have to face up to the fact that there are some relationships you never get over."

"Not even with professional help?"

"Not even with help."

"I thought you had gotten past this sort of nonsense."

"I'm working on it," she says solemnly. "But I could be working on it for the next fifty years."

"Let's get out of here," I say.

"You sure? I could grab a cab if you need some time to yourself."

"Not tonight."

"I'm in your pocket," she says.

We run the good-bye gauntlet of handshakes, back patting, and shirt-collar kisses. Even Emily offers up a cheek and begs us to return. She calls: "You'll have to stop in and talk to me about what you are looking for, Mr. Flood. I see thousands of slides every week. Literally thousands."

I find this departure scene amusing, which is unfortunate. The smile on my face freezes with unpleasant effect as I turn toward the street and almost run down Marie and Richter Lawrence. He's dressed in a crumpled tweedy hat and a wrinkled tan mac, and has about him a monochromatic, "Father Knows Best" aura. Marie, in contrast, is dressed for a bank heist: sunglasses at 8:30 at night, a white polyester head scarf edged with blue snowmen, and a bulky black coat with the shaggy pile of a freshly washed cocker spaniel.

"Jack!" she cries. "What's it like in there?"

"Packed to the rafters."

"Tell the truth."

"I'm serious. It's been a great success."

"Is Angie a mess?"

"She's a battleship."

"Jack, thank God you know better than to be honest with me. I'd turn around and get right back in the car. She must be dying. Why does she put herself through this? Why does she put *me* through this? Do you know what my day has been like?"

I can guess: she has offered up a number of fifteen-decade rosaries, the big ones that nuns wear as belts, to the patron saint of gallery openings. She has lit candles at Little Flower, imploring God, the Virgin Mary, and a host of long-dead relatives to see to it that Nina has a respectable turnout. Marie's biggest fear at events like this is that no one will show, followed closely by the worry that no one will buy. With those anxieties dispatched, she is forced to confront what, for her, is the most troubling aspect of this whole business: the paintings themselves. It will jangle Marie's already jangled nerves to stand in that brightly lit room, surrounded by Nina's work. I think all those unhappy characters and the odd scenes and perspectives leave Marie with the sharp feeling that she has failed as a mother.

At Nina's last show, I found Marie huddled in a corner, madly slicing up a wedge of Gouda. "I raised them all the same way," she said hotly. "Boys, girls—didn't matter. I shouted at each one. I didn't play favorites. My Angie was a sweet little girl. She was going to be a nun. But then she stopped going to church. And now she doesn't pray—she told me that herself. She stopped praying. She went to art school. She started living in sin. And what happens? She stops painting horses and trees and starts looking in garbage cans for things to paint. Why? I ask her. The only thing you find in a garbage can is garbage."

"Doctor, Marie," I say, "I'd like to introduce you to Kate Baldwin. Kate: Nina's parents, Richter and Marie Lawrence."

Kate offers Marie a hand, but Marie retreats into the collar of her coat. Richter, an Instamatic in his right hand, shakes awkwardly with the left.

"Well," I say, "I guess we'd better be off."

Richter touches his hat, giving us a little salute. Marie nods gravely. In this light, the down on her lip looks woolly. Her expression is commissar grim.

WHERE THERE
IS NO VISION

Two days later, my answering machine is blinking like a signal light. Nestled between a complaint about a frost-buckled brick patio and a pitch from a guy who has been hounding me to buy penny mining stocks is a message from a woman with a sultry voice: "Jacques, I zzimply must zpeak vith you. Thees is Babette LaDoux. I em zzure you half my noombair."

Immediately I dial 622-7891.

"*Infida!*" I say.

"*Qual voce!*"

"Und vhat iss da problem, madame?"

"Well," Nina says slowly, "it was sort of a social call and sort of wasn't."

I wait.

"Are you angry with me, Jack?"

"Whatever gave you that idea?"

"I *knew* you would be."

"But I'm not."

"You were one cool cucumber when you left the gallery."

Responding honestly to this comment would result in a disastrous downhill slide in the conversation. So I hold my tongue.

"Please don't wear me down with the Marty routine." This is a reference to my father, who is a master at keeping his mouth shut when it's his turn to speak. "What are you doing tomorrow?" she asks.

"Tomorrow we build a retaining wall with cobblestones pirated from the streets of Georgetown."

"What about in the afternoon?"

She has a way with me. Even at my stuffiest, Nina can unstuff me at will.

"Where?" I ask.

"Museum of American Art."

"Why?"

"A plea that must be delivered in person."

"Whose plea?"

There is silence. I study the pot of African violets on the telephone table and shift in my seat, a cube-shaped wooden frame wrapped in fifty or sixty yards of leather strapping, giving it the look of a box kite. Once the chair may have been comfortable, but now, with the leather stretched, my rear end is hanging a mere two knuckles above the floor. I feel like a little boy in the throes of toilet training.

"I come on bended knee," she says.

"You didn't answer my question."

"Well, the answer is sort of complicated."

"Why didn't Marie call me herself?"

Nina's sigh suggests that I, of all people, should not have to be told that Marie, like God, works in Her Own Mysterious Ways. You don't question her method. Marie has a message for me and Nina is the hook.

"Let me guess: another family crisis?"

"Of course."

"Give me a hint."

"Only if you promise to meet me."

"Of course."

"Nonna has been asking about you."

God bless that old woman.

The National Museum of American Art is at 8th and G, across the street from the Martin Luther King Library. Chance does not take you to this neighborhood of wig supply houses and heavily fortified jewelry shops, and the granite steps of this museum have not exactly had grooves worn into them by the shoes of vacationing Vermonters and Texans. NMAA patrons tend to be a pretty serious bunch. I watch them push through the revolving doors, faces stern as Federal marshals. They need no floor plan and don't pause for even an instant to survey the listing of exhibits. These are people who know the precise location of the painting before which they will park themselves for the next hour. As does Nina, who at this moment might be planted on a velvet bench on the third floor in front of Romaine Brooks's *Le Trajet*. Or at Yasuo Kuniyoshi's *Strong Woman and Child*. Or, if she's in a campy frame of mind, she's sketching Lilly Martin Spencer's *We Must Both Fade*, the painting of a young woman in a blue gown and white shoes, standing at a mirror holding a rose.

As for me, I find it almost impossible to make my way past the lobby of this museum. Tucked in a corner is an American masterpiece that takes my breath away. Here is what a handout has to say about the 177 objects covered in gold and silver foil that constitute James Hampton's *The Throne of the Third Heaven of the Nations' Millennium General Assembly*:

Little is known about Hampton, a quiet man who had few, if any, close friends. Born in rural South Carolina in 1909, he was one of four children of a black gospel singer and itinerant preacher and, around 1928, moved to Washington. He was a short order cook, served in the Army and, returning to Washington, was a janitor for the General Services Administration from 1946 until he died of cancer in 1964. At some point in his youth, he believed God had come to him in a vision and, until his death, he continued to receive visions. His massive Throne is a moving testament to his spiritual dedication and faith.

In 1950, Hampton rented an unheated, poorly lit garage and there he built the Throne—which he may have begun earlier. At midnight, after finishing his janitorial duties, he went to the garage for five or six hours and believed that God visited him there to guide him as he worked. With discarded materials—old furniture, cardboard, bottles, kraft paper, desk blotters, sheets of transparent plastic, burnt-out light bulbs, aluminum and gold foil—he fashioned his intricate objects. Some suggest traditional church appointments—a throne chair, pulpits and offertory tables; each unit is one of a pair and each has its assigned place on either side of the center throne chair.

Presumably, the work is unfinished but, from Hampton's explanatory labels, the basic scheme is discernible: to the viewer's left, the objects refer to the New Testament, Jesus and Grace and, to the viewer's right, the Old Testament, Moses and Law. Crowning the throne chair are the words "Fear Not" and tacked to Hampton's bulletin board is the inscription, "Where There Is No Vision the People Perish."

I wish I had met Hampton. I wish I had met him and had had the guts to apprentice myself to him. For all we know, the objects in front of me might amount to a tenth of what he had planned. Right now I could be working in an unheated garage on N Street. I could be making Art under the guidance of a man who conversed with God.

The display space is small, but no smaller than a single-car garage. I wonder if Hampton had *The Throne* set up in his garage. If so, where did he work? Maybe, like painting a floor, he started in one corner and worked his way out, leaving a foil-covered crown here, an angel with a light-bulb head there.

I am studying what look like foil-covered drumsticks hanging from the front of one of the offertory tables when I become aware of someone standing behind me. A pair of hands cover my eyes. I smell Varsol. A sweetly pitched voice that I recognize says, "And so the landlord says to himself, 'Darn shame about James, though he sure was a lonesome fella. Wonder what he was up to in that old garage. Don't think he had a car, least I never saw him drivin' it. Maybe he was jest fixin' it up, never got it on the road. Strange guy. A little too much hell and damnation for me. Better'n liquor, ennyhow. Well, guess I better open'er up and see what kinda mess he left for me to clean up. Hope it's a T-bird. Maybe he thought he was Noah and was building hisself a boat. That'ud fit.' And so he opened the door"—Nina uncovers my eyes—"'Good lord, James! So you was a crazy fella!' "

I want her to keep talking. I want to continue to feel her breath on my ear. She has eaten an orange, and after that, a wintergreen Tic Tac.

"You know the guard keeps track of people who spend too much time staring at this," she whispers. "They keep a video file at the FBI. Pretty soon they'll be talking to your elementary school teachers and checking to see if you belong to subversive organizations like the ACLU."

I wave the handout in her face. "It says here he's dead, but he's alive. Hampton's alive, I tell you. I see him all over town."

"Sure he is. I've seen him, too. Now let's find a water fountain so that you can take your Thorazine."

Nina is wearing blue jeans and a black turtleneck, dangly turquoise earrings. I study her face, looking for clues. She looks, well, fired up. Maybe it's the effect of Lorser Feitelson's *Genesis #2,* maybe it's the bracing December air, maybe neither.

"You're a sweetheart to meet me here," she says. "And listen, despite how I behaved, I'm really glad you came to the show. It meant a lot to me that you'd come without an invitation. Even if you did bring that woman." A smile.

"Big success, I take it."

"Between me and you, I would've preferred to have taken the cash and run. The whole production was a little weird. I don't have anything against lesbians, but after three solid days with those two I felt like an overcooked carrot in a pot of soup."

She takes my arm and we begin to walk. We circle the four marble columns in the lobby, wending our way past the information desk, past Daniel Chester French's sculpture, *The Spirit of Life,* a winged woman holding up what looks like an old feather duster and an inverted construction helmet, all the while discussing our respective families, the health of Dan, the state of the planet in the twilight of the Republican age of greed. We could do this for hours. We could do this until the guard booted us out at closing time. Truth is, I am avoiding the subject that so preoccupied me the other night.

"So what's new in your life?" I ask.

There is a long, long pause.

"Computers," she finally says.

"That's it?"

"They're leaning on me to learn the Macintosh."

"I thought you were quitting to paint."

"I'm thinking about it. Meanwhile I'm supposed to become a computer graphics wiz. No more pencils and paper, no more scissors and rubber cement. It makes me crazy to spend the whole day designing things without being able to hold anything in my hands."

"But it's fast."

"Sure it's fast. It also fries your brain. And the screen gives me a headache."

"No reason to have to suffer from headaches these days." Silence. "Is there?"

"Jack," she says, "I suppose you realize that next Sunday is Christmas."

I nod solemnly.

"And Christmas Eve, as you may recall, is in the Catholic tradition an evening of celebration."

"A sacred fête."

"The family gathers together to welcome the arrival of the Christ child."

"Bearing poinsettias and Paco Rabanne."

"Will you come?"

The sudden question and the plaintive tone of voice startle me.

"You want me at your folks' house for Christmas Eve dinner?"

She nods.

"Why?"

"Because I do."

I wait.

"Marie wants you there, too."

"Oh."

"She begged me to beg you to make an appearance for Nonna's sake. She was planning to ask you herself outside the gallery, but then she saw Kate and lost her nerve."

"Not Marie!"

"Apparently it's true. She stayed at the opening for a total of eleven minutes. Never even made it up the stairs. The next day she called me and suggested that I might want to talk to her priest. Jack, will you please come?"

Last year when Nina and I cancelled our wedding plans, no one bothered to tell Nonna. The week before we were to marry, Nonna took to bed with what she claimed was typhus but turned out to be a bad case of the flu. When she recovered, she asked about the wedding, and Marie, for reasons known only to herself, described the beautiful ceremony right down to the groomsmen's boutonnieres.

"Um, maybe it's time Nonna knew the truth about us, so we don't have to go through this every year."

"Jack! The news would break her heart."

I seriously doubt that. Nonna has a few years on her frame, but her heart is as tough as a catcher's mitt.

"So what does England have to say about this?"

We are standing at the revolving door. Nina is looking out at what appears to be the foil-covered cupola of an orthodox church across a parking lot.

"It just so happens that Michael will be out of town on Christmas Eve."

"You didn't tell him."

"For your information, I am not obliged to tell him everything that happens in my life."

"And since we're just doing this for Nonna, there isn't anything to explain."

"Exactly."

We stand there like statues. All that's missing is a title plaque at our feet, *Domestic Bickering and Museum Fatigue.*

"So, will you see Kate's psychologist?" she asks.

"I don't know. I haven't decided. What do you think? Do I need it?"

"Without a doubt."

"Maybe I should talk to Liza."

"She only handles lapsed Catholics."

"I'll convert and then drop out."

"It doesn't work like that. You need a secular shrink, Jack. In the worst way."

"I know people crazier than me who seem to get along fine without professional help."

"Name one."

I think.

"Whatever possessed you to tell Michael that Kate is Ray's widow?"

Frankly, it's a little embarrassing to have a story like that thrown back in my face in the clear light of day.

"I had to say something to make him stop talking. It was the first thing that popped into my head." I shrug. "Anyway, I never mentioned Ray."

"He's so impressionable, Jack."

She makes it sound as though I'm responsible for England's naiveté.

"He bought it, huh?"

"He talks about it constantly. I don't have the heart to tell him it isn't true."

"Poor England," I say.

"He's not a bad guy, Jack."

"He's a wonderful guy. A tad too predictable on the court, but solid as the Hoover Dam. I'll bet he could've gotten Ivan Boesky *and* A.H. Robins completely off the hook. You can't say that about everybody."

"You know, he's a little afraid of you."

"Me?"

"He thinks you're a little too *un*predictable."

It's true. I am. Especially with him.

"To look at him," she says, "you might think he's had everything go his way. But he hasn't. He feels like he's had to fight every step of the way for what he's gotten."

"I hear it's a bitch getting from Andover to Yale."

"You're so literal," she says.

"What's he afraid of?"

"I don't know."

"Is that part of his appeal?" Again, we become statues. "I withdraw the question, Your Honor."

"Last night, he told me that he was interested in learning more about the Church," Nina says.

"And you wonder why I have it out for this guy."

"Who was it who read the entire Bible and the Baltimore Catechism after he started going out with me?"

"I was patching up a hole in my education. You can't understand the simplest reggae song without grounding in the Bible. Anyway, my interest is metaphysical. England's just padding his résumé."

"The thing is—" She stops.

"Out with it."

"Forget it," she says.

"Not a chance."

"Promise me you won't laugh."

I nod, bite my lip.

"Lately, he's started coming on like a freight train."

"What did I tell you?"

"Why do guys do that, Jack?"

"Sometimes we can't help it. Even when we know it's going to mess everything up. Just another thing to blame on testosterone, I guess."

"It's upsetting is what it is."

I should be gloating, but it pains me to imagine the degree to which England has begun to make an ass out of himself.

Nina says, "I had a nun in fifth grade who said that any woman who reaches thirty without a husband should resign herself to a loveless marriage."

"I won't go for separate beds," I say.

She smiles. I want to kiss the mole that I know is resting in the hollow behind her left ear.

"Will you come, Jack?"

She is holding my arm like she used to hold it, her fingers curled tightly to the elbow.

"So it's over between you and England, only he doesn't know it yet."

"Can we please talk about something else?"

"Is there something still there?"

"There's something there." It sounds as though she's referring to a gob of bubble gum stuck to the bottom of her shoe.

"I knew this was going to happen. I knew it from day one."

"Knew what?"

"That you'd stay with him until you slept with him and then he'd get weird on you."

Her neck flushes. I am expecting a frosty silence in this public space, but get a brief, moving aria instead. "For the last time, whether or not I have slept with or will sleep with Michael England is *none of your business*."

A woman at the information desk bows her head and begins writing furiously. The guard at the revolving door is clicking his clicker, though no one is entering the museum.

The deed is done—of this I am certain. I can see in Nina's eyes the exhaustion of conquest. She made the glorious climb up the side of the mountain only to sprain her ankle on the final ascent. Life can be so disappointing.

"Have you two ever argued?" I ask.

A shake of the head. "Michael's not much of a fighter," she says.

"England's not a fighter?"

"He prefers to work out disagreements through discussion."

"He should meet Ellen."

"He's not a bit like Ellen."

"Um, what sort of disagreements have you had, if I may ask?"

"As a matter of fact, we haven't had any."

"Not *one?*"

Another shake of the head.

"Doesn't that tell you something?"

"I figured we just needed time."

"You and I were screaming at each other on day two."

"We were special, Jack." She smiles.

"Have you met England's mother?"

"No," she says. "But I've talked to her on the phone."

"What did you think?"

"Nice enough. A little overbearing. But then, Michael's the oldest, so I guess you'd expect that."

"A *little* overbearing?"

"Okay, she's a dragon. What are you getting at?"

"Never mind."

"What is it, Jack?"

"This is none of my business."

"Let's have it," she says.

"Hoops gossip, nothing more."

She squeezes my arm.

"Innuendo," I say.

Her fingernails dig in. "Out with it."

"He goes home on the first Friday of every month," I say.

"I know that."

"But do you know *why?*"

Nina shakes her head. "I've always assumed it was some sort of religious reason."

"The story is that England and his mother are in therapy."

"The whole world is in therapy, Jack."

"It's called confrontational therapy. England and his mother do it together. They scream at each other. The two of them go to a shrink once a month and let each other have it for an hour and a half."

Nina looks stunned.

"He never mentioned it?"

She shakes her head.

"It's true," I say. "I asked him about it. He told me himself. He said that it's cathartic. Afterward they go out to dinner."

"Poor Michael," she says.

Dear reader, this is not the effect I was intending.

I am seated at the glass table in Ellen's kitchen. Mrs. Stubbs stands at the dishwasher, leaning against the counter. Her arms are crossed. I have just delivered a sketchy account of recent events in the roller-coaster life of Jack Townsend, but Ellen cuts to the heart of the story as deftly as she slices apart the piece of turkey in front of her.

"Let's start at the beginning," she says. "In the first place, we need to know why you even went to the show. Whatever were you thinking, hon?"

I wasn't thinking at all, that's the point. In hindsight, considering how that impulsive act has complicated my life on all fronts, I would have to admit that crashing the opening was a mistake. Why *did* I go? Would I have blundered into that gallery had Nina sent me an invitation? Or if, say, England had broken the news about the show as we were jogging up the basketball court? I don't know. For some reason, getting word as I did caused me to act recklessly. I couldn't begin to explain this to Ellen.

"I guess I was curious," I reply.

Mrs. Stubbs lays her strong hands on my shoulders. "Let me tell you somt'ing, dearheart. Curiosity is what kills aivery old cat."

"I didn't want to be left out. I wanted to show everybody that I was a good sport."

"And did you?" asks Ellen.

"Not really."

"Why in heaven's name did you bring Kate with you?"

As embarrassing as this grilling is, the question must be asked.

"I told her what I was doing and asked her if she wanted to come along. She said yes."

"Hon, do you understand the concept of politesse?"

"I think she really wanted to go. She was curious, too. For different reasons. She wanted to see this scene for herself." A sip of wine and Ellen fixes her gray-green eyes on me. They beckon. She wants more. "Look, Kate and I have talked about Nina from time to time. I guess she wanted to put a face with the name."

"Three years living together and you don't own a photograph?"

"It was her decision. She seemed to enjoy herself—she said so afterwards."

"And what telse is the young lady suppoased to say?"

Ellen says, "Jack, it sounds as though you didn't think this through before discussing it with her. You didn't leave her a way to refuse without sounding insecure. People don't always mean what they say. You should take that into consideration."

"Kate means what she says. Always."

"Kate is as rational as anyone I know, but that doesn't mean she always makes the wisest decision."

"You lairn to swim by stepping into the water a bit at a time, dearheart. Not by jumping in over your head all at twonce."

"What was Nina's reaction?" Ellen asks.

It was Act III of *La Traviata*, the party scene. I don't say this of course. Nor do I suggest that I think I know what's coming in Act IV. Instead, I describe Nina's effort to hide out in the upstairs gallery. I recount our first conversation—without a word about the electricity that was zapping the two of us the whole time. I don't mention the conversation in the storage closet either. Nevertheless, Ellen seems to be getting the picture.

"And while you and Nina are catching up, Kate's wandering around all by herself?"

"She handled it. She talked to everyone."

"Honestly, Jack. Just because she *can* doesn't mean she should *have to.* If you want my opinion, this does not sound like a smashing date."

"You think maybe we're not right for each other?"

"I wasn't suggesting that for a moment."

"Well, sometimes I wonder. And I get the feeling Kate's wondering about that, too. The truth is, I don't know why she agreed to go along. If I had suggested to Nina that we make an appearance at Kate's art show, she would've gone through the roof. Not Kate. She didn't seem to mind at all. I really think she enjoyed it."

"Please don't criticize people for being able to act mature."

"And doan't be all the time trine to read a young lady's mind."

"So you arrive at Kate's house," Ellen says. "Then what happened?"

"I turned off the engine and started to get out of the car. But she took my hand."

Ellen waits.

"And we talked."

"About what?"

"About whether or not she has too much shade in the back-yard for an herb garden."

"And?"

"I told her that herb gardens need a lot of sunshine."

Ellen frowns.

"I doan't think your sister is asking about the herbs, dear-heart," says Mrs. Stubbs, pronouncing herbs with a hard *h,* in the Rastafarian style.

"Well, it just went on from there," I say.

Ellen says, "Jack, we've got to know *everything* if you want us to help you." And Mrs. Stubbs: "Doan't be shy wit' me. I have been livin' on this eart' for a long enough time, darlin', to see everyt'ing once and hear about the rest of it t'ree or foar times. You won't be shocking me on this lovely afternoon."

"We sat in the car holding hands, talking about the different varieties of basil. Then we talked about a business idea Kate has come up with. She's thinking about selling prepackaged herb window boxes. Basil, parsley, dill, thyme. You could buy the whole set or buy them individually. She has even registered the name Kitchen Garden."

"Jack."

"Then she yawned and I apologized for keeping her out so late and we talked about the show. Kate could recall every one of Nina's paintings."

"She has a good mind," says Ellen. "I told you that."

"She told me about her conversation with Joanie Lawrence—it seems Joanie asked Kate if it bothered her that there is an arrest warrant out for me in South Carolina."

"That woman!"

"It was a joke, sweetheart."

"Don't be jokin' 'bout the law. Not 'round here."

"Then Kate asked me a few questions about Marie Lawrence."

"Asked you what?"

"Asked what her story was. Marie was acting kind of strange when Kate and I bumped into her outside the gallery."

"I hope you changed the subject."

"It changed itself. We went from Marie to the difference between Catholics and Episcopalians to the need for religion as a way of coping with the reality that we will all die someday. To Ray."

Ellen looks stunned.

"It was a wonderful conversation."

"Oh, no," she says.

"I told her about the funeral."

"How could you tell her about the funeral? *You* didn't go."

"I told her why I didn't go. I told her about that awful minister swilling coffee in the kitchen and running on with that crap about how important it is for us to accept God's wisdom in calling His children home. I told Kate about buying a fifth of Wild Turkey and driving to the mountains and stumbling down a slope and camping on the open ground beside a stream, and about getting home late the next night and finding a new lock on the front door. I had to sleep in the backseat of Ray's Impala. Do you remember that?"

"I remember being worried sick about you and I remember seeing you asleep in the car."

"You don't remember the new locks?"

"Oh, everything about that week is a blur. I suppose Mother must have had that chore on her mind and was just keeping busy."

"Funny, I always assumed it was a gesture directed at me."

"Well, she wasn't happy that you weren't there. I do remember that."

"She was furious. She didn't talk to me for months."

"She needed support, hon. You didn't come through for her."

"You want to know what I think? I think that deep down she blames me for Ray's death."

"I hope you didn't give Kate the idea that there are psychological problems in the family," says Ellen, without a trace of irony.

"You mean because we moved from Ray to Evan?"

"Jack, honey! Why?"

"I think the connecting thread was the cruel hand of fate." Her head is shaking. "It's news, El. Every lawyer in town is talking about it."

"I think that's called gossip."

"Not with Kate and me. We're thinking about you. We're both worried about you."

"And I'm worried about the two of you. If I recall, that's what this conversation is all about."

"How come you change the subject whenever I ask how you're holding up?"

"Because I wouldn't be giving the subject a second thought if people like you weren't bringing it up all the time. Ev's a lawyer. Litigation is what he does for a living. How many times do I have to explain that as far as we're concerned this is just one more case?"

"He's not the lawyer on this one. He's the defendant. He's being tried for mail fraud. He's being sued for more than two million dollars. If he's convicted on the criminal charges, he'll go to jail."

"If, if, if. Honestly, Jack, you're starting to sound like that pesky reporter who's been hounding us day and night. We had to take an unlisted number and still he calls. If you want to discuss my problems, that's my real problem."

No aggravation in life so vexing it can't be remedied by a more sophisticated answering machine: "You have reached the home of embattled Evan Barton. If you are employed by a federal prosecutor, press one. Print and television journalists, press two. Lawyers looking to purchase a share of a flourishing K Street practice, press three. Evan Barton Defense Fund contributors, press four, and have your credit card ready. Literary agents and movie producers, press five. Friends and neighbors who wish to enquire about my well-being should dial 1-900-GO-4-IT-EV. The message is updated at seven A.M. and noon; the cost is two dollars, and may be tax deductible."

"I take it Evan's still bearing up," I say.

"Oh you know Ev. This is just one more ball to keep in the air. He loves that. Work makes him happy."

Ellen is standing at the sliding-glass door, gazing into the backyard. Mrs. Stubbs, seated across the table, touches my hand and shakes her head slowly.

"Sometimes it's good to talk," I say.

Ellen brings a fist to her mouth and begins to tap it gently against her lips. "Jack, do you remember the trip we took across country when we were kids?"

Who could forget it? Ray was ten, I was fourteen, Ellen had

just graduated from high school. We fought the whole way. Ray stole the men's room signs from a dozen gas stations between Chicago and Coeur d'Alene. Ellen had to be at a telephone at eight P.M. eastern time to call a boyfriend back home. I snapped the antenna off our rented car with a bullwhip that I bought in the Badlands. My father whistled for seventy-seven miles at one stretch.

"Sure," I say.

"I'm thinking about taking the kids out to Yellowstone this summer. They're still a little young for it, but Ev's never been there, so I thought, why not? I haven't mentioned it to him. Knowing him, he'll be too involved with this case to think about a vacation."

"Then I'll go."

"Oh you and Kate will probably be engaged and living together by the summertime."

"I don't think so, El."

She tries to look surprised. "But everything sounds so open and honest between you two. And you genuinely care for each other. Anyone could've seen that the evening you met."

"It's not that."

"Then what is it?"

"I get the feeling something's missing."

"An' maybe wha' tis missing is a diamond ring, dearheart."

"Mrs. Stubbs might have a point," says Ellen.

"I don't think Kate and I really understand each other."

"How much more is there to understand? You seem to have discussed every unpleasant subject under the sun."

"We think differently."

"I should hope so."

I shake my head. Ellen sits. She pushes the plate of turkey bones to the side. "This is the other night? After Nina's show?" I nod. "What happened?"

"It doesn't amount to much."

"Talk," she says.

"Well, we started to get cold in the car so we went inside. We sat on the couch, not saying much. For some strange reason it felt like it does sometimes after you've had a fight with someone you care about. Both people are sorry it happened. The storm cloud is gone and you're looking for ways to patch things up. But still, you're at a loss for conversation."

"Hon, did it occur to you that in Kate's mind, you might have *had* a fight?"

"A silent fight?"

"Lordy, Jack, the kettle can be aboiling without the lid popping off."

"Kate sat next to me, and it was really nice to hold her. It was relaxed for once. She talked about the future. She's really set on retiring early from the government and living near the ocean."

"What did you say?"

"Mostly, I listened. In a funny way, I felt closer to her right then than I'd ever felt. She's always been honest, always said what was on her mind, but somehow I never got a glimpse of what was going on inside. So this was a new side of her, and I was glad to see it."

"And then?" asks Ellen.

"And then we moved to the next phase of the evening and everything got confused."

They lean forward like veteran police interrogators and I am instantly sorry that I didn't wrap up the evening for them with Kate and me smooching on the couch.

"It's just us and the four walls," says Ellen. "Our lips are sealed."

"Well, I guess I expected the evening to end with a peck on the cheek at the front door—that's where we were headed. But all that talking and somehow we got sweet on each other. And . . . well . . ."

"And you found yourself sleeping in the young laidy's bed," Mrs. Stubbs says grimly.

"I didn't exactly sleep there. That was part of the surprise."
Ellen polishes off the final sip of wine. "You left?"

"I departed. It wasn't exactly my idea."

"Explain," she says.

No way. From me Ellen gets the expurgated version. I tell her
that the cuddling led to kissing and the kissing to some rather
acrobatic moves on the overstuffed couch, which led to a chuckle
or two, and then to the stairs. As in the movies, here we dissolve,
and pick up the principals as they light up metaphorical cigarettes.

In Kate's bed I sighed the sigh of an exhausted man. She
rested her head on my chest and whispered, "I hope you won't take
offense that I want to sleep by myself tonight."

My eyes popped open.

Of course not. In fact, at that moment, sleep was the farthest
thing from my mind. It filled me with inexpressible joy to don cold
crumpled clothes and push out into a black, black night with the
air temperature, measured by a front porch thermometer aligned to
Herr Fahrenheit's scale, at fourteen degrees.

"She was angry," says Ellen. "What did you expect? A
woman Kate's age wants a sign of commitment. She wants to know
where you stand."

"And she doasn't want to go gallyvanting off to the old one's
party, shuurrly."

No. Anger and jealousy, while justified, were not part of the
equation. This was a different woman in bed with me. This Kate
was someone I didn't know at all. Kate the straight arrow was
sublime; Kate the talker, silent. The acrobatics were left behind in
the living room and I was being led by the hand by a woman I'd
never met before. She lay beneath me with her eyes closed, the
vaguest hint of a smile on her face. There is nothing more erotic
than this. Every time nature urged me on, Kate would slow me
down. Her eyes stayed shut. Her lips were parted just a fraction,
showing a thin row of white teeth. She ran the tips of her fingers
down my back, held fast to my waist. She sighed and sighed.

Thinking back on it, it seems we lay together for an hour. It felt like an eternity. And immediately afterward she asked me to leave.

I cranked up the van at two A.M. and drove home with the scent of sex on my hands and a film of perfumy sweat freezing to my brow.

"Has she called you?" asks Ellen.

"Not Kate."

Ellen's eyes pull together. "Nina called you? What did *she* want?"

Given my sister's nose for the truth, I confess straight out Nina's dinner invitation, minus the embarrassing business about Nonna believing that Nina and I are married. That bit of Calabrian subterfuge Ellen would never understand.

"She just called you out of the blue and asked you to Christmas Eve dinner at her parents' home?"

"Not exactly. She called me and asked me to meet her at the Museum of American Art, and while we were there she asked me."

"I thought she had a new boyfriend."

"He'll be out of town."

Ellen and Mrs. Stubbs exchange dark glances.

"It's not like that," I say. "Christmas Eve at the Lawrences' is a tradition. Nina wants me there for old times' sake."

"But you turned her down," says Ellen, a note of desperation lifting her voice into the ragged range. "Isn't that right, Jack?"

"Um, no."

"And what did Kate have to say about *that*?"

WASHINGTON'S HAMLET

I am a coward.

Soon, no doubt, I will confess to Kate my Christmas Eve plans. The thing is, I haven't found the right moment. I'm waiting for us to find ourselves on the subject of the holidays (heavy traffic, presents to buy, office parties, whatever), so that I can steer the conversation around to the birth of the Christ child and slip in an offhand "Oh-by-the-way-looks-like-I-have-something-going-on-the-twenty-fourth" remark. It's a gutless approach, I admit. And the only defense I can offer is as weak as the scheme: I grew up in a family that placed a premium on avoiding unpleasant issues.

Tonight Kate and I are taking Jason to see the national Christmas tree and I am late. Not five minutes late, in which case I would find Kate and Jason bundled in coats, hats, and boots, inside, sitting on the stairway beside the front door, but twenty minutes late, which means I find them outside, parked like refugees on the dimly lit stoop of a darkened house.

"Car trouble," I say. "Gunk on the battery terminals. Took me a little while to get them cleaned off." This is a white lie. The truth is that I just had to whack the positive terminal once with a wrench.

"Your phone was busy."

"Must've been the machine."

"For ten minutes?"

"A couple of calls, I guess."

Kate stands. "I thought it might have something to do with Evan."

"No news there—at least no public announcements. I saw him yesterday. He looks terrible. He's lost fifteen pounds."

"I spoke to a friend in the U.S. Attorney's office. Off the record, Jack, they think they have him. Right now they're wearing him down. It looks like it's just a matter of time before he accepts a plea bargain." And more quietly, "He's going to jail. Ellen needs to realize that."

"Deep down I think she does. She's talking about taking the kids out to Yellowstone."

"How does *she* look?"

"She's tougher than you'd think. She's got my father's self-preservation instincts. You don't have to worry about Ellen playing stand-by-your-man on this one."

"Do you think she needs to talk to someone?"

"She talks to Mrs. Stubbs."

I pick up Jason and start toward the van but Kate calls, "There's ice on the roads. Let's take mine."

She obeys the speed limits on Reno Road; on Massachusetts Avenue, we roll past the darkened embassies in silence. While we're stopped at a light in front of the Watergate, she says, "Think we'll find a parking space at the Ellipse?"

"Let's try."

Jason, too, is quiet. This sneakered boy of many questions asks just one the entire trip. At Constitution Avenue, the brightly colored lights of the tree come into view and Jason leans forward. "Do the people who live outside get the presents that are under that tree?"

Kate gamely tries to explain the difference between *that* tree and all the trees that people have set up *inside* their houses, but Jason is more interested in determining if the people who live *outside* have Christmas trees, and if they don't, just exactly where Santa leaves their presents.

Soon Kate gives up. She grips the top of the wheel with both hands and squeezes it. "Jack, why don't you explain it to him."

"This year the people who live outside don't get any presents," I say.

"Jack!"

The lights of a parked car in front of us come on. Kate pulls to the side and brakes sharply, throwing me into the seat belt strapped across my chest.

"Were they bad?" asks Jason.

"No. But the President spent all of Santa's money buying guns, so Santa couldn't buy any presents for the people who live outside."

"Why'd he do that, Mr. Townscnd?"

"Because he likes guns more than he likes people."

"Honey, Jack is teasing you."

Jason says, "They don't look like they got any presents last year either."

Not for the past twelve years anyway. Not so much as a lump of coal.

When Jason runs ahead toward the colored lights, Kate says, "That really wasn't like you."

"I suddenly felt a need to be honest."

"Make that crabby." She takes my arm. "He's a little young for sarcasm, don't you think."

"I guess I ran out of gas. Sorry."

"Is that it? I'm sensing hostility directed at me." Jason spins around to find us and Kate calls, "Over here, Jace!," then turns to me and says, "The other night must have seemed pretty confusing to you. I sure sent some mixed signals." Jason waits at the curb and we cross the street together. Two older children run past us, and he racewalks after them.

Kate says, "At first, I didn't know what to make of it myself. I didn't plan any of it, that's for sure. It just happened. I lost control"—I smile—"Yes, me," she says. "It was the best that it's ever been for me, Jack. That scared me. I needed to be alone to try to figure out what it all meant."

"Sort of wish I had stayed."

"Oh no you don't. I probably would've started crying and gotten clingy and you would have made a beeline for the door. It would have set me back years."

"You know what I thought? I thought you were trying to teach me a lesson. I thought that was punishment for my dragging you to Nina's opening."

She looks at me with total surprise. "I wouldn't have missed that for the world!"

I regard the mass of quilted coats gathered at the base of the tree and recall Ellen's latest postcard, *The Stranded Boat,* by Martin Johnson Heade. The inscription is from Christina Rossetti: "This downhill path is easy, but there is no turning back."

"Mom! Mr. Townsend! Look!" Jason is pointing at the huge Christmas tree in front of us.

Tinsel covers it like fur. Huge lights and silver globes the size of beach balls hang from its branches. Nearby, extending in two lines, are fifty small state trees. Everything looks as if it was decorated by someone who does windows at a shopping mall. Christmas

Muzak fills the air, a Yule log is smoking somewhere down the midway. The White House, behind us, is lit up like a wedding cake. We are surrounded by Nigerians, Sikhs, a group of Finns or Latvians, a British couple in tweed. Kate shakes her head as we take in a scene that fairly screams the message of peace on earth and goodwill to men.

"It's enough to turn a holy man into a sinner," I say.

She takes my arm. "You know, sometimes I get the sense that you really do believe in God."

"Sure. Why not?"

"What do you mean, sure, why not?"

"Well, as I see it, you start with the idea that there is or isn't a God. Either way it's a guess, right? I happen to like the thought that He's up there, so I'm leaning that way. It's just a hunch, the flip side of my belief in the profound insignificance of the human race. Just because we made up the idea of God doesn't mean He doesn't exist."

"I'm just not comfortable with the idea of someone else pulling the strings. But sometimes I wonder. It's one of those questions that really frustrates me because there's no getting to the bottom of it."

"You need faith," I say.

"Tell me about faith," she says.

"Nina once told me that a nun told her that faith was the black space between the stars."

"We're supposed to believe that there is a God because of the existence of the universe?"

"Not the universe, the black space. This is according to a nun who later dropped out of the Sisters of Charity and got thrown in jail for pouring a bucket of fake blood into a Minuteman missile silo."

Kate looks at the sky and shakes her head. "A belief in the inherent goodness of mankind is all I can muster," she says.

It happens that I don't have an ounce of faith in the inherent goodness of mankind—who could, I wonder, living on this planet?—but I keep the thought to myself. Kate rests her head against my shoulder. I strain to get a reading of the situation. I've never seen her so subdued. She's humming a Christmas carol, her eyes on Jason. He has his face pressed to a chain link fence at the reindeer yard. Beyond him, a park ranger is addressing a small crowd. Shortly they break up and Jason comes running toward us.

"Mom! The ranger said that the reindeer are sick. They've got worms."

Perfect. A sign from God if there ever was one. It's morning in America and Santa's reindeer have worms. I am tempted to shout the news at the top of my lungs. This whole scene depresses me. I wish Kate and I could have this conversation somewhere else—someplace *real*. Beneath the "We Cash Checks" sign on the boarded-up storefront at 18th and Florida, say, or sitting on *The Exorcist* steps in Georgetown.

After two circuits, after we have warmed our hands at the Yule log and ascertained as best we can that the national tree is real, Jason announces that it is time to go home. Today is Tuesday, a Mommy night for Jason and a Palisades night for Mr. Townsend.

Kate says, "Jack, would you get the car? I need to make a quick telephone call."

Of course I don't see what's coming. I'm screwed so tight to my desire to confess my Christmas Eve dinner plans that I don't see the ground in front of my shoes. Holding Jason's hand as we search for Kate's silver Honda Accord among a thousand silver Honda Accords parked around the Ellipse, I catch myself thinking about Nina.

Regarding the White House, Jason says, "Mr. Townsend, why doesn't the President let the people who don't have a home stay at his house? It sure looks big enough."

"Because he never learned to share."

The answer satisfies him. We keep walking, scanning license plates until Jason points out Kate's. He climbs into the back seat of the car and gives me detailed instructions on the proper way to cinch him into his seat belt. He wants the strap tight. He reminds me to fasten my own.

"Are we all set?" I ask.

"Roger."

"Prepare to launch." I crank up the engine.

"Mr. Townsend?"

"Yes, doctor?"

"Maybe you should spend the night at my house tonight."

"Something to think about," I say.

"You could sleep in my room."

"Well, that's a generous offer."

"And tomorrow we could play. And you could stay over tomorrow night and the next night. And next week you could marry my mom."

"Whoa, kid. Before you marry someone, you have to talk and talk and talk. It's better if you're not living in the same house."

"But if you're living in the same house you could talk *more*," he says with the force of conviction.

What happens after childhood that causes us to shade what we say to such a degree that we lose the ability to say what's really on our minds? Blunt can be rude, but polite is so often dishonest or utterly beside the point.

"The thing is, you have to spend a long time becoming friends before you can even think about getting married," I say.

"Why?" Jason wants to know.

"Well, it's a very serious decision."

"Like when my father bought me a bike?"

"More like buying a car. You're going to have to live with it for a long, long time; day in and day out. So you have to think about everything very carefully. You have to be sure to ask a lot of questions."

What a crock. You go with your gut. I should tell him that

it's more like skydiving. You leap from the plane with the confidence that your chute will open. Sometimes it doesn't.

"So you and my mom won't ever get married," he says.

"Sometimes people meet and fall in love right away; sometimes they start as friends and don't fall in love until much later. So you never know. But listen, even if we don't get married, that doesn't mean we won't be friends. And friends are good to have, don't you think?"

I have bored the kid into silence.

Kate is standing at the U.S. Park Service information kiosk, telephone receiver pressed to her ear. She is looking up at the night sky—at the stars, I suppose. After a time, her head starts nodding rapidly and she hangs up. I toot the horn. She crosses the street and climbs into the passenger seat; she drapes an arm around my seat and gives Jason a smile. I start toward Independence Avenue, but she directs me the other way.

"Where to?" I ask.

"Tobe's," she says quietly. To Jason she adds, "Honey, tonight you'll be staying with Daddy."

"But today is Tuesday," Jason says.

To date, Jason's Mommy and Daddy schedule has been sacrosanct. Something serious is in the works. The kid senses this, too.

Kate says, "Daddy said that he wants to see you tonight and I told him that it was okay with me."

"But you called him," Jason says. He's too old for this. And too smart. Someday, he too will ace his GREs and LSATs. In the rearview mirror, I see his lower lip extend as he begins to pout.

"It's important to learn to be flexible," Kate says, and there the conversation ends.

Tobias lives in Adams Morgan. Kate directs me to an apartment building on Columbia Road, an eight or nine-story behemoth with elaborate scrollwork and a horseshoe-shaped driveway covered by a huge portico. It's the sort of place that needs a doorman.

"Say good night to Mr. Townsend."

"Good night, Jack," snaps Jason. All the rules of etiquette have been suspended.

I watch them walk toward a stocky man in a khaki jacket standing inside the lobby. He is rubbing his hands as though warming them. He and Kate peck each other on the cheek as Jason is passed from one protective arm to another. The kid seems resigned to this life, but neither parent does. The smooth exchange is heartbreaking to watch. The conversation continues. Tobias glances over Kate's shoulder. At me. In the end he follows her through the door; her posture says that this show of bonhomie—or whatever it is—was not part of the plan. There is a meaty hand at my ear. I lower the window.

"Jack, Tobias Aronson. Listen, I just want to take a moment to say that Jason has had a lot of nice things to say about you. We really appreciate the attention you've paid to him. I can't thank you enough."

Another clue sails past me, so distressed am I by the sudden realization that during these past months I have been standing between a father and his son. I nod, but then get the sense that a nod won't do. Tobias wants me to say something. His mouth is open, his eyes beckon. There are moments in life when I would give anything for a script.

"He's a good boy. You have a right to be proud of him," I manage.

"We feel very fortunate."

"Tobe, it's already past his bedtime," Kate says. For an instant, I think she's talking about me.

He looks at his watch. "Righto. Well, 'night now. Take care of yourself, Jack."

Clue number five or six.

Kate throws herself into the seat. "Sorry about that. He just broke off a relationship a few weeks ago and I think he's a little starved for adult conversation."

We pass a playground and a park, separated from us by an endless line of parked cars.

"I guess you must be wondering what this is all about," Kate says finally.

"Seems there are a few things to talk about," I say.

"Too many."

She leans against my arm as we pass the statue of General George Brinton McClellan, America's Hamlet. At the corner of Florida and Massachusetts, I watch the lights of a distant plane skim along the tops of the trees as it descends into National Airport. Kate rests a hand on my leg. My mouth goes dry and suddenly I can't bear the weight of her tenderness.

"You know, we haven't talked about Christmas," I say.

"Strange, isn't it? Considering that it's five days away." She touches the side of my face. "I guess I've been reluctant to bring up the subject. Jason and I are spending the weekend in Pelham."

"I wish—"

"Oh, I wouldn't put you through that again. Ever."

We pass the statue of Robert Emmet, skulking in a grove of trees.

"Kate, I've been doing some thinking."

"I guess I've been doing some thinking, too."

Acutely aware of the hand resting on my thigh, I lose my nerve. "So what have you been thinking about?"

"Same as you," she replies. "About us."

Is it possible that she knows exactly what I want to say?

"Jack, I have an apology to make. The other night I shouldn't have asked you to see Judith with me."

"Funny, I was thinking that it might be a good idea. I mean, maybe she could help us sort things out."

"It was premature. For some reason, I jumped off the deep end. I got way ahead of myself."

"It couldn't hurt to talk."

"But is that what we need? Are we there yet?" She thinks we aren't. "Judith and I have been talking about the request. We've come to the conclusion that my desire to have you see her with me is a manifestation of something else."

"What's that?"

"At some level I think I'm looking for her approval."

Winston Churchill, on the grounds of the British embassy, throws his *V* for victory sign toward the Kahlil Gibran Peace Park.

"Surely that's not the whole story."

"It's enough of the story that the rest seems superfluous," she says.

Thirty-fourth Street is a dark corridor of frosty pavement and rolling hills. We pass a bike rider speeding down to Porter Street with a scarf wrapped around his or her head, leaving a slit for the eyes. Kate continues to gaze out the passenger window until we roll to a stop in front of her house.

"Everything is so confusing," she says. "I've never felt closer to you than I did the other night, yet what did I want immediately afterward? To be alone. Suddenly there was a wall between us and I wanted it there. I put it there." She shakes her head. "The more I think about it, the more I realize that the request to see Judith didn't stem from my desire for us to get to know each other better. It was an expression of anxiety about our relationship. A cry from the heart."

"Still—"

"Trust me on this. I'm beginning to understand my motivation. Judith and I spent the last three sessions talking about us."

I sense that all-too-familiar scrotal ache. Had I only made the effort to learn Nonna Romano's ear-tingling technique, none of this would surprise me. I kill the engine, figuring the cold will soon force us into the house. This conversation desperately needs a change of venue. But Kate doesn't budge.

"Actually, we only spent two sessions on us," Kate says. "The third session was about you."

Oh dear Lord.

"She asked me about my perception of your relationship with the important women in your life."

The ache becomes a throb. "Did you tell her that I'm still working on my spontaneous answer?"

Kate smiles. "You may have a long way to go in some areas, but not in the humor department. Don't lose your sense of humor, Jack. I'm really going to miss it."

"Shouldn't we finish this conversation inside?"

"I don't think so. I prefer serious talks in automobiles. It's the right scale, don't you think?"

Some cars. I have a theory about the dangers of conducting intimate conversation in perfectly designed Japanese cars, but it hardly seems appropriate to sketch it out right now.

"Where was I?" she asks.

"You were about to tell me about my problem with women."

"Are you angry, Jack? Are you surprised?"

"No."

"Not at all?"

"We seemed to have stalled at Thanksgiving."

"Wasn't that really just a symptom?"

At this cold moment I have not one iota of curiosity about what went wrong between us. Tomorrow I might spend the whole day mulling it over, but right now, with Kate beside me, I'd rather listen to a sad country-western song or a broken-heart blues number and not say a word.

"Have you gotten over Nina?" Kate asks.

Another opening to discuss my Christmas Eve dinner plans, but it hardly seems relevant now.

"I'm sure I haven't."

She leans against the door, her head cocked analytically. "What does it tell you that you haven't known that all along?"

We are strangers now. In the space of thirty minutes, we have mutated into different human beings. The only thing left of the old Jack and Kate are the wrinkled clothes that hide our nakedness.

I'm not angry. To tell the truth, I am relieved. I saw this coming, but had no idea that Kate would act so decisively. I admire her resolve. From the look on her face it seems that she could shake my hand right now and march off into the crackling-cold night, feeling positive that she has done what she set out to do, said what she wanted to say.

But she doesn't leave. Not yet. Kate hasn't finished her list of particulars.

"Has Nina gotten over you?" she asks.

"I don't know."

"I do. The answer is no."

"Maybe she and I ought to look into joint counseling," I say.

"It would be time and money well spent."

"Of course we won't."

"Don't decide that too quickly. You might want to try Judith."

Why not? She knows me. Nina and I wouldn't have to start at square one with Dr. Judith. No doubt Kate has given her a better introduction to Jack Townsend than I could ever hope to. Probably to Nina, too. Perhaps the good doctor has already made a diagnosis. I should ask Kate about this. It might save us a trip.

"Any insights on territory we ought to be sure to cover?"

"So you are angry."

"Whatever gave you that idea?"

"Please don't be hostile."

"Why not?"

"I don't think there's any call for it."

"Of course there is. You're breaking up with me. Even if your reasons for doing so make all the sense in the world, I'm still allowed to sputter and bitch and slam my hand against the steering wheel a couple of times. That's only fair."

"It doesn't sound very rational to me."

"I'm feeling sorry for myself, for God's sake. Slamming my hand against the steering wheel suggests that no matter how mismatched we are, the fact that it's over between us is causing me pain. Which means we had something. Which means I lost something and ought to be allowed to grieve a little bit."

"Judith said—"

"I don't give a damn what Judith said." Kate freezes. "If you want to know the truth, I'm not real excited about the fact that she has been getting a transcript of everything we say."

"It can't surprise you that I talk about our relationship with Judith."

"I guess I was under the assumption that the main reason you go to see her is to talk about yourself."

"I do," she says. "We *were* talking about me. We were looking for patterns in my life. 'Trying to understand the mosaic,' as Judith says. You see, I have this tendency to get involved in unhealthy relationships. I'm trying to get a handle on that. Ultimately change the pattern. That's what this conversation is all about."

It seems to me that at some level all human relationships are unhealthy. Which is what makes them so interesting. Anyway, what's the alternative? The folks who carry on about the joys of solitude have always seemed to me to be a pretty grim bunch.

"For instance," Kate goes on, "with both you and Tobias, it evolved that I was responsible for managing certain aspects of the relationship. Deciding where we went to dinner, how we spent the day, that sort of thing. With *both* of you. It's curious, don't you think?"

No. There are any number of ways to explain the coincidence: Kate is a control freak, Tobias and I are twins separated at birth, the water in Friendship Heights is tainted with some chemical that induces passivity. (Kate drinks Evian.) Anyway, what difference does it make? Why are we obligated to take the blood of a failed romance and spin it in a centrifuge to separate its component parts? Whatever happened to the era of raised voices and tears and slammed doors? At least that way you leave with the good memories intact. I'd rather recall Kate in the odalisque pose she assumed in bed last Friday night as I was pulling up my pants to face the subarctic chill. As it is, she'll be forever fixed in my mind hunkered down in the passenger seat of a goddamn Honda, a fingernail picking at the armrest.

She takes my hand. I mean she really takes it, squeezes it, traces the lines of my fingers like a doctor feeling for broken bones.

"Don't get me wrong," she says. "There were many positive things, too. Many positive things."

I don't want to hear the list. It's bound to be short and disappointing.

"In the interest of closure," I say, "might I be allowed to know what you have determined is the precise nature of my problem with women?"

"Judith thinks it might have something to do with your relationship with your mother."

"I haven't said two words about my mother."

Kate nods gravely. "That might be an avenue to explore, Jack."

The kiss materializes like a barroom punch, a fluttery jab that lands high on the cheek. It's the same kiss Tobias got. Kate pulls the key from the ignition.

"You take care of yourself," she says. "Believe it or not, this is really hard for me. I wish it had worked out differently. I wish certain issues had come up earlier, when we might have had the opportunity to deal with them But that's water under the bridge. We can't change the past."

Maybe we can't change the past, but we can stomp all over it like a barrel of grapes and pack it away in an oaken vat and pray that someday it will be transformed into something wonderful. We can become obsessed with the people who once meant the world to us, thereby forsaking the formation of new relationships. Forget what the duly accredited helping professional might say about whether such behavior is healthy. In this crazy world, fidelity to one's character should count for something.

"I'll miss you, Jack."

"I'll miss you, too."

Kate was my window to the world of the patently normal. She has an awfully light touch for a GS-15. And a fine dry sense of humor.

"Stay as long as you like," she says. "Just do me a favor and lock up when you leave."

It grieves me that neither of us is crying. What good is a breakup without a few tears? This isn't a cowboy movie or a sands-of-North-Africa war flick—still, she salutes me from the stoop like Montgomery at El Alamein. And then she's gone.

It takes time for me to summon the courage to face another bitterly cold night in Friendship Heights. The van looks sinister parked in the shadows. Dan, bless his heart, is asleep on my seat and has warmed it to the temperature of a hot-water bottle. He is unhappy about being roused, and lets out a throaty groan as he stumbles into the back and collapses on his bed.

I can see my breath. I can hear every spring and bolt in the vehicle cry out as I shift around and lock up my seat belt. This past fall I spent $700 for a new clutch, new starter, and new brakes. Still, I can't shake the sense that there are other dogs in this beast to be fed. In cold weather they howl like wolves. I step the gas pedal to the floor three times, insert the key, offer a brief ejaculation to the patron saint of ignition assemblies, and turn the key.

Nothing. Not a chug, not a pop, not a click.

O HOLY NIGHT

Snow is falling, a light dusting sweeps across MacArthur Boulevard; two or three inches of white powder cover the roadside. The weather report promises twelve inches of snow, maybe sixteen!—or ten and freezing rain if a warm front stalls in the mountains for any length of time. I listen carefully to the details of the latest weather report, ignorant of the most basic principles of meteorology. The announcer counsels everyone to stay home. His voice is edgy. I don't understand why Washingtonians work themselves into such a pitch during snowstorms. I see a heavy snowfall as a piece of good luck, an opportunity to stay home, act like a kid again, burn off a few calories, throw out my back.

The rear end of the van slips as we glide through a turn. Dan's mustard-colored eyes implore me to slow down. I am cautious and sober but the tires on this vehicle are bald. I was thinking about buying a new set of Dunlops as a Christmas present to myself, but then I had to spend $76 on a new battery and cables. So the tires will have to wait, and we will slide.

The tree branches crisscrossing the road that climbs into Mohican Hills are covered with snow. Weighted down, a tall slender pine looks like a rocket. I barrel up Tuscarawas, swerving around a snowy scrum of bamboo that has collapsed into the roadway. Dan is whining as we pick up speed to make the hill in front of us. We slide through the sharp turn at Wehawken like a truck in a cartoon, then ride the roller coaster to Winnebago Road. Richter's château, sitting behind a matchstick stand of tulip trees, is a Yuletide scene of wafting smoke and amber light.

The cars parked every which way in the driveway suggest that something illegal is going on inside—a crap game, say, or a cockfight. But the makes of the autos are all wrong. Instead of Camaros and Firebirds, I see Richey, Jr.'s Porsche, Joey's restored Karman Ghia, Liza and Bruce's rusty Subaru wagon, Barb and Zalman's shiny Volvo, Richter's vintage Ford truck, Joan's '66 Mustang, and Marie's bullet-riddled Toronado. Nina's Citroën is nowhere in sight.

The temperature has warmed a few degrees, the wind has died down, and the snow is now falling in clumps. I shake like a dog at the front door.

Joan greets me. Her color is high. The sly smile she is wearing announces that tonight she is my accomplice. "The gate is unlatched," she whispers. "Saddle the horses."

"How can you be sure?"

"A feeling, lad. A strong feeling. Remember, I've been there myself." She kisses me hard on the lips, wrenching my neck. "Merry Christmas, Jack! Welcome back!"

In the living room, not a creature is stirring. From the feel of things, this could be the game room of a nursing home. The fire crackles, a small train plods a tedious figure eight on a green sheet of plywood at the base of an artificial Christmas tree, a football game progresses silently on the TV in Richter's study. Liza and Barb sit together on the couch; Zalman, in a cream-colored cable-knit sweater, stands behind them. Father Bruce and Patrick are seated at a card table studying a chessboard. Richter and Richey, Jr., are bent over maps and blueprints. I hear Anna in the kitchen. It sounds as though she's singing an old Tony Bennett number—something about a moon in June that rises like a helium balloon. Nonna I almost miss, seated in a wing chair in the corner. She gives me a big smile and seems to be weighing my head with her outstretched hands.

"Ah, Jack!" she calls. "My Marie a told me that you were coming, but I a wasn't sure. Come over here an' a let me see you!"

I kiss her cheek. Her skin is like paper.

"Annowa you get me something to drink," she whispers. "A litta red wine."

I make the rounds, bussing cheeks and shaking hands and shaking my head in amazement at the amount of time that has passed since my last supper under this roof. Nonna sits there like a bird, her eyes twinkling like the colored lights of the tree, sipping Gallo Hearty Burgundy from a huge goblet.

Nina and Joey, I learn, have been dispatched on a culinary mission. Marie wanted smoked salmon for hors d'oeuvres, but refused to pay delicatessen prices. So she called the Ramada Inn in Bethesda and talked to the Sunday brunch director and got the name of his salmon connection. Thus, at this moment, Joey and Nina are plowing around the Beltway, trying to make a six P.M. rendezvous at a dumpster behind a nondescript warehouse near the state prison in Jessup, Maryland. They have the cash; a guy named Bill will have the fish.

"What do you think of the site, Jack?"

Richter wants to show off the parcel of land that he is looking to buy. He likes to think he has a nose for Washington real estate. It takes him weeks, sometimes months, of agonized thought before he will plunk down his money on a new piece of land. Yet he always does. And in the end he always comes out ahead. The real-estate market in this town just goes up, up, up. This scheme is a little different, however. On this property—a gently sloping cliff, really—Richter is planning to build a new house from the ground up. A sixty-year-old man working on a sixty-degree grade sounds to me like a recipe for disaster. I would never say that to him, of course. It would only strengthen his resolve.

"Can't miss," I say.

"Can't miss? In the name of sweet Jesus, man. Why, if we don't bolt the house to that hill, the first storm comes along and the whole shebang slides down onto MacArthur Boulevard!"

"I figure that an engineer like yourself would be sure to have that covered, Doc."

"There are a thousand ways to go wrong. This isn't like planting trees, Jack."

This from a man who has not planted a tree in his whole life. I could call him on this, but then Richter would act wounded for the rest of the evening. Instead, we study his topographical map and argue about the drainage patterns on the MacArthur property. Twice he tells me that he has decided to back out of the deal; twice he rejects that idea.

There is a rumble on the stairs like the sound of a bowling ball descending. Marie sweeps into the living room in a peach-colored Zsa Zsa Gabor–style gown.

"*JAACK!* Bless you for the flowers! Irises in December! You must have paid a fortune for them." A big kiss on my cheek.

In fact, my Christmas gifts—a red, white, and blue scarf for Marie and English Leather Soap-on-a-Rope for Richter—are under the tree. The flowers are from Zalman, who sends a beautifully subtle and ironic smirk in my direction. Barb, though, is steaming.

"Ma, the flowers—"

"Just beautiful. Could you put them in a vase, darling?"

I say, "Marie—"

"Don't just stand there, Jack. Help me with this table."

We drag it into the center of the room and Marie covers it with a lacy tablecloth.

"What are we setting up for, Ma?"

Anna is speaking. She stands at the kitchen door wearing an "I'd rather be fishing" apron. She is a younger version of Nina, a startling sight.

Marie says, "A little surprise, kids. My Christmas present to all of you."

Barb immediately becomes suspicious—with good reason it seems to me—when Marie sets Zalman's flowers and a line of mismatched candlesticks on the table. She has transformed this nondescript sidepiece into a miniature altar.

We hear a car, not the throaty roar of Nina's Citroën, but the rattly hum of an old VW Beetle.

"Right on time," says Marie brightly. "Now everyone be-have."

The front door is thrown open and snow blows into the hallway.

"Welcome, Father," Marie calls. "We're all so grateful to you for coming out on a night like this."

"Neither rain, nor snow, nor the dark of night," comes a cheerful reply.

Barb has turned a deep shade of crimson by the time a stamping of feet heralds the arrival of a reed-thin man with an incongruously large waxed mustache. Beneath a tan suede coat he is wearing a black shirt and a starched white collar. Marie's gift to the family, it would seem, is forced participation in Christmas Eve Mass. Father McLucas makes a priestly entrance and circles the room, greeting everyone with a freezing two-handed shake. Nonna gets a blessing over the head as well.

"Well now," intones Father McLucas, in a booming cathedral-sized voice, "before we begin, maybe we should have a little chat." He paces around the makeshift altar, rearranging the candles and flowers. "Christmas Eve," he muses. "Christmas. Christ Mass. Mass, from the Middle English *masse*, meaning feast day, a celebration." His hands are held prayerfully at his chin, fingers touching his lips. "Patrick, what exactly is it that we are celebrating tonight? Why don't you tell the family what Christmas means to you."

What has been merely odd suddenly becomes annoying. This isn't fair. What sort of twisted soul would turn the spotlight on a kid whose only hope of surviving the hormone-wracked years of adolescence depends on the ability to make himself invisible at moments like this? Patrick has nothing to say to this man, nothing to say to any of us for the next two or three years.

"Uh, the birth of the Baby Jesus, I guess," he manages, his eyes focused on a chess piece in his hand.

"The birth of the Baby Jesus!" McLucas should be a game show host. "Joan Anne, tell us about the significance to your life of the birth of the Baby Jesus."

Joanie says sweetly, "Father, I think it would save some time if we went straight to what *you* have to say on the Baby Jesus subject."

"The Baby Jesus subject!" He laughs, fiddling with his mustache. "Quite right! It certainly has become that, hasn't it. Our whole economy depends on the gifts that are given in the name of Baby Jesus. I think it's fair to say that the Baby Jesus subject has become an important subject indeed."

I could quote the entire warm-up homily, but what's the point? There is no escaping the feeling that McLucas stitched together this little talk on the drive over here. It probably started with an ad on the radio for Raleigh's or Sears. I can see him stopped at a light on Massachusetts Avenue, wiping the condensation from the windshield of the Beetle with his left hand, thinking: "Consumerism, Materialism, the Meaning of Christmas—that's the ticket."

The meaning of Christmas isn't about shopping malls, he explains. They didn't even have shopping malls in Bethlehem in those days. Or outlet shops. "I'm not talking about Bethlehem, *PA*, mind you," he says, chuckling.

All the while he is unpacking vestments, kissing each piece of cloth before donning it. Soon he looks as radiant as a fruited tree. "The meaning of Christmas," he says, "is the meaning of Christ. What does it tell us that God sent us His only begotten Son to take away the sins of the world? What does that loving act suggest about our responsibility to answer the call of His Church? To find the image of Christ within ourselves, to nurture this image in our children? I will leave you with one thought tonight. The first Commandment applies to Jesus as well as to his Father. 'I am the Lord thy God, thou shalt not put strange Gods before me.' My dear friends, we must open our eyes to the One True Church. In order to secure a place in Our Father's heavenly kingdom, we must believe in our heart and confess openly our Catholic faith. Thus, we shall. In the name of the Father, the Son, and the Holy Spirit."

We're off. The Mass has begun. In the past, Nina dragged me to a couple of bootleg Latin Masses. Not understanding a word of the proceedings stimulated within me a peculiar enjoyment of the ritual, for the same reason, I suspect, that a shouting match in the streets of Naples, Italy, would seem much more interesting than, say, a restaurant spat in Georgetown. The Mass in English is stripped of all mystery. It seems, well, banal. Apparently I'm not alone in this assessment. Joanie is counting ceiling tiles. Barb has turned into an Old Testament pillar of salt. Richter glances surreptitiously at the television in his study. His lower jaw tenses as a halfback takes the pitch and scampers around left end. Of the younger generation, only Father Bruce and Liza are participating fully: he's out on the floor serving as acolyte; she's sitting beside

Marie on the couch, shielding her mother from the scolding glances of her children.

Father McLucas asks for a show of hands of those who will receive communion, and six go up.

Joan, on the couch next to me, can't resist the occasional comment: "This is like something out of *Brideshead Revisited.*" A moment later: "Make that Monty Python." And later: "Might have a new fella, Jack. Met him at the Bethesda Food Co-op. He runs an organic farm in Pennsylvania."

"A match made in heaven," I whisper.

"Except that his name happens to be Josh Cohen."

"Oh my God. Restore the Inquisition."

"Marie's reaction exactly. She threatened to take my name out of the family Bible."

"Pretend that you never existed—"

"—in the eyes of God."

We are both working to control the expressions on our faces.

"So what's with this Judeo-Catholic attraction?" I ask. "Some sort of Old Testament/New Testament thing?"

Liza scolds us with a glance.

"The oddball factor," Joan whispers. "Two sides of the same coin. Plus, both camps are raised on bizarre rituals and strange smells and weird food rules. And don't forget that our guy used to be one of theirs, so there's the rivalry aspect, too."

"A Harvard-Yale thing?"

"More Redskins-Giants," she says.

"So why isn't Mr. Cohen here tonight?"

"I asked him, but he didn't seem too excited about the idea. Said he might show up at midnight." And, a moment later: "What happens if this creep gets snowed in with us?"

More worrisome, as far as I'm concerned, is the chance that Nina and Joey might get snowed *out*. I watch the heavy flakes batter a column of exposed windowpanes between the drapes. When Father McLucas asks the Lord to hear our prayers, mine is a rather specific request to bring to my ears the whooshing sound of a front-wheel-drive Citroën careening sideways into the yard. In time I do hear it, just moments before Father Bruce rings the brass dinner bell. The host is raised as the front door opens. Nina, radiant Nina, appears in the doorway and drops to her knees with such grace you'd think it's something she does every time she enters the living room. I can hear the first notes of the tender Mimi theme; Joanie must hear it, too, given the force behind the elbow she throws into my ribs. The wrapped salmon is passed from hand to hand across the room, so deftly it seems part of the Mass. When it reaches Anna, she crosses herself and spirits the big fish off to the kitchen.

Nina sits beside me, squeezing my wrist. I am looking for the tiniest clues to her state of mind, but the sight of this sacred ritual being performed in her parents' home engages her fully. Wearing a black silk shirt, black leather skirt, black stockings and boots, she could easily be mistaken for a widow mourning the loss of her biker husband. Her face, however, is beatific. It is the face of a woman who, through divine intervention, has just beaten the odds on a snow-covered highway.

"What in heaven's name is this about?" she whispers.

"Marie's Christmas present to the family."

Nina: "Her *what?*"

Joan: "I would've told her to go for the gas grill."

The Mass is in the homestretch. Father McLucas is blessing everything in sight. He kisses the tablecloth and tells us to go in peace. Everyone stays put, everyone except Marie, who sweeps off to the kitchen and returns with a tray of salmon and Stoned Wheat Thins surrounded by goblets of wine. Father McLucas bolts one glass as he packs up his vestments. As suavely as any maître d', he takes the folded bill that Richter slips into his hand and tucks it into a breast pocket as he heads toward the front door. "Good night," he calls. "And God bless." We listen to the VW roar to life and die, roar to life again, and then rattle off into the night. In a moment,

Patrick stands up and says what's on everyone's mind: "That's it. He made it up the driveway. He's gone."

Nonna is asleep.

Father Bruce and Richey, Jr., carry the wing chair that she is occupying to the dining-room table as the rest of us seat ourselves, musical chairs fashion. I find a place between Anna and Nina. The conversation is subdued—that is, almost nonexistent. The talk tonight does not touch on the suspicious death of Pope John Paul I or news of a new weeping Madonna in Krakow or Pittsburgh. Instead, it's focused on getting plates of food passed from the right and left.

Marie takes the seat closest to the swinging pantry door, ostensibly, one might guess, to be close to the kitchen. But after the meal has begun she doesn't budge. Instead, when food or drink is needed, she barks out a command and one of her daughters (Anna or Liza, Joan on rare occasion, Nina if she's in a mood to escape, Barb never) responds. This time I join in, not to make a statement, but to spend a few moments alone with Nina. Such disappearances are allowed, encouraged actually. All serious family discussions are held at mealtime in the kitchen.

"Tartar sauce," Marie calls.

Nina disappears. I follow. The clock ticking, I don't have time to fashion a neat segue from talk of tartar sauce to a discussion of, say, Tartars and other Old World emigrés to more immediate concerns.

"So what happened with England?" I ask.

"The fridge," she says. "Door panel. Top shelf."

"Joanie said that it's over between you two."

"God, she has a big mouth."

"Potatoes," Marie barks.

"Did you dump him?"

A platter of baked potatoes covered with preternaturally orange cheese flashes past my eyes. The door to the pantry swings open and shut. I am left trying to coax a half teaspoonful of tartar sauce into a cereal bowl. It hardly seems worth the effort. Nina returns.

"We'll have to make some more," she says. "What's in this stuff?"

I read from the label: "Soybean oil, distilled vinegar, sugar, pickles, high fructose corn syrup, salt, egg yolks, lemon juice concentrate, onion powder, xanthan gum, calcium disodium EDTA, polysorbate 80—"

"Enough!" She dumps a scoop of mayonnaise, a spoonful of diced sweet pickles, a dollop of mustard, and a few pinches of onion powder into the bowl and stirs it before my eyes.

"What do you think?"

It's a tad yellow. "I think the key is polysorbate 80."

Nina stirs in another teaspoon of mayonnaise. Again she holds it up for my inspection. "Taste it," she says.

"Not on your life."

"Wine!" Marie calls.

I grab Nina's wrist before she can disappear.

"A hint," I say.

She flashes the sort of grin I've waited six months to see. "This has to work both ways, you jerk."

"My presence here is proof enough that I am ready to give up the throne for the woman I love."

"Well, pardon me for assuming that there are still complications with a certain attorney who lives in a certain cozy little row house in Friendship Heights."

I smell jealousy. I smell late-night egg rolls and stale coffee and the pungent odor of a brand-new pair of binoculars.

"How did you find out where Kate lives?"

"I hope you finally got the engine started."

"You were there?"

"The van is a little obvious, Jack."

"So where were you headed at midnight?"

"Home."

"In such a hurry you couldn't jump an old friend?"

A top-notch, old-time Nina smile. "It would have been . . . well, uh . . . a little too complicated," she replies.

The mock tartar sauce disappears through the swinging door.

"So what happened to the Galloping Gourmet?" Marie asks.

"*JAAAACK!* Are you going to join us?"

"In a moment."

I hold my ground, forcing Nina to return.

"Am I to take it that you weren't alone?" I ask.

Her averted eyes answer the question.

"Did he see me, too?"

"No."

Honestly, England is the sort of guy who could drive coast to coast with his blinker going.

I fill a carafe with purple wine. "Sounds like you two were in a pretty big hurry."

She turns her head, but not before I see the light in her eyes, the lust of the *conquistadora*.

"You didn't!"

"It is absolutely none of your business, Jack."

"You did."

"Not another word," she breathes.

She grabs my arm, but I play Errol Flynn as Captain Blood, holding fast to the mainmast—in this case, a greasy oven door handle. I pull her into my arms and plant a juicy kiss on her lips. She swoons. Her eyes become saucers. We part, both of us grinning.

"I don't know what happened," she whispers into my sweater. "He seemed like a perfectly normal guy at first. Then bingo, he turns into a creep. It's awful. Just awful. The worst part is that he's been trying to make me feel like all of this is my fault. Like I'm some sort of investment he made that hasn't panned out. He's been calling me in the middle of the night. He hangs around outside my apartment. He had flowers sent to me at work. What do I do, Jack?"

"What do you want?"

"I want my life to be normal again."

"It can never be normal," I say with a Wellesian flourish. "The man has become unhinged. The thought of losing you is driving him mad. The only thing for you to do now is quit your job, move into the countryside, take on a new identity, wear a disguise. And that's not all."

"What else?" She is smiling.

"The Citroën will have to go."

"I'll never sell that car."

"Even so, he would probably hire a private detective and track you down. There will no escaping him." I cross to the microwave and pivot. "Unless—"

"Unless what?"

"Forget it. It's probably too late for that." With that, I depart.

The dining-room scene has changed completely. Joanie is massaging Nonna's shoulders. Barb's and Zalman's seats are empty. They're gone, vanished. No explanation for their disappearance is offered or requested. It happens all the time. Barb might have created a scene on principle—a delayed response to her mother's gift of the ritually crucified Christ—or Marie might have driven them out by launching into her standard Yuletide homily about how she has spent a lifetime feeling *sorry* for Jews, sorry that *they* had to be chosen to be the forgotten people, still waiting for a savior like a crowd of unfortunates gathered in the driving rain awaiting a canceled D-6 Metrobus.

Soon Nonna becomes fired up. Is it the massage? The strong coffee she insists on drinking with every meal? Perhaps she has just marshaled her energy to briefly assume the role of matriarch. Her elbows are planted on the table as she begins to lecture, Calabrian style, a forefinger swinging like a metronome. The topic is taken from the Book of Numbers. Nonna is exhorting her grandchildren on the importance of procreation. Another homily on the meaning of Christmas.

"Ana without the little children, there is a no joy in the house."

Joan lifts a lock of Nonna's hair and pantomimes speaking into a microphone. Anna drops her gaze to the empty plate in front of her. Patrick's lip curls slightly. Richey, Jr., looking straight at Joan, sees nothing. Liza and Father Bruce listen intently. Richter has a faraway look in his eyes, a most mellow expression. Chances are good he has just had a breakthrough in the scheme to anchor his cliff dwelling. Marie leans forward on her elbows, projecting her bosom out over the table. Nina, standing behind me, jabs me in the back to underscore each of Nonna's points.

"An I remember the night that your mother was born. The pain was a something terrible. An still afterwards I get a down on my knees to thank God for this baby. She was a beautiful. An her cry could awake up the dead. I didn't sleep for two, three days. But I thank God anyway."

The Catholic families I have known have all turned out children like machine-tool parts on an assembly line, a new one every 15.68 months. As a kid, I was appalled by this procreative zeal. Filling up the world with their own seemed downright selfish. I wasn't thinking about the fate of the planet, but I did have a microcosmic view of the global problem. The houses of the Catholics I knew were always a mess, the noise level tremendous—my first visit to Richter's château left me reeling. It seemed ludicrous to expect one house to accommodate so many different personalities. Now I can't imagine this family without all of these people. Even the most recalcitrant character seems *essential* to the whole. Even absent Barb.

"Is that Danny I hear?" Nina asks.

I don't hear a thing, but a sharp tug at my belt loop prompts me: "Maybe I should take him some table scraps and tell him to knock it off."

Nina says, "I'll go with you."

"Who wants dessert?" asks Marie.

Anna is already in the kitchen cutting up Mrs. Smith's pies.

Nina and I don boots, coats, and hats, and trudge out into the snow, ducking our heads to keep the blowing flakes out of our eyes. The night is dark and quiet. No sound of cars, no incessant jet noise overhead. No barking dog for that matter. Barking isn't Dan's style. If he got frustrated, he'd be more likely to spend an hour or two trying to scratch a hole in the door.

But he's asleep, curled up in the cedary recesses of his denim bed. Nina and I sit up front, gazing at the snow-covered windshield. The side windows are etched with ice scribbles. The atmosphere in our makeshift igloo seems to take us back thousands of years. I wish I had a bearskin to wrap around the two of us so that we could turn in for the night.

I do have *Il Trovatore*. I could pop the cassette into the tape deck and force Nina's hand, but I don't. Instead, I wait. I wonder where the jealousy that I've been nurturing like an exotic mushroom all these months has suddenly gone. I'm not feeling hurt or angry or vengeful, not feeling anything except a sharp post-Lawrencian-dinner ache in the pit of my stomach.

"So," she says. "Did you get this thing started the other night?"

"Roll started it," I reply, recalling the unpleasant task of muscling this frozen machine down 41st Street to the slight hill on Jenifer Street.

"Seemed kind of late to be going home."

I have a sudden image of Nina passing Kate's house regularly, like a birder keeping tabs on a bald eagle nest. I wonder if she figured out the Wednesday-through-Saturday Jason schedule.

"I wanted to stop," she says. "You looked like something was wrong."

"Bad battery."

"Seemed worse than that."

"Bad battery and a wounded ego."

"Jack, tell me what happened."

I do. I tell her the whole story, from my trying to work up the nerve to confess my Christmas Eve plans to Kate, to the scene on the Ellipse and meeting Tobias, to the denouement with Kate and her observations about my problem with women, including my mother.

"God," says Nina. "She has some nerve. You want to talk about men who have trouble with women? Ask *me*. Compared to Michael, your problems are *zilch,* Jack."

I kiss the side of her face. "Thanks, lady."

"You need a shave," she says, sending a fingernail against the grain of my whiskers.

"Maybe you've forgotten that I *always* need a shave."

"You want to know something weird? Michael shaves twice a *day.*"

"Poor old England."

"People don't ever change, do they, Jack?"

"Not without personal trainers."

She has idly begun to sketch what looks like a nativity scene on the fogged front window.

"Remember that time you came to my apartment and the place was so clean?" she says.

I nod.

"That was because Michael was cleaning it every time he stopped by. I couldn't stop him. He'd disappear into the bathroom and the next thing I knew the toilet water was blue. I never even saw the bottle."

"You should've rented him out."

She shakes her head. "The first time we went out he got indigestion from a plate of spaghetti. A simple marinara sauce. How could I have missed so many clues? Last week he gave me a folder of articles about the dangers of eating sushi. A whole folder."

Dan yawns, a high, piercing sound.

"And you know something else, you were right about Michael and his mother going to a shrink to yell at each other. I just don't get that. I asked him what happens when he feels like calling her up and yelling at her and it's not a first Friday of the month and you know what he said?"

"What's that?"

"That it doesn't happen."

"Maybe it doesn't."

"Oh, come on. What about their telephone conversations? What about the nights he stays with her when he's working in New York? Are you trying to tell me that they *never* get irritated with each other then? Only in a doctor's office?"

She has a point.

"People in therapy are trouble, Jack. There's something human missing. From one day to the next you never know which way they're headed. Just one cockamamie conversation with the shrink and all of a sudden they start getting after you because you haven't talked about your mother. Why do people do that to themselves?"

"It's all very logical. You work through the trouble of the past so that you can get on with the future."

"Has this woman ever *met* your mother?"

"No."

"God, she's got nerve. Are you wounded?"

"Only my pride."

"She's not worth it. I'm not saying that she's a lousy person, but anyone who would say something like that before she met Louise just isn't playing with a full deck. It's not my place to say it, but it sounds to me like this Kate person wouldn't know a good man if he bit her on the nose."

To illustrate, she bites my nose, and we quickly end up on Nina's seat doing a shaky rendition of the Iwo Jima memorial. O holy night! Were it up to me, I would take this moment to pop the clutch and let the van roll backward into the gauzy darkness. But it is not up to me. Nor is it up to Nina. Not yet anyway.

The lights at the front door flick on and off a dozen times and Marie's voice pierces the snowy fastness: "Should we call an ambulance? Is there anyone still alive out there?"

ACT IV

Nonna is standing in the door-
way draped in the skins of long-dead animals. She sniffs the air and
draws the fur coat around her; from where I stand it looks as though
the two vulpine heads perched on her shoulders are nibbling at her
ears.

Nina and I have been conscripted to walk Nonna home. Nina
takes her grandmother's left arm and I take the right. Nonna is short
and slight, but strong. She resists any attempt to guide her down the
snow-filled driveway, pulling us instead like a well-bred husky. My
heart is light. Nina invited me to dinner tonight because she
wanted me here. The suggestion that my presence was needed to
placate a failing old woman is bunk. Nonna will be with us for
years.

"So, Jack," she calls out. "Maybe I a see you again before next Christmas? Maybe I a say a prayer to Saint Jude an' then you gonna come aroun' a litta bit."

I look at Nina over the top of Nonna's rabbit hat. She averts her eyes.

We climb to the street and kick our way through a snow bank, walking downhill in the middle of the freshly plowed road. Nina fiddles with the key at Nonna's front door, then flicks on the outdoor lights, illuminating the front of the yellow bungalow. Inside, Nonna grips my face with cold gnarled fingers and kisses me on both cheeks. The grip I recognize: Joanie has inherited it.

I repair to the kitchen while the ladies clomp around upstairs. This room is newly renovated but still decidedly Old World, with a huge cast-iron kettle projecting like a bowsprit from the stove, a Sacred Heart of Jesus calendar, a half-filled bottle of Chianti on the red-and-white-checked Formica table. Squint your eyes and you're transported to the back room of a little *caffè* on a side street in Napoli.

I help myself to a glass of wine and glance at a newspaper laid open on the world's largest cutting board. It's the *Post* Metro section, the obituaries. It's easy to imagine Nonna standing here with her morning coffee in hand, glancing down the page for her name, and, not finding it, pouring another mug, buttering a piece of toast, and getting on with the day.

Some time ago, the *Washington Post* instituted the annoying policy of identifying by profession everyone who gets an obit. Thus, Walter F. (Slim) Waters is a "Concrete Inspector." Harold P. Grafton gets dual billing as "Navy Admiral/Dairy Farmer." Claudio R. Villalobos is listed as "World Bank Economist," though the obit goes on to say that he devoted all his free time to coaching a kids' soccer team. Why not "Soccer Coach?" Why a listing of professions at all? Is it for them or for us?

How about this: "John H. (Jack) Townsend, Landscape Architect." To tell the truth, I don't much like the sound of this guy already. Ray's obituary read like a sketch of the fine young man my parents wished he had become. They had him described as a varsity football player and bassoonist who died in a swimming pool accident. *Bassoonist!* This, to describe a kid who six months earlier had pitched his bassoon into the uncharted waters of Dickerson quarry. I wish my folks had been more honest, for everyone's sake.

"Ray Townsend killed himself at two A.M. last Sunday morning while attempting a backflip into the shallow end of the River Road Community Pool. Strictly speaking, this was not a suicide: Ray was said to have performed the same stunt at ten area pools, each time under the influence of alcohol. But this time he miscalculated, severing his spinal column. Mr. Townsend leaves behind a family that largely misunderstood him. In fairness to them, Ray was difficult to understand. Though he had not yet found his way in the world, he knew himself well enough to realize that he hated the hunger for power and influence that is so celebrated in this town. Shortly before he died, he revealed to his brother, Jack, an ambition to write. Mr. Townsend had just finished reading a biography of Lincoln Steffens and hoped to become a muckraking journalist. Friends consider him one of the most generous young men they knew, as well as a real entertainer. His brother related a story. . . ."

That is an obituary I would read. But who would write it? I could write Ray's obituary now, but not then. Over the course of these last months, my memories of Ray have lost their brittle edge. These days he comes to me less like a howling wind and more like a gentle ghost who sometimes finds his way into my room in the dead of night. Ray smiles at me in the darkness. I reach out from my groggy sleep and touch his knee and recall a cool Saturday morning in April, a couple of months before he died, when he showed up unexpectedly at my apartment and asked me to drive him out to Rockville for a gonorrhea test. He wanted company. We joked around a little about sexually transmitted diseases—those were the days when there was still some humor in the subject—but didn't say much else. I recall watching Ray fiddle with the radio dial as we drove out the Pike. In his view, all of life's important moments needed to be accompanied by the right music.

Tonight Ray is back. He is gently tapping his fingernails against the windowpane. I turn on the outdoor light and watch the snow piling up in the backyard. For once, the National Weather Service is right: snow is general all over the Washington area. It is falling on every dark alley of Silver Spring, on every empty lot, falling softly on the still Potomac and farther westward, softly falling into the dark mutinous valleys of the Blue Ridge. It is falling, too, upon every part of the lonely churchyard in Kensington where my little brother is buried.

Nina's arms encircle my waist. I cross my arms over them.

"You looking for someone?" she asks.

"Saw him. Had a quick word with him."

"How's he treating you these days?"

"He's calmed down. Calms me down."

"I'm glad to hear that."

"Liza would probably say that I am moving toward acceptance, but I honestly feel as though this change has more to do with him than with me."

"He could have hardened up."

Not Ray. Not in the end. What I feel in my heart is sorrow, sorrow that I can't get into a car with him and take a ride through Rock Creek Park. I see Ray hanging by his knees from a jungle gym, telling me about the first game of softball he ever played. He was five or six. First at bat he got a hit. But he ran to the pitcher's mound instead of first base. And he wouldn't leave. "The point is, I beat the throw," an upside-down head explains. "I was *safe*." Thank God I have finally arrived at a place where I can hold this little brother of mine in one corner of my mind and still enjoy leaning against a dark-haired beauty whose lips have found the corner of my jaw.

"What was the last word from Nonna?"

"Not there yet. She's working on a rosary."

"She could be at it all night."

"She's offering it up for us."

"Then she'll be asleep in five minutes."

We are as quiet as mice. Nina is standing on my shoes, her back to the tiled wall. Soon I am pressed against her. She pushes back, giggling under her breath.

She whispers. "The scene in *Il Trovatore* when Leonora shows up in the dungeon and begs Manrico to leave."

"I'm not budging," I declare.

The lights go off—exactly how I cannot say—and Nina's legs lift, gripping my thighs. She is almost as tall as I am, but holding her now she is as light as a bird. We smile at each other in the darkness, not daring to speak. I swing around and seat her on the edge of the table.

"Downstairs," she whispers.

The beast with two backs staggers into the front hallway, descends five steps to the family room, stumbles across the shag carpet, and collapses upon a huge sofa. Articles of clothing fly off or are urgently pushed to the side, and shortly Nina and I look like two people who have been trapped in a spinning clothes dryer. "Did you bring anything?" she whispers. "You mean like a chocolate eclair or *pommes frites?*" "No, not like either of those." "Right here," I say, producing the foil packet. She bites my chin. "You cocky bastard. I can't believe this." "Believe," I say. A spring buried deep in the sofa cries out, a lone sentinel alerting God to the activities of two joyous sinners. So we slide to the carpet and make love among the shaggy worms.

The sound of footsteps freezes me. Upstairs, the kitchen light flickers on. I grab for clothes and shoes and press them between us like a cooking waffle, and, with superhuman effort, lift Nina and scuttle toward the guest bathroom. Her warm face is pressed to my neck as we sink to the tiled floor. I start to withdraw, but she grabs me by the collar and whispers fiercely in Italian. Under the influence of Mistress Nina, I can block out the noise of a radio call-in show blaring from the kitchen. Nina locks her legs to my calves and soon begins to roll like a pitching boat. I become as expressive as a one-celled organism. The knocking that I hear as I am overcome by the *petite mort* I assume to be the crown of Nina's head tapping against the base of the door. I collapse on top of her and float as if on the ocean. The knocking continues.

Nina whispers, "Front door." "Christ," I breathe. "I doubt it," she says. Soon we hear Nonna's heavy tread.

"Good evening, Mrs. Romano."

Half-naked, heaving, one ear buried in the tangle of Nina's hair, I recognize England's voice immediately.

"Sweet Jesus," she says. "This is a thousand times worse than I thought."

The conversation comes through as clear as a bell. England goes to great length to explain that he was just over at the Lawrences, and Mrs. Lawrence told him that Nina had walked her grandmother home, and he thought he would hurry over to see if she was still here, blah, blah, blah, blah, blah.

"She put me ina bed and then I don't see her anymore," Nonna says. "But I a don't sleep so I come downstairs to make a some warm milk. How about I make you some cocoa?"

"Hot cocoa would taste wonderful," he says eagerly.

He's preparing to camp. I can feel it in my bones. England is just the sort of guy who, as a last resort, would try to woo his beloved via her grandmother. While he cools his heels in the entranceway, Nina and I sort our clothes by touch. My underwear goes on inside out and, first time around with my pants, I pull them up backwards. The cocoa is served before we are fully dressed. There's a bra left over; I stuff it into my pocket as Nonna and England make their way down the steps to the family room. Outside the bathroom, a lamp blinks on.

"Mrs. Romano, this is delicious. It really hits the spot after a long drive."

"So you a come alla way from New Jersey ina the snow?" I whisper, "I thought she wasn't supposed to know about him."

Nina: "She wasn't."

England: "Oh, the highway wasn't bad at all. And anyway, I've got top-of-the-line Michelins. They held the road pretty well."

"Ana what part of New Jersey are you a from?" asks Nonna. "Frank Sinatra, he was a from Hoboken. You know Frank?"

"Well, not personally. I've been to Hoboken, though. My family lives more to the west."

I whisper, "We could be trapped here for hours."

Nina: "She'll get tired. And he'll get tired. Please let's just let this end quietly."

I sigh inwardly as Nina rests her head on my shoulder. I feel like singing. I want to play out the famous double scene in *Aïda,* when the two priests move the stone slab over the tomb while Radames and Aïda sing their final farewell. *O terra addio!*

Nonna says, "An tell me why you drive back in the snow in the middle of the night."

"I wanted to see Nina," England says, a bit testily. "I was hoping that we might have some important news to announce. You see, we have discussed becoming engaged."

I give Nina my strongest look of reproach.

"He kept bringing it up," she whispers. "I didn't say yes."

"It sounds like you didn't say no either."

"I was hoping the subject would go away."

If only she had played basketball with England, or watched him play, she would have realized that such a tactic was hopeless. Subtle gestures don't reach a man who is willing to put his head down and try to drive through five guys to get to the hoop.

The conversation in the family room is growing serious. Earnest England has begun to unburden his soul. I should be interested in what he has to say, but there's no pace to his tale. He's telling Nonna the story of his whole life. We get to hear about the sense of abandonment he felt when he was sent away to boarding school, about his relationship with his divorced parents. It's so deadly dull I have to consider the possibility that what we have here is a new twist on the *Arabian Nights*: to win Nina's heart and vanquish his rival, England has the task of boring me to sleep.

"My parents are dead set against the marriage," he says unhappily.

Me, in a whisper: "Now it's a marriage."

Nina: "Sometimes Michael gets ahead of himself."

Nonna, her dander up: "Whatsa matter, they don't a like my Nina?"

"Oh no, Mrs. Romano. It's not that. It's just that they're against mixed marriages."

"Itsa difficult life I can a tell you."

"You married a Jew?"

"A Sicilian. It didn't work out. But he died. It was a the will of God."

Quiet reigns, an uncomfortable silence punctuated by a mug-draining slurp of cocoa.

"Mrs. Romano," England says finally. "I need to ask you a question. Does Nina still love Jack?"

There is a long pause. With the cracked-open door facing the steps, Nina and I can't see either of them.

"Oh," says England.

Nina: "Was that 'oh yes' or 'oh no'?"

"You don't know?"

"Of course I know. I just want to know what she thinks."

Nonna: "How about I make you a litta more cocoa."

England: "Please."

Me: "Prepare the shower stall."

England begins to whistle while Nonna is upstairs in the kitchen. Whistling, of all things! I'd like to pretend that the tune is "The Lass of Aughrim," but it sounds like a shaky rendition of "Silver Bells."

Nonna returns. "I tell you something funny, Michael. Everybody ina the family thinks that I think that Nina and Jack are married." She laughs and laughs.

"They do?" He is shocked. "Why?"

"Because I got a sick when they were making plans an I asked my Marie about the wedding that is supposed to happen while I am in the hospital an she tells me it was bee-you-ti-ful."

"Your own daughter lied to you?"

"What else is she agonna do?" Nonna says sharply.

"When did you realize that they hadn't married?"

"The first time I see them. I look at their faces. I listen to the words that a come out of their mouths. Too much *passione*. An no rings. An no pictures. An no sign of the baby. I tell you, those two are crazy for each other, but they don't a wanna get married. I can't say why, but I understand. Maybe I tell my Nina too many stories about a my Enzo.

"But a you," she continues. "A man like you needs a good wife. You need someone to make you cocoa. An my Nina don't cook so good. Not even a pan of milk and chocolate."

"She makes a wonderful marinara."

"The marinara she picks up at my kitchen door."

"That's *yours*?"

"I'm an old lady, Michael. I'm not agonna live forever. An my Marie, she don't cook too much. She uses a Ragu."

I lean against the towel rack, straining to picture the scene on the other side of the door. They talk at length about the kind of woman who would be right for England and the sort of man who would be right for Nina. England sounds much too eager as he pumps Nonna for information about me, the Lawrence family, Nina, himself. Pretty soon he'll be hitting her up for advice on how to handle Judge Lambertini of the Fifth Circuit.

I know that I shouldn't say a word about my erstwhile rival, but cooped up in this damp bathroom, I can't stop myself from whispering, "Just what did you see in this guy?"

"He's really very sweet," Nina replies.

Sweet! "Is sweet enough?"

"I thought it was."

"I would like to point out that you just spoke in the past tense, madame."

"Oh Jack, it is. But let's don't make Michael out to be some kind of nut. He's just a little different. Everyone has odd qualities. Even you."

"My odd qualities are endearing."

"To whom?"

"You?"

"What about that Baldwin woman?"

"She went from appreciating my differences to respecting me for them. That's the kiss of death. It turns out that I'm too judgmental for her."

"You? That's nuts. She wants judgmental she should take a ride over here and meet my mother."

"More cocoa?" asks Nonna.

"No, thank you, Mrs. Romano"—Nina and I both sigh— "but could I use your bathroom?"

"Oh, Michael," Nonna says sadly. "I gotta tell you something. You an me we understand each other. Itsa crazy world. Nothing makes sense. People who are married are not married, but they live together. Why? The priest, the judge, they don't a matter anymore. Nobody listens. Nobody takes the good advice. The family, Michael, the family is what's important. Especially at Christmas. You stay with them. You go to midnight Mass with them. But you don't a leave them in the middle of the night to drive alla way from New Jersey in the snow an for what?"

"I thought I made it clear—"

"I hear allota words, Michael. I turn on the TV and get the

same thing. Allota words. What do they mean? I'm an old woman, Michael. Who can tell me something I don't know?"

"I was hoping—"

"Don't a hope. You take what God gives to you and you say thank you. You want a litta more, you go to church and pray."

"There are two sides to this story, Mrs. Romano. You haven't heard mine. I have legitimate grievances. I will grant you that everything wasn't spelled out in my last conversation with Nina. But I think I should be allowed to draw some conclusions—"

"Ah, forgive yourself, Michael. Everybody is wrong sometimes. It happens."

"I'm not wrong." Silence. Nonna might be picking lint from her bathrobe or making the sign of the cross. Maybe she shut her eyes. "I expected rationality, Mrs. Romano. A little common sense. I was trying to help Nina find that. But all I got was that temper of hers. She has no self-control."

"Asshole," whispers a voice beside me.

"And I tried to help her with that, too. If the law teaches you anything, it's logic and control. Maybe I didn't always say the right thing. Maybe I didn't always understand her motivations—"

"Ah, Michael. Don't be so hard on yourself."

"I'm not finished," he says sharply.

"Itsa sad. Such a big world, so many people who look for somebody to love, ana still so much unhappiness."

"So much dishonesty," England says.

"Don't a criticize your business, Michael. Itsa bad luck."

I glance at Nina. Her glare could set the room on fire.

It's over for England. He's history. I have to admit that he had me worried for a few moments, displaying an impressive amount of recklessness rushing back from Short Hills in the midst of a driving snowstorm. But his entrance was all wrong. This petulant "Rumpole of the Bailey" act has finished him.

England says, "Tell Nina that I stopped by. And tell her that

I am sorry it had to end like this. I expected more from her. A little more maturity. Tell her that I hope she learns a lesson from this and that in the future she'll have cause to—"

"Itsa too much to remember already."

"Tell her I don't understand her at all."

"Who can understand my Nina?"

"My mother thinks she might need professional help. I disagreed with her at first, but now I'm inclined to think that she's right."

Nina goes rigid with indignation. "Those two have to hire a doctor to scream at each other and they think *I'm* the one who needs help?"

"Let's just let this end quietly," I say.

"On Halloween he wanted me to dress up like a cabaret singer in pre-war Berlin, which just happens to be where his mother grew up."

"Poor England," I say.

"Hold me tight, Jack. Hold me tight and promise you won't let me do anything I'd regret."

I do. I do.

As soon as England departs, the house goes dark and we throw open the bathroom door.

"She knew we were here," Nina whispers.

"Nonsense."

"She knew. We didn't fool her for a second. She knows the whole story."

"The *whole* story?"

Nina nods solemnly.

"I'd like to know where this story ends," I say.

"We go to the kitchen door and throw ourselves headfirst into the snow."

This we do. But instead of lying there to await the cold kiss of death, we struggle to our feet and brush the wet flakes from each other's hair and trudge past the snow-toppled mounds of bamboo sitting like yurts in Richter's gully.

The Lawrence house is dark.

"Your side or mine?" asks Nina, as we approach the van. She is resurrecting a wager we often made about which front seat Dan would be occupying. So far this winter he has favored mine. But Dan is clairvoyant and anything but predictable.

"Mine," I say.

"I think you're wrong."

We creep up to the driver's window and brush off the snow. The little bastard is curled up on Nina's seat. He lifts his head; an inch of dry tongue protrudes from his closed mouth. When I open the door to let him out, he surveys the snowy ground, gauging, it would seem, the urgency of the need. Finally he exits, walking gingerly. Off the roadway, he sinks to his chest. He turns and looks at me.

I hear a window crank open.

"Who's out there?" calls Marie.

"Just us, Ma," says Nina.

"Who's us?"

"Jack and me."

"Thanks be to God, Angie. That Jewish boy was here after you left." From her tone of voice, you'd think she discovered England reading the Torah on the front steps.

"I *know*. Why in heaven's name did you send Michael to Nonna's?"

"It's where you went, young lady, if I'm not mistaken."

"Ma, I guess it never occurred to you that his showing up at Nonna's might put me in an awkward position."

Nina's voice is still under control, but growing shrill. Marie is with her step for step. No scream therapist will ever be needed for these two.

Marie says, "Well, he saw Jack's van. He asked where the two of you went. What was I supposed to do, lie to him?"

"It wouldn't be the first time."

The gloves are coming off. I stand off to the side, near Dan, who is lifting his leg on a snow-filled wheelbarrow.

Richter's voice comes up. "For God's sake, Marie, we don't need to heat the entire neighborhood."

The casement window shuts with a bang. Marie is not one to waste #2 heating oil, nor duck an argument. Another window winds open, the bathroom window: "Just what was I supposed to do, Miss Know-it-all?"

"*Anything!* Anything except sending him after me!"

I'm reminded of the scene in *Il Trovatore* when Azucena turns on Count di Luna and warns him that an angry God is going to strike him dead. I wish we had that opera playing right now. I wish I had England's sound system in my van; I'd wake up the neighborhood.

If this story were true opera, then this would be the final scene. In Verdi's hands, the result would be depressing. England, assuming that Nina had gone back to me, would have gulped a bottle of poison. His body would be found in a storm-runoff drain, lips as blue as the sea. In the course of this screaming argument, Nina would discover that Marie was not her real mother: Marie would reveal that she had stolen baby Nina from someone else's crib. *My* crib, in fact. Nina and I are twins! Wracked with guilt, Nina would curse Marie, curse her fate, then do herself in with a dagger produced from her purse. Marie would shriek to the heavens. I would have no choice but to climb Richter's scaffolding, sing a rousing *non vivendi sin tumulti!* and then throw myself to the ground beside my incestuous lover.

But this isn't opera. This is Washington, D.C. Nobody sings for love here. Passion is something that comes in a perfume bottle. England has no doubt gone home; right now he is probably sorting his mail—a time-share deal at Williamsburg, a Mastercard offer from a bank in North Dakota, a postcard with a photograph of a missing kid attached to a bar of soap. If Nina had a pearl-handled dagger in her purse, she wouldn't use it on herself—she'd probably throw it at her mother. As for me, I'm completely exhausted from my exertions. Climbing scaffolding is out of the question.

"Young lady," calls Marie. "You always have to have it *your* way. Someday that's going to catch up with you. Mark my words. You keep lighting the candle at both ends and you'll end up burning your fingers!"

"Well, one reason I invited Jack tonight was because YOU begged me to."

"So I'm to blame for that as well. Fine. What else? No reason to stop there. Did the conversation at the dinner table displease you? Any complaints about the meal?"

"The fish was overcooked by about three minutes," I call. "And the bird needed another hour with the oven cut back a hundred degrees."

"That's enough out of you, wise guy!"

"Good night, Mother," says Nina.

"You're leaving us?" Marie's voice suddenly is filled with maternal worry. "With the snow, at this hour? Where in heaven's name will you go?"

"I have an apartment in the city, if you recall."

"Massachusetts Avenue is probably a sheet of ice."

"Then we'll skate."

"Don't be smart."

"We'll go to Jack's house."

Marie makes the sign of the cross. "The kids'll be so disappointed tomorrow morning. You told them you'd be here to open presents."

"I'll stop back."

"What time?"

"I don't know. I'll call."

"We might be off to Mass, Angie."

"You've BEEN to Mass," she screams.

I call, "Good night, Marie."

"Merry Christmas, Jack. Are we going to have the pleasure of seeing you tomorrow?"

Nina says, "She wants to know if we're back together."

"Are we back together?"

"I guess it sort of looks that way."

"You two!" Marie bellows. "Your hands all over each other—in the Holy Land, you'd be stoned for such things—and still you don't know whether or not you're back together!"

"Marie," I say. "Let's just say that we've achieved conjugal American bliss."

"And what is that supposed to mean?"

"We couldn't live with each other, and now we've discovered that we can't live without each other."

She disappears, but her voice comes through loud and clear: "Richey, our baby is going to get married!"

I expect faces to appear in all the windows. Bing Crosby, Julie Andrews, Andy Williams, Claudine Longet, The Osmonds, Perry Como, each knocking out a verse of some maudlin Christmas favorite. Instead, the front door flies open and light floods out of the foyer. Then Marie appears in hairnet and shocking pink bathrobe and red quilted booties.

"Our Lady of Mohican Hills," Nina whispers.

"The two of you expect the world to stop turning because you're in love again," she shouts. "You expect miracles. You're spoiled rotten, that's what you are. If you ask me, you deserve each other. Who else would have you?"

Nina takes my arm. It feels as though we're part of an evolving modern rite, the marriage of the Catholic wedding and shock radio. The blessing will include epithets. The attendants will shower us with personal observations.

A short whistle gets Dan's attention. "Where's your friend? Where's Marie?" I point. "Go see her. Go see your friend."

He takes off, cutting a swath through the snow. Approaching the front door, his whole body begins to wag, the tip of his tail and tip of his nose swinging left and then right. Marie retreats into the doorway. Only her lips show through the crack, but the diatribe continues.

"You think you know everything. Nobody can tell you how it went for them, because with you it will be different. You *exhaust* me. I'm tired of getting my hopes up for the two of you. I don't ever want to hear another word about your troubles."

Nina says, "You know something, Ma? Nonna knows that we aren't married."

"Oh for God's sake, Angie! I know *that*."

"Then why have I spent the last two years pretending?"

"You were doing that for *me*."

Nina puts her long arms around my shoulders, planting me like a fence post. "Jack and I are going to live together. We're never going to get married. Definitely not in the Church, anyway. You'll have to get used to that. Our children won't be baptized. And I won't stand for you sneaking them off to Mass every time you baby-sit them."

Marie addresses the gold-plated statue of the Virgin Mary in the foyer: "Now I'm accused of planning to brainwash the nonexistent grandchildren. Who put such ideas into her head?"

"You've been practicing on other people's grandchildren."

"Penny *asked* me about the Baby Jesus. She *wanted* to go to Little Flower."

"Ma, she's four years old."

"Well, I had her for two whole hours. What was I supposed to do, wreck my voice reading books to her the whole time?"

On and on. We are caught in the grooved surface of a thousand old conversations. Nina and Marie could carry on until dawn without pause. I am cold. Dan, weary of the shouting, is scratching at the door to the van. I open it and let him in.

"Merry Christmas, Marie," I call.

" 'Night, Jack. You take good care of my darlin'. And you

come see me tomorrow. You're the only one I can talk to. You're the only one who tells me the truth anymore."

The engine cranks exactly once before catching. I smile.

The truth is that I don't have a clue as to where Nina and I are headed. All I can say for certain is that tonight we are sleeping side-by-side in the old pattern: facing west, my right arm draped around her waist, entwined in her hands. After a few hours in this position, we execute a 180-degree shift. The noise awakens Dan beneath the bed. He thumps his way out, shakes off, and collapses atop a pile of laundry. He begins to snore loudly. His whinnying nightmares rouse us in the early hours of dawn and we whisper the pros and cons of waking him or letting the anguish play itself out.

"Must be dreaming that he's a dog who runs with wolves," I say. "Or maybe about his last visit to see Dr. Nancy."

"What if it's us? He's so darn sensitive. I feel awful for putting him through this. Psychologically, he's probably a wreck. Maybe I should give him a bowl of milk."

"Save up your money and buy him a herd of sheep."

"A plate of Milk-Bones is as far as it goes."

"Adopt a kid to throw Frisbees for him all day long."

"Jack. I'm serious. Something's wrong. Listen to him."

As if on cue, Dan sighs and falls silent. We fall silent, too. I hold Nina's hand to my lips and watch the western sky turn gray, then winter yellow. I listen to the sound of her breathing and listen to the wind. I daydream about the morning. Some snow shoveling, a long march to Georgetown for raisin bagels, ice-skating on the canal perhaps, Yuletide pilgrimages to Cleveland Park, the Water-gate, Mohican Hills—to the moon, for all I care. An argument, of course. About what? About which wise man brought the best gift, say. (I'll vote for the gold and Nina will no doubt make a strong case for frankincense or myrrh.) Some barking to settle the conver-sation when it grows too heated, some laughter, more barking, talk, talk, talk, a new recording of *Simon Boccanegra.*

And *La Bohème.* Maybe.

ACKNOWLEDGMENTS

For their support and encouragement, I would like to express my heartfelt thanks to Marjorie and Karl Ackerman, my parents; Gail and Bill Gorham, my other parents; Mary Frances Veeck ("The Aunt"); Barb Wahl; Chuck Ossola ("The Commissioner"), David Allen, and the rest of the Monday night hoops group; Nan Graham; Sage Parker; Mary Johnson; Josh Astrachan; Kate Renko, who first read the completed manuscript; Suzanne Gluck, who saw its promise and found it a home; and George Witte, whose suggestions have improved it immeasurably.

Special thanks to two fellow writers, Jennifer Ackerman and Christina Bartolomeo, who read and commented on the novel at every stage.

Finally, to Danny—the real Dan—climber of mountains, chaser of Frisbees, swimmer of oceans, a salute and sad farewell.